True North

Also by L. E. Sterling

True Born

True Storm

L.E. STERLING

TRUE NORTH

TRUE BORN TRILOGY

This book is a work of fiction. Names, characters, places, and incidents are the product of the author's imagination or are used fictitiously. Any resemblance to actual events, locales, or persons, living or dead, is coincidental.

Entangled Publishing, LLC
2614 South Timberline Road
Suite 105, PMB 159
Fort Collins, CO 80525

Entangled TEEN is an imprint of Entangled Publishing, LLC.

Visit our website at www.entangledpublishing.com.

Edited by Liz Pelletier
Cover design by Michelle Fairbanks
Interior design by Toni Kerr

Print ISBN: 978-1-63375-595-6
PB ISBN: 978-1-63375-915-2
Ebook ISBN: 978-1-63375-600-7

Manufactured in the United States of America

First Edition April 2017

10 9 8 7 6 5 4 3 2 1

For my grandmother, Catherine,
And in honor of her mother, Emily,
Who in part inspires this story

I

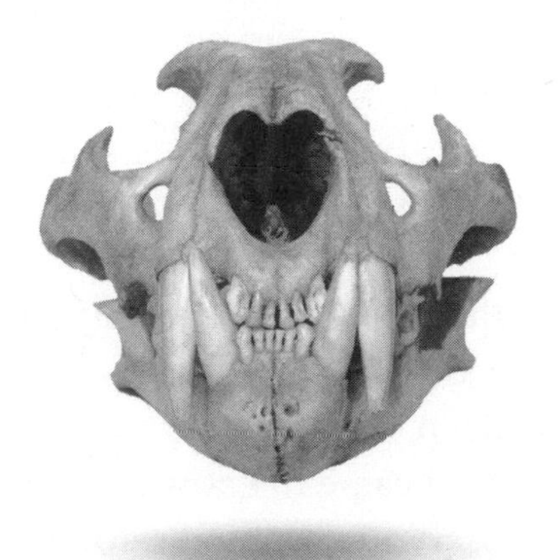

Sometimes flesh and bone are as inexplicable as magic. I was but seven years old when I first realized that the song of blood-to-blood could hold sway over death. Margot was out with our driver that day. I don't recall the why now, except to say we were always uneasy to be separated, and more so that morning. Jenks was our old-timey driver with the bushy eyebrows. He wore a black cap tilted on an angle over his thinning hair. His suits were always a touch too large. I'd noticed, in a child's offhand way, that those suits were getting larger. When the Plague bit into him that morning, his foot stuck on the accelerator. He drove wildly through the town, drowning in wave after wave of agony, while Margot clung to the backseat like a burr.

At home, they tell us, and miles apart, I was hysterical. No one would listen to me. Not the staff, nor our mother or father. Desperate, I ran out of the house and started one of our father's many cars. I'd go after my twin on my own.

I thank all the gods in Dominion that it was Shane riding the gate that day, our father's man who knew us well—knew we were different. By the time Shane had a dragnet stop my sister's car, poor old Jenks had cut a swath of destruction through the town. He died before they delivered a tear-stained Margot home. Bruised and shaken but miraculously not hurt, my twin looked at me as though she'd seen through the veil.

They were halted thirty feet from the lake. Just thirty more feet and they'd have been underwater, my sister's flesh tangled with the deep.

That was the day I came to know the power of our bond. If we listened closely to our bones, fought hard enough, showed the world we'd not back down, my sister and I could pull each other from the jaws of fate. I learned my lesson that day as my raging grief clawed back the tides of death—that the only thing worse than feeling my twin's suffering was the fear of not feeling her at all.

It was a hard and terrible and wonderful lesson, and I learned it well.

I squat at the roots of the giant tree, sliding into the bark a long, thin pipette to gather a sample. The slim tube fills, and I add it to the sample case, counting off vials along with how many months it's been. *One, two.* I imagine this is a new game Margot and I have devised: the game of the missing sister. *Three. Four.* The air buzzes with the sound of machinery. Startled, I look up, trying to sight the choppers whirling overhead. The sky stays white and blank, though the sound rises and falls. Rain slicks my face and runs down my neck to pool at my collar.

"It will be dark soon." Beside me, Doctor Dorian Raines packs away her tools. "We'd better finish up or Storm won't let us come back here for a month." One of her springy curls defies the rain and gravity to stand on end. A spade lands at my knee. "Make sure you get a proper sample from under the root this time," she teases me.

She has reason to, I reckon. Over the past months, Doc Raines has had to teach me a great deal. The first time we'd come to take samples of the massive, unnatural thing known across Dominion as the "Prayer Tree," I'd pulled vials of broken asphalt rather than the loamy soil from which the tree sprang.

I'd been tired and distracted and suffering from "too much glitter," as Margot would say. But all that glitter—the parties, the meetings, the endless social events—was robbing me of sleep. And what dreams I did have were shadowed with what glitter hid. But my life these days isn't so much about digging for soil samples as digging for answers.

I'm on a hunt for my sister.

Four short months ago my world—and Dominion City—had been very different. The glitter had been my everyday, though of a different variety. Coming from one of the most prominent families of Dominion's Upper Circle, my sister and I were expected to attend social events, to play hostess for the rich and powerful. That had all come to a crashing halt the night of our Reveal. That night, our world had exploded. The Lasters, led by the crazy preacher man, Father Wes, led a revolt on our house.

So many had died that night, so uselessly. And I had been left alone. I reckon I could have gone with my parents and Margot and the dark Russian aristocrat Leo Resnikov, who held sway over them. I opted to remain behind in Dominion—I'd wanted to stay with the wild-eyed Jared Price and the rest of his tribe. I wanted to get as far away from the corruption of my father and his ilk as I could, trusting that the True Borns and their enigmatic leader, Nolan Storm, would help me get Margot back.

I gave myself a choice: I could curl up in a ball and let the Plague take me. Or I could have faith in the magic buried deep in our blood and bones.

I chose to believe.

Four months on, things haven't worked out quite as I'd expected. I'd hoped to forge a home here in Dominion City, a place to bring Margot back to. Instead, I reckon I feel as I did all those years ago, when I first thought my twin would be taken from me. Helpless. Lost, as though my body and my world had been ripped in two and the better part of me vanished. The True Borns are helping, or so says Nolan Storm, though there has been no progress to speak of. And I'd trust Jared Price with my life, though he doesn't make it easy. Ever since that terrible night, Jared has been the perfect merc: cold, professional, distant.

Still, I'll not soon forget the moment I decided, when he looked at me and the masks between us fell.

Stay with me, Lu.

I shiver at the memory and idly tune in to a rising tide

of chatter from around the tree. Childish voices scratch at the air. Something like the song of a bird grabs my attention. It's unnatural, out of place here. I glance up. From this short distance, you can see the bits of silver and red and white flashing from the tree's lush canopy. Grown in mere hours from the seeds of a so-called "magic bomb," the deciduous now dwarves the intersection it's eaten—a place the Lasters have renamed Heaven Square. It crows over the red-graffitied buildings of Dominion City's wasteland. And this is where Doc Raines, Nolan Storm's semiofficial clinician scientist, and I, her assistant, dig for answers. Literally.

The birdcall sounds again, this time from another direction.

"Oh, bother," Doc Raines mutters under her breath. She swipes a lock of hair from her eyes with the back of a gloved hand. "Not again."

"You think?" I say, trying not to sound too excited.

Doc Raines picks up the pace of her packing. "What else could it be?"

The swarmings happen fast. Before you can blink, the kid gangs can arrive en masse and strip you of money, clothes, the gold from your teeth. We've protection here, courtesy of Nolan Storm, but that's of little comfort. A team of thirty or forty could overwhelm us. There's no shortage of little thieves in Dominion.

"Hurry, Lucy," Doc Raines calls impatiently.

"Just one more sample," I tell her, crawling deeper under a bough.

The sounds rise, more like a warning than harmless birdsong. I can sense, rather than see, small bodies maneuvering around the buildings plastered in a mess of graffiti. Everywhere you look, the red tags appear: the same two circles, conjoined in the middle like a pair of crossed eyes. EVOLVE OR DIE is scribbled beneath the best of them, sometimes even spelled right. The dying part is easy enough to understand in a city like Dominion. Thanks to the Plague, people here are dying by the bucketful. But how can anyone think a place like this can evolve?

A shout. It's Derek, one of our guards for today. Then I hear it: a shrill battle cry that raises the hair on the back of my neck. It comes at us from every angle. I push my way closer to the trunk. It would be hard to attack me under the tree, I reason. But the shelter also fulfills another need of mine.

"Lucy!" Derek yells. "Stay where you are!"

The sounds grow louder, more ominous, chilling the blood in my veins.

Derek shouts over to Penny, our other guard. If the gangs think they've hit an easy mark here, Penny—whom I affectionately call "Mohawk," though not to her face —will have them thinking twice. I imagine her grinning sharp teeth at the children, scaring them silly just before she laughingly tears one of them limb from limb.

Doc Raines whispers something urgently at me, but I'm too far out of range to hear. I creep farther into the deep, reaching out my fingers until I touch bark. The kids' shrill sounds fill the air like a screaming murder of crows. I can't think, can hardly breathe.

And suddenly I'm not alone.

A dirty head pokes out from around the trunk, with a pair of brown eyes that shrewdly size me up from under a shaggy bit of hair. *Alone*, I think to myself, and wonder if the kid was sent to rob me—or worse. It cocks its head and sidesteps over to me like a curious bird as I riffle through the bag strung over my shoulder.

I fish out an apple and hand it to the filthy creature, trying to speak loudly enough to be heard over the violent calls. "What's your name?"

The kid eyes my hand. "Marta." Her voice croaks like she hasn't used it in a while.

"You with this gang?"

She nods, sidesteps a bit closer, like a wild animal. Up close you can tell. Not just dirty—this young thing has likely seen far worse than death. Death is easy here in Dominion. Cheap and plentiful. It's the living that's hard. And if you're in a kid gang, swelling with the orphaned castoffs of the Plague, I reckon it's even harder.

Quick as lightning, the apple disappears from my hand. The girl munches away at it, crouching against the base of the tree.

"You stay around here?" I venture.

The girl doesn't reply but cocks her head at me as though I've asked if she's from the Upper Circle. I ask, quiet-quiet, "Who runs your pack? Can I talk to them?"

There's a method to my madness. The kid gangs go everywhere. They flitter here and there and everywhere. If anyone will know things—for instance, which direction the Fox family may have fled four months ago—it's the leaders of the kid gangs.

I've made a mistake. I see this immediately. The girl quits her munching. She cocks her head and looks around wildly before bolting around the tree. But by then I've clued in that it's not my question that has her running rabbit.

I hear it, too.

Silence.

And then I understand why.

"She's unguarded?" Jared True Born Price snarls. The few songbirds in the trees go silent.

I peek out from the safety of the tree to catch a glimpse of Doc Raines going head-to-head with the charming but psychopathic loafer who heads my security—the man who makes my heart gallop more wildly than a swarming kid gang.

"Now hold on just a moment there, big boy." Doc Raines glares back at him, hands on hips. "We're not responsible for ordering the damned security details. We're just going about our work. As we do every day, I might point out." The doc isn't afraid of much—not swarmings, anyway. Nor even a murderous True Born who, when provoked, picks his teeth with men's bones.

Jared lets out a long hiss of breath. "If you're attacked, you're not going to get very much work done, Doc," he counters reasonably. I watch with too much curiosity, my heart pumping furiously, as the True Born sighs and runs his hands from his neck through his golden curls so they stick up like exclamation points. I reckon my time is short. I may have thirty seconds, maybe less.

It's hard to turn away from the sight of him. For a moment I'm transfixed: Jared Price is sinew and gold, a pacing jungle cat with flashing eyes. And like the cat he shares his gen code with, there isn't a single inch of Jared's lean frame that isn't tailored to hunt and kill. I'm mesmerized all the more by his tender side, though—in many ways wilder than his beast—and how his fierce eyes turn soft when he looks at me.

Still, I won't likely get this chance again. *I need to do this.* I get down on my hands and knees and crawl a few feet around the base of the tree. I can't see Marta any longer, but that doesn't necessarily mean she's gone. Reaching into my bag, I toss another apple as far around the trunk as I can manage.

"Marta," I call softly. "Marta, I'm Lucy. Come back in two days, right? I'll bring you more food. Look for me." I hold up two fingers, though I doubt the dirty little thing can see them. "Two days. I'll have more eats."

As far as bribes go, this one is supposed to be a sure thing. Food is guaranteed to make you friends in Dominion—or get you killed. It's in scarce enough supply that for some, it trumps Plague Cure. No sense living through the wasting disease if you're just going to starve to death. Granted, I wouldn't know much about starving—aside from staring at it in the gaunt planes of the girl's cheeks.

"Oh, *Lu*-cy. Come out, come out, wherever you are. I'm not going to bite," Jared purrs.

I snort in disbelief but decide to come out anyway, knowing with every cell in my body that Jared Price is scenting the air, fixing on me like a bloodhound—though panther is more like it.

Backing out from the shadow of the tree, I hit something as hard as tree bark. I glance up. A blond man with the face of an angel looms over me. His bulging arms cross over one of a never-ending supply of stupid T-shirts. This one has a cartoon moose drawn across it. I notice a vague resemblance to my so-called guardian, Nolan Storm. My hands rest on his long bare toes that he's shoved into some fragile-looking leather sandals. There's a rip in the left knee of his trousers, and where the threads pull apart, I spy a freckle I've never seen before.

"Find something interesting down there?" Jared's eyebrow cocks up under a shag of blond curls. I hate it when he mocks me.

"Yeah." I hold up the small vial of dirt and asphalt like a shield. "You really need a new pair of pants."

He bends low over me, taking the dirt. So close I can smell the cinnamon scent of his breath. "I thought we had an understanding, Princess. You know the drill. Does this look like a good neighborhood to go prancing around in alone, making yourself a target for these idiot kids? Have you forgotten about all those nice preacherfolk who want to skin you alive?"

I huff indignantly. "I was *not* prancing."

I blink and look around. In the short time I've been under the prayer tree, Heaven Square has emptied out. The air has turned still, the swarming kids gone to ground. Even the handful of Lasters who usually hang around day and night, praying to all the Gods of Dominion to be saved from the Plague, have disappeared. I doubt it's because they realized only Splicers can be saved—Upper Circlers with money enough to visit the Splicer Clinics, where they can have new DNA sewn in to replace the bad. Maybe one day the Lasters will pray to the True Borns, instead. They say True Born DNA jumped back in time, reasserting the genetic traits of our evolutionary ancestors. Some wear gills, other feathers. Some, like Jared, are a breed apart and able to wear their animal selves. They can't get sick—no True Born has ever caught the Plague as far as I am aware. But in Dominion the

True Borns are feared and loathed. People would just as soon believe that as their DNA returned to our primordial roots, the True Borns became not gods, but monsters.

I peer up and extend to Jared a hand almost as filthy as the Laster kid's. His nostrils flare in annoyance, but he takes it and hauls me to my feet, none too gently.

"You scare everybody away again, True Born? What happened to Torch?"

Ignoring my taunts and question about Derek, who prefers the name "Torch," Jared wrinkles his nose and drops my hand as quickly as he can. "Rolling in the dirt again, Princess?"

"I save that for when I'm with you," I throw back teasingly. But my merc is clearly not in a teasing mood. Derek stands off to the side with Doc Raines, looking upset. "Tore a strip off him, did you?"

"Not yet I haven't. Merely grazed him."

"Go easy."

"Now wait just a minute there, Princess."

"Save it," I say, waving my dirty fingers in Jared's face. "Security is your thing, not mine. I'm not stupid enough to argue with you."

"No, but you're stupid enough to hang around Heaven Square without a proper security detail at your back." His words drip with condescension. Behind Jared, Torch blanches.

Red gathers behind my eyes. "Don't you *dare* call me stupid, Jared." I poke the hard chest before me. "*You're* supposed to be in charge of making sure I'm safe. So instead of blaming others, *do it yourself*." I turn on my heel and stomp toward Nolan Storm's waiting van, just catching a quick pang of hurt flashing across Jared's face. I've hit home and I know it.

"You forgot your little thing of dirt, Princess," he calls after me. But I won't turn around, won't dignify his behavior with a reply.

Doc Raines and Torch fall in behind me as I climb into the car.

"Brat," Jared mumbles under his breath, clearly intending for me to hear. The engine rumbles to life.

"Bully," I mumble back, just as loud. It's surely not my most mature moment, but it feels as satisfying as a kick to the shins.

Jared slows his walk as we approach Nolan Storm's meeting quarters, tucked away in one wing of his enormous penthouse suite. Here, the dimly lit hallway curves and branches off into either the game room or the meeting quarters. Still, it's narrow enough that in order to squeeze by Jared's massive frame, I'll need to get close to him. My prickling nerves don't think they're up to the task.

He places his hand on my arm, where it burns my cool skin like a coal. "Hold up a moment. We need to finish our conversation."

I pointedly look down at his hand before giving him a hard stare. To Jared's credit, he's never been cowed by my ice-princess routine, though lately this has become a bit of a problem for me. "Fine," I tell him in the crispest of tones, crossing my arms. "I'm willing to hear your apology."

Jared's indigo-blue eyes widen under his shag of curls before he tips his head back and laughs, as though I've just told him the funniest joke in Dominion. He actually scrapes a tear from the side of his face. "Ah, Princess. You sure are hilarious."

I glare back. "That's not funny."

"Ha-ha-ha! You just keep doing it!" He slaps at his thigh. "Seriously, though, did your parents ever tell you how hysterical you are? If this whole Plague thing dies down, you could bring stand-up comedy back to the masses."

I ignore the sharp jab of pain—it's a low blow to bring up my parents, and he knows it—in favor of studying the True Born who stands just inches away from me. His mouth is smiling but his eyes have gone cold and flat. *The eyes of a predator*. I'd do well to remember that this man isn't just a man. He is trained in the art of war, instincts sharpened to points as fine and deadly as his claws when he draws them. And like the massive hunting cat he shares his genetic code with, this man likes to play with his food.

My hands go to my hips and I open my mouth to give him a blast of wintry hell when Nolan Storm sails past us and into his meeting quarters. A handful of his True Borns arc in tow, notably a tall, striking woman with red hair that curls over one shoulder. She flicks her fingers at Jared, who immediately straightens up and walks into the room without so much as sparing me another look.

"Sorry, kid. This meeting's for the grown-ups," Kira tells me with a mocking trace of regret. I hide a pang of hurt as the rest of Storm's cabinet of True Borns file inside. The young man who calls himself Torch shrugs unhappily as he scoots by Kira and me.

"I'm the same age as Torch!"

"Well, now," Kira purrs. I instinctively step back as

she sidles closer. Kira looks like a runner-up in the Miss Dominion pageant. Should she ever partake in that particular competition, her talent would surely be "killing." As one of Storm's most accomplished assassins, Kira isn't someone I'd like to cross, let alone cross paths with. I've seen this slender woman drive a spiked heel through a man's throat without mussing a hair. "I can see your point," she tells me calmly as she flips back a glossy red lock. And then she drives the dagger home. "But you're not a True Born."

Ouch. I feel the sting of her words, though there's no denying it. I still don't know what I am, but I know I'm not True Born. Not even by half measures. Even if I am helping them. In the Upper Circle, "True Born" is bandied about as an insult of the harshest proportions, making my hurt over Kira pointing out that I'm not one all the more ironic. I do not truly belong here in this world. I am the outsider, the freak.

Funny how perceptions change.

2

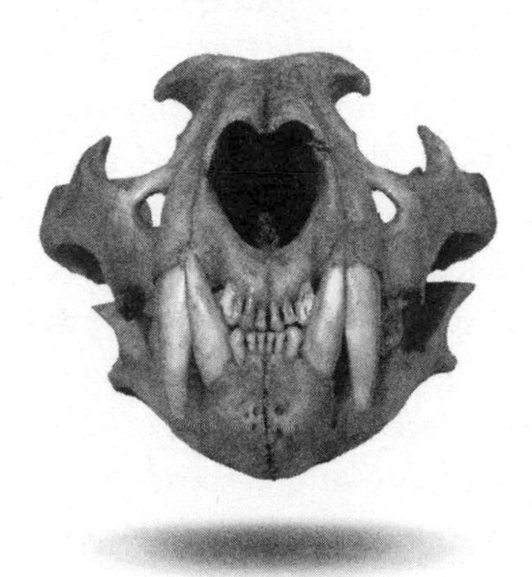

A swift, insistent hammering sounds at the bedroom door.

"Come in," I finally grouch to the insistent knocker. It isn't my bedroom—not really. But while Nolan Storm has it in his head to play my guardian, I'll not argue. I have nowhere else to run.

I've made it cozier since officially moving in after my home was destroyed. Now freshly cut grasses sit in a vase on the little table near the window, and I've placed a bright-red throw cushion on the chair across from the bed. Still, I'm not just sitting around on my once-rich thumbs, redecorating.

Coming from the elite Upper Circle, I have access to networks of power that Nolan Storm needs. And, despite the fact that my parents haven't been seen since the night our home was destroyed by magic bombs, the Fox name still carries a certain cachet. My father is chief diplomat of Dominion City and a beacon of influence across Nor-Am, though perhaps no longer serving his city. I use his reputation to help the True Borns' leader. I know how to sashay across a room and dip into the perfect curtsy before foreign dignitaries, after all. I've stood before kings and titans of industry. I've smiled and danced my way into the good graces of many. It was my duty and I did it well. My parents had drilled into me the importance of working on the behalf of the family's interests.

I'm no longer sure I believe in those interests—especially now that my family is gone. But I believe in Nolan Storm. Nolan serves the interests of the True Borns, and that's good enough for me. So now I attend these parties for him. Like a spider, I weave my web, listening for vibrations of power among Dominion's elite. I crawl through their ranks, preying on those members of high society who still feel so entitled, so safe to share their secrets with one of their own. I am small but deadly. I am relentless. I'll not stop until my questions have answers.

Where are my parents? Where is my sister?

In the hush of night, Nolan Storm squires me—or rather, I squire him—around Dominion's Upper Circle supper clubs, its dances, its balls. Together we attend gallery openings, recitals, operas, and ballets, always accompanied by the charismatic Jared Price. As I play my part, Storm plays his: always officious and kind. Gentle, too—yet I've seen him rip a body in two.

One day Dominion will bow to this leader of True Borns, though for now they try to ignore him. They can't yet ignore me. I take great delight in pushing him forward into a society that would like to shun him, despite his influence in their lives. I introduce him to the nebulous power brokers of Dominion, though to me they are as familiar as the toys of childhood. I bring him into the inner sanctum of the Upper Circle, where until now no True Born has tread.

And during the day, though tired from the night's adventures, I hunt my own mysteries. *Where are you, Margot?*

And yet, in all these months working on behalf of the True Borns, I have made no progress. No one seems to know where my parents, who I am convinced will lead me straight to Margot, have gone. And we're no closer to figuring out why Father Wes and his followers, the Watchers, are so keen to get their hands on Margot and me. In four months, I have learned nothing, I realize with disgust. I am growing restless. While I would have jumped on a boat or into a plane and hared off to Russia anyway, the homeland of Leo Resnikov, Storm manages to convince me to stay a little longer, to give our intel system time to work. *You'll find her more quickly if you know where she is, Lucy*, he's told me again and again.

He might even be right, but my patience hit its limit some time ago. I've decided to cultivate my own sources of information—which is why I now volunteer to work with Doc Raines at the Prayer Tree.

I tug at that extra sense I was born with, the thin, invisible string that tethers me to my twin. The bond I share with my sister, my lifelong companion, has remained inert since the night she left.

Wherever they've taken Margot, I reckon she's far, far away.

Storm ducks his head as he enters. He carries out his usual trick—the one where he seems to fill up all the space in the room. Around him the air crackles and blurs, especially around his head where the faint blue outline of an impressive set of antlers rises and tangles like a crown.

He's a handsome man. Handsome in a way that Jared Price could never be. Jared is a bum to this man's prince. And he's been good to me. In fact, Nolan Storm has been a better parent to me than my own, taking me in and becoming my guardian when I had nowhere to turn. Yet when I am in a room with Nolan Storm, when he looks at me with those eyes that shine like liquid metal, some part of me shivers and cowers in dread.

"You'll need some more new dresses. I'll send you out shopping with Kira." I try not to flinch as I mentally tally what I will owe Nolan Storm. I reckon I don't hide it well enough.

"We had a deal, Lucy." He says the words gently enough, though I don't miss the note of impatience.

It's not quite a Faustian bargain that I made, but it's close. I live in Storm's fortress at the top of the massive sky rise in the lap of luxury. Here I am surrounded by True Borns who will—no, *have*—protected me with their very lives. And without his *patronage*, as he's reminded me a time or two, I could no longer afford to breathe the rarified air of the social circle I was born to inhabit.

But that's just it—I don't like to be beholden to anybody. Certainly not for dresses. Nor for patronage. The Upper Circle can fall to the Plague for all I care.

I came here with my own agenda. And that agenda isn't being met.

I pull my features into the indifferent mask of the diplomat's daughter, the role I play so well, and square my shoulders at him. "I have not once complained about it."

Storm's lips curl in amusement. "Well, that would be out of character anyway."

"And what kind of character am I, exactly?"

I can tell he doesn't expect the question. His eyelashes flutter down over those exquisite, molten silver eyes. He folds his arms across his chest as he leans against the wall, regarding me for a long moment.

"I have no desire to make you do something against your will," he finally says.

"You have the wrong sister, you know," I throw back after a beat.

In the shallow light of the room, Storm's face has turned all lines and dark planes. "Do I?"

"You know you do. Margot is the one who enjoys the new dresses. I'm happier in my old school uniform."

"Funny, I didn't get that impression from her."

"Well she wasn't quite herself, was she?"

It's true. When Margot first met Storm, we'd been rescuing her from the Splicer Clinic where she was being held captive. I still don't know who was behind her capture, nor everything they did to her while she was there—save for what they stole.

Potentials. That's what the Splicer docs call the eggs they harvest for in-vitro births. And maybe that is what they stole from my sister—her potential—since she struggled so hard afterward to imagine living her life again. And then she was stolen once more.

Only this time it was a kidnapping sanctioned and abetted by our parents.

"Lucy—" Storm begins.

I cut him off. "You misunderstand me." I fold my hands in

my lap and stare at the well-groomed, overlapping fingernails. "I don't mind what we're doing. In fact, I'm enjoying it."

"Then what's troubling you?" Storm waits for my answer patiently.

But what can I tell him that he'll understand?

They say the Upper Circle live by another set of rules altogether from regular folk—and they're right. While the rabble survive on scraps and tear their houses down to cook them, Margot and I have always dined on fine china dipped in gold.

That doesn't tell the real story, of course. No one will admit it, but the Upper Circle is its own hell, a prison where everyone is watched from all sides. We Fox sisters may not have starved or watched our family sicken and die in the streets, crazed from pain as the Plague quickly ate its way through their insides, but the Upper Circle has its own brand of ugly. Children of the Upper Circle are pawns in a game much vaster than I can fathom—not even from the great height of Nolan Storm's sky-rise tower.

Splicer. Laster. True Born. They say when you know, when at your Reveal they finally tell you how your genetic code will unravel your fate, there's a vast sense of relief. Margot and I are now four months past our Reveal. There's been no relief.

We're still waiting.

We were connected as we entered this world, Margot and me. One flesh, one blood. All that's left of that time are the dark maps drawn across our toes where we once joined. Mine is brown in the shape of a blotchy lock. Margot's is long and thin with little teeth that make it look like a key. As kids we used to joke that the day before they cut us apart was the happiest day of our lives. Today, I'd mean it.

There is a great deal I still don't understand about us, my sister and me—such as why all through our childhood, our parents looked at us as though we were strangers visiting from another planet. But Margot and I have other secrets we've spent a lifetime pondering: like how whatever sensation she experiences seeps into my skin as though it is happening to me. And how is it I can practically write into a book the names of those about to be stricken by the Plague?

But those are our secrets, Margot's and mine.

Then there are the other, bigger secrets hidden away in our blood. As Doc Raines has so eloquently put it, how is it that two creatures who shared the same blood for nine months have different DNA markers in their bloodstreams?

These children will be our salvation, the preacher man, Father Wes, had told us as he captured my blood in vials and his mercs tried to murder us. *We can draw a path to the future with their blood. For blood is the answer, blood is the divine holy river, the Flood that shall deliver us.*

They say we're different. But now that she's been stolen from me, all I feel is lost.

What does a lock do without its key?

Keep its secrets.

It's on the tip of my tongue to tell Storm, *I miss my sister*, when there's another sharp rap. Kira's preternaturally beautiful face appears in the doorway.

"Serena and Carl are in the elevator," Kira says.

Storm lets out a breath and ponders me for a long

moment. "We'll continue this conversation later. Come and meet us when you're ready."

"Fine," I reply with a casual flip of my shoulders. Truth be told, I'd love to avoid this conversation as long as possible. It would be hard, if not impossible, to explain to Storm that I have simply replaced one prison for another.

By the time I've pulled myself together and found my way back to Storm's meeting room, it's near dark. Outside the floor-to-ceiling windows, small fires ring the city like twinkling beacons lighting the way to hell. The Lasters have begun their nightly ritual of setting the garbage bins on fire. All around those fires, the rabble will shove their sleepy babies into car apartments—cars stacked on parked cars—and lay down to sleep with one eye open and a prayer on their lips that they last through the night.

Serena appears like a ghost in the reflection of the glass. Her long ash-blond hair hangs down her back, a lazy river against her slender form. When I enter, she turns sightless eyes on me. Serena may be blind, but she sees me just fine.

She can clock me in a room of thousands, she says. Each one of my veins stands out to her, liquid silver to her dark sight. To her I'm as unique as a snowflake, something she's never seen before. Different even from my sister, whose faint webs of silver flow in a different direction.

"Lucy." Her face lights with a smile as I walk over to hug her. "You look well," she says.

I may want to yell and scream, but my impeccable breeding can't be ignored. "I am," I say faintly. "And you?"

Serena turns impish. “Carl and I just can’t stay away.”

“To be fair,” says the large, marmalade-furred man perched on Storm’s sofa, “the vittles here are very good.” The cat man takes a sip of something that smells like gasoline and pauses, a purr lifting his bowed lips. A messy mop of cream hair sticks up from his head like an ill-wish doll. Bullet belts crisscross over his shoulder and run down his furred chest. He looks content enough now, but he can pull a gun faster than any lifer merc I’ve ever seen.

Carl isn’t your average True Born. The Upper Circle has been hard at work making it impossible for most of them. But while True Borns with less flamboyant genetically expressed anomalies—a small fin or some gills, say—might be able to hide their differences and get by well enough, Carl is all cat. And he isn’t afraid to show it.

Splicers hire Carl and Serena to find things. Sometimes objects, sometimes people. They’ve lived so long in the Black Market they’ve forgotten how to let go of their wildness. But while Serena’s elegant beauty lends her more to being an Upper Circle queen, Carl is an alley cat. I’ve overheard Storm’s people joke that they work well together because Serena can’t see him.

Salvagers like Serena don’t mix with other True Borns, either. The salvager mutation represents the rarest form of True Born—so unique I’d thought they were just a bedtime story. Even Serena has never come across another. Like a genetically enhanced bloodhound, a salvager can sniff out True Born mutations. It’s the kind of gift that makes other True Borns nervous, knowing they can be exposed. I’d as soon have her on my side, though, if it meant she and Carl could sniff out where my sister has been taken. I’ve wished, more than once these past few weeks, that those mutations left trails like scents.

But these days, we are all after a different quarry.

"Any luck?" I nod to Carl, whose smile fades at my words.

"Sorry, kid."

Serena sighs. "The streets have gone blank."

"What does that mean?"

"It means," Carl breaks in with his gravelly voice, "all the preacher's mice have scurried away to their little hidey-holes and won't come out." He waggles his fingers.

"Where? You mean the old tunnels?"

Carl shrugs. "Could be the subways. Who knows? Maybe they've found their way in with the rats."

"Can't be," I say. "Those have been sealed off for years now." Carl's sharp look tells me I'm wrong.

Disappointment ripples through me. Father Wes has played a major hand in my current fate. If you count bringing an army of Lasters to my family home and destroying it with magic bombs, that is. I reckon he'll have yet a bigger part to play in the days to come, if my instincts ring true. It's not just my life he's made miserable, either. Serena's mother was once in the hands of this preacher man. It was she who told Father Wes a fortune-teller's tale about twin girls who would save Dominion from the Plague.

Serena's mother was never seen or heard from again.

My voice turns tight and coarse. "We have to do something."

I might have gone on if my own personal shadow didn't saunter into the room at that second, in that particularly feline way of his, and lean up against the door. I used to think Jared was a slob, casual and detached in his sandals and ripped trousers and funny T-shirts.

I know better now.

"We are doing something." His words are casual but his shoulders are tight, his eyes glittering almost to green so I know he's on edge. "We're keeping you away from him, Princess. When you do your part."

"It's the funniest thing," I throw back. "From where I'm standing it looks like you're sitting on your thumbs and throwing orders around."

Jared grins wide. "I think of it more as a casual toss."

I groan and glare at him, not completely over this morning's disagreement. "You're impossible."

"Glad you think so, Princess."

"Oh, stuff it, Price." Serena snorts. "As if any of this is Lu's fault."

"Do I really need to go through security protocols with you, too, Serena?"

Carl hisses low in his throat. "Do I really need to make you eat a fur ball, kitty?"

"Ripe coming from you."

Fur standing on end, Carl rises. He may not be very tall, but he's thick, a wall of marmalade muscle and fur. But Jared is deadly. When he uncrosses his arms, I know there will be trouble. I cross the room to stand in front of Jared. As I near, his nostrils flare and his eyes flash. I watch as he blinks, my nearness temporarily short-circuiting him. I take advantage of this and quickly push Jared into the hallway, shutting the door behind us.

"What the hell is wrong with you?"

A shine of green parades across those beautiful eyes

of his. A subtle shift crawls across his face. I become aware that my hands still press on his chest when I feel the heavy thread of his heart beneath my fingers. I start to say his name, to try to get us beyond this awkwardness, but he stretches a finger across my lips.

"Don't ruin it," he says with something darker speaking through his eyes.

"Ruin wha—"

I'm shushed when his lips brush down over mine, just light enough to electrify every square inch of my flesh. He presses his forehead to mine. Then breathes deeply, as though he's run a race, and stretches his hand lightly across my mouth. But he says nothing more. Just holds me there, as though it's the most exquisite torture. Which it is, for me. Jared has gone out of his way not to touch me, not to get too close, since the day I came to live in Storm's keep. His kiss feels like a drug I've long been denied. And whether I admit it or not, I am addicted to Jared Price.

My heart pounds a drumbeat against his chest, and my head spins with confusion. Up close I can see lines of strain around Jared's eyes. The fine lines striating his perfect, slightly parted lips. A small scar near the side of his mouth from a long-ago encounter. I can smell his skin: baked heat from the day mixed with that scent of his, cinnamon and forest.

Jared licks his lips. "You need to listen to me, Lu. For your own safety. Not because I'm telling you to. Do you get that?"

I nod, but truth be told, my brain has been taken offline. Under his fingers my mouth grows parched, my body an electrical wire. I start to say something in reply. Jared's eyes, which had gone vague and faraway, sharpen tightly on me as though I've pulled a gun.

A moment later, he spins away and disappears down the hall. My body revolts from the loss of him. I slump down the wall and wait for my legs to grow bones again.

The shadow that has eclipsed my heart has run away from me once more. I want to be angry with him. I want to chase him down the hall. I want to scream at him to never touch me like that again. I'm not the type of girl who becomes obsessed with men who ignore her, and I don't intend to start now. I used to pity those girls, Margot among them. But this feeling—the one I get every time he looks at me and touches me or says my name—it isn't rational, it isn't logical. And as much as he tries to suppress it to focus on his job, I know Jared feels it, too.

3

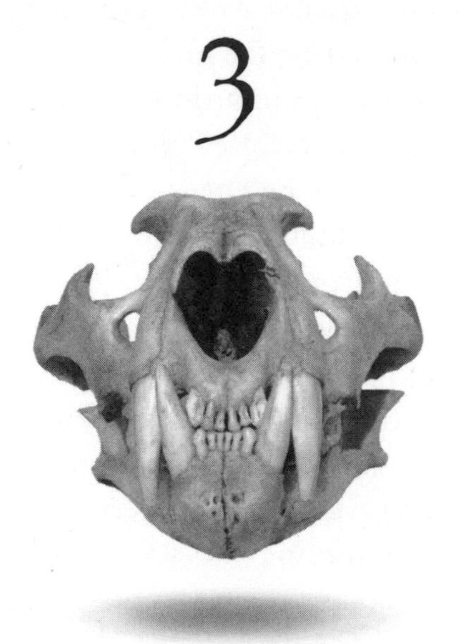

I haven't been back to my former school, Grayguard Academy, since everything happened. Haven't seen or spoken to anyone from the school in weeks. Still, I find myself crossing paths with that old life more times than I care to.

I'm making a difference, I remind myself as I stare into the beefy jowls of Colonel Deakins. I've known the colonel since I was a baby. His son, Robbie, is—*was*—one of my oldest friends. Had everything not gone as it did, I believe that my father might have eventually agreed to let Robbie court Margot, though perhaps not marry.

We're in the living room that the colonel is fond of telling people is an *exact replica* of the house in Africa his ancestors owned. An antlered deer stares moodily down at me from its perch on the wall, resting beside a stuffed and mounted zebra that tosses its decapitated head in perpetual dismay.

It reminds me so much of Mohawk that I wonder why it doesn't buck loose and go on a rampage. Here and there are long-limbed wooden figurines that look smooth as silk. Two Zulu spears cross over a shield on the far wall, just next to a tartan plaid and an oil painting of a bald, rotund man with a monocle in Victorian British fatigues. How much did it cost the Deakinses to remodel their history? Even the air smells like a British colonial house: dead animal and cigar smoke and that strange, crepe-like smell of age and the stench of unholy power.

I reckon my mother would know.

Colonel Deakins has gone all out for our visit; he's donned his black and scarlet military uniform for the occasion, the bright gold braid woven tightly around his inflated shoulders. Robbie let it slip one day that the padding is extra thick. The colonel had a bout of the Plague when we kids were still in Primary. It chewed through his shoulder and a good part of his chest before the Splicing took hold.

Beside him, perched on a gilt and zebra-hide colonial chair, is Robbie's mother. Margot and I haven't met her more than once or twice. They say the colonel likes to leave her at home as often as he can.

"Can I get you something else, dear?" she asks in a friendly enough voice. Fiona Deakins's eyes are large and blue and faraway. Her skin sits like parchment across her bones, dotted here and there with early liver spots. They say she's been ill, though they didn't say what of. Now that I'm seeing her again—and despite the bulk of her gold and cream receiving dress—I can tell it was more than bad manners that had Colonel Deakins leaving her at home.

"Thank you, Mrs. Deakins, no." I smile and indicate the

half-drunk cup of lemonade perched in my lap. “Mr. Storm should be returning in just a moment.”

I’m dangled in front of them, my good manners and better breeding on display like a rare animal in a zoo, with nothing but my bodyguard behind me. Granted, I can feel the sizzling heat of Jared’s eyes as he mercilessly sweeps the room crowded with hunting trophies.

It’s all part of the plan, of course. And the Deakinses fall headfirst into the trap.

“Your man seems a right-trained Personal.” The colonel takes the bait, nodding at Jared as though my True Born defender is both deaf and blind.

He may be as smart as cardboard when it comes to people, but the colonel can read training. Robbie’s dad spent a lifetime in the military before settling down with a wife and an important position in Dominion’s defense cabinet. Though until now I have always wondered why they bothered to spend money on armies when the real enemy is within us, ticking away our lives with all the power of a doomsday clock.

My smile widens as I indicate with a finger the man behind me. “Oh, Jared? I almost forgot he was there; he’s so quiet,” I confess in appallingly high tones. I add a giggle for good measure, just in case they aren’t getting the message. “I don’t know much about mercs,” I prevaricate. “Our father kept us away from them as much as possible.” I throw in a stern look, showing them in no uncertain terms this is the best way, the only way, to raise proper young Dominion ladies. “But these True Borns do seem rather frightening.” I shiver delicately before placing the crystal cup on a side table and grasping my elbows as if the cold has seeped into my bones.

It's not all an act. Storm had me dress for the occasion of our visit, meaning I'm wearing an evening gown with a low-cut bias and no back—and a harassed-looking servant took my wrap at the door. Dominion has been unusually cold since the last Flux storm, with more bouts of rain and even sleet than usual, especially for the spring. Save the giantess in Heaven Square, none of the remaining few trees have begun to sprout, turning the world starker.

"Oh, you dear!" exclaims Mrs. Deakins, who pops up to call in a servant. The servant casts a short look at Jared's impressive build before scurrying over to whip up the fire.

In the larger houses, there's still wood to be had for fires, though it leaves you with a mark like Cain's.

"Aren't you afraid of attracting...the wrong kind of attention?" I say the words delicately. My gloved fingers curl over my lips as though it's too much to bear. I don't call them by name, but the colonel knows exactly who I'm talking about. The Upper Circle has been in a tizzy since the insurrection at my family's gates, led by the preacher men and followed by hundreds of desperate, hungry Lasters.

Behind the colonel, Fiona Deakins tuts and shakes her head in commiseration. "Poor darling," she coos. The colonel kicks back, crossing and uncrossing his skinny legs as though he's about to tell a good story.

"Oh, those. Don't worry about *those* people." He says it as though it's a secret he's sharing. One Upper Circler to another.

I make my eyes go wide and guileless. "Why not?"

His fist bangs the armrest of his high-backed chair. "We've routed those godless bastards," he says smugly. I'm surely not the only one who catches Fiona Deakins's sidelong glance of disgust at her husband. But even I'm a bit shocked at the casual way he blasphemes the holy ones.

"George," Mrs. Deakins warns in a low voice, but I busily paper over it.

"Please, Colonel. While my parents are out of town I just don't— If you know something..." I let my voice trail off like wisps of smoke from the funeral pyres.

The colonel trains a pair of watery, triumphant eyes on me. I suddenly notice how much he has aged in the past few months since I last saw him, though if he's been heading to the Splicer Clinic, I haven't heard.

"My dear, I don't think we'll have to worry about the preachers and their ilk for a long while to come. We've issued warrants for them all. Shaking in their boots, they are, the whole miserable lot."

"Warrants," I manage to get out. "On *all* the preacher men?" I am genuinely flummoxed.

The colonel sits back in his chair and preens while Fiona busies herself with something on the mantel. So, not a popular decision in the Deakins household. Then again, Fiona Deakins wasn't born to the Upper Circle.

Fiona Deakins was born Laster.

Half an hour later, I breathe a heavy sigh and strip off my hot cotton gloves outside the Deakinses' large colonial home.

Jared taps his ear and murmurs, "Get what you needed?"

Storm's white teeth gleam in the darkness. "We make a good team." He grins easily and hands me into the black-windowed van that pulls up. Mohawk sits behind the wheel, showing us her sharp teeth and exotic hair. Today she's even added white stripes to the complicated mess of zigzagged lines shaved into her head, topped off by a swath of longish hair that sports the odd braid here and there.

I slip into the backseat, boneless and tired. It takes only moments for Jared to vent his ire.

"It was a stupid plan. Can I kill him? Please? I'll do all the dishes for a month."

"It was an acceptable risk," Storm argues reasonably, "and it worked." There's no mistaking the note of finality in Storm's voice. Then again, listening is really just not in Jared's skill set.

"It was *not* an acceptable risk," Jared growls. "Clients stay out of the line of fire. Period."

"She's not a client any longer, Jared."

"So what, we're just going to throw her to those wolves?" The growl in Jared's voice ramps up, along with my ire.

"*She* is right here," I break in, crisp as apples. It does the trick, bringing two pairs of unnatural eyes to heel. "Don't speak about me as though I'm not present. I can handle a meeting in an old friend's living room, Jared, I'm not fine china… But you know, I think you raise an excellent point," I continue in what Margot calls my boarding-school voice, turning toward Nolan. "What exactly am I to you, Mr. Storm? A pawn? A tool?" I'm getting fed up working without results. This little spider may soon bite back.

"A friend. A ward." He says it quickly, surely, with all the confidence of the lord of the jungle behind it. But of course, Nolan Storm has no natural enemies.

I hear Jared murmur from the darkness of the backseat,

"Friends don't make friends play in the Upper Circle."

I chuckle and wonder to myself whether Jared has a T-shirt with that slogan. I think about the other lord of the jungle I grew up with, the king of the Upper Circle—my father. What would he say of this particular juncture? Probably something like: *Opportunities should be snatched like the last piece of meat on a Laster's block.* I calm myself. Now is not the time to show my hand.

"Another good point," I say after a moment. "So now that we know the government is handling the preacher men, we can think about where we go next. Right?"

A hand brushing across his chin, Storm nods slowly. "You think the colonel can be trusted?"

"I think…I think he believes what he says."

"Good," Storm says, though this can be taken in a number of ways. "I think you're right."

"You think it's not true, then?"

"No." Storm turns the full force of his attention on me. I fight not to squirm in my seat like a little girl. "I think you're right that he believes what he says."

"Then you agree—"

"I didn't say that."

"I don't under—"

"He's a fairly minor player in the cabinet, Lucy. There may be people in the government plotting against the preachers, but it's sure as hell not the colonel. The right question to ask is *why?* Why go after the preachers now? It's been months since the insurrection."

Storm has a point. I sink back into the upholstery, disappointment sapping me, and meet Jared's eyes in the rearview mirror. Not hostile or mocking, as I'd anticipated.

He just looks curious, absorbed. I look away as quickly as I can.

"But why wouldn't he be telling the truth? And if it's true, then maybe we can move on to the next objective..." I don't finish my thought.

Storm knows what I'm not saying. He knows what I want. *I want my sister*. And the fact that he doesn't answer is as good as any answer. If there's anything I've learned from all these years in the Upper Circle, it's that people will rarely admit an inconvenient truth. I hear more of my father's words, raising a shiver down my back. *When they stop filling the air with bullshit, your deal is finished. Then you walk away.*

I clear my throat slowly, sitting forward until the light from nearby houses catches my face. The words are mild, but I throw a little Fox behind them. I want Nolan Storm to know that I'm serious.

"So that's how it is, is it? I reckon we've got some renegotiating to do, Mr. Storm."

It's only later, in the relative safety and darkness of my room in Storm's soaring sky-rise tower, that I realize the enormity of what I've locked myself into. I've been helping Storm with his agenda for weeks now. Somehow it didn't feel as official as it does now. *Maybe it would have been better to take my chances with the Upper Circle*, I muse before erasing the thought.

Outside my bedroom window, Dominion City looks as though it's resting in peace. The odd house still has power. A few months ago—feels like years already—the Lasters took out the power station in Dominion's north end. From my room I can see the ocean of blackness stretching out before me, the occasional high-rise cresting the darkness.

Storm's bunker perches on the top floors of a massive apartment building. The elevator still works, as do the lights, which means it's one of the premium buildings in Dominion. It also means Storm pays a pretty penny for utilities. Most of the sky creepers, as they're more affectionately called, stand empty in an emptied core. The ones that are unguarded see their furniture stolen, wood paneling and tiles stripped and pocketed for fuel and black market trades. In Dominion, you're taught at an early age to watch above you. Sometimes they punch the heavier desks through the windows, only to get stuck. We've heard stories of the unsuspecting having their heads lopped off when the heavy objects are finally blown loose during a Flux storm and hurl down from the heavens like a blast of holy Plague fire.

I'm jolted from my train of thought by a knock on my door. The knob twists before I can even say *get lost*.

"Lucy," says Jared Price, trying on a reasonable tone to start. His blond head glints as he crosses over to me, tossing a wavy lock from his eyes. He looks like an avenging angel in this light. Perfect lips and chiseled cheekbones accenting eyes that would make the gods swoon. Beautiful and deadly. And with two words, he shatters the peace: "You can't."

So, Storm has told him, then. A burst of anger grips me. "Can't what? Just what can't I do?" I ask, wrapping my voice in that same reasonable tone. It's a calm I don't really feel.

"Stop this, Lucy. While you still can."

I push at his granite chest, the huge googly eyed *O* on his ridiculous T-shirt rubbery beneath my palm. "No, *you* stop it. Who do you think you are, barging in here and telling me what I can and can't do?"

I've caught him by surprise. His eyes flare green before banking back to blue. But he doesn't touch me back. "You have a choice," he says finally, flatly.

"What choice is that?"

"You can go back. Stay with the Uppers."

I suck back breath like I've been punched. It hurts that he wants me to go back— that he would even suggest it. To go back…that would mean I would disappear from his life. *Doesn't that matter to him—don't* I*?* I know he only wants to protect me. Somehow Jared has convinced himself that I'll be safer surrounded by my own kind, the rich and suffocated ranks of the Upper Circle. Still, his careless words make my heart hurt in places I didn't know it had. I rub at my chest as if it will help and bark a laugh. "You think I can just call up one of my old pals—maybe Senator and Mary Kain, eh?" I say, and watch him flinch. He remembers full well the last time I saw Mary Kain, when I all but realized the Kains knew of my sister's kidnapping. The night Mary Kain slapped the daylight out of me. "You think I can just go on the way I have before…as a houseguest?"

I shake my head in disgust. Jared knows nothing about the Upper Circle. If he did, he'd understand that they'll never truly permit me, now a penniless refugee abandoned by her family, to cozy up in their ranks. Oh, certainly, while people are trying to decide whether my father will return, they'll be very polite to me. They'll still tell me things, because they can't help themselves. But they are all talking. Weighing my fate. Waiting.

Nolan Storm doesn't know how bad a bargain he's really made.

"You can't keep doing this," he says again stubbornly.

My back sags, the fight gone out of me for now. "How can I not?"

I can handle being the tool Storm uses in his meetings, his entrée into the glamorous and cold world of the Splicers. I can sit beside him, using my skills to uncover the information he needs. I can sell my dignity and my freedom. But only for the price of our bargain: my sister. Margot's rescue is more important than my comfort or humiliation.

Lock and key. What happens when the key goes missing? *The lock doubles the bargain.*

I can't keep this up, I'd told Storm earlier that evening, hating the way my voice had trembled as I spoke. I'd already shoved my hands behind my back so he couldn't see them shaking.

"I see," was the entirety of Storm's reply. He paced the room, his footsteps slow and measured across the white shag rug.

"Unless you help me get Margot soon, I'll—I'll go back to the Upper Circle." It was a foolish bargaining chip but one of the only I had.

Suddenly he was before me, eyes blazing. I stood there, holding my ground despite the aching desire to hide. "And what makes you think you have anything to go back to?"

Honesty is always the best bargaining position, my father had told us often enough. I nodded. "You're right. Maybe I don't. But I'm sure I could convince someone to help me look for her."

Storm considered me for a long moment. "All this—this

isn't enough?" He swept his hand out, encompassing not just the luxury of the room but maybe the dark diamond of Dominion down below.

But no, it wasn't enough. We'd made no progress. And I was out of patience.

"You know better," I chided him.

His bony crown dipped, hiding a small smile before he looked up at me, eyes lit with amusement before turning serious again. "She went willingly."

"No."

"Yes. Lucy, your sister left of her own volition. She wasn't kidnapped."

I chewed on my lip in frustration. He didn't understand. "What does that even matter? She wasn't bound and gagged, no. But was she coerced? You know she was. I'll not pretend to know what my parents are up to, Storm. But Margot is a pawn in this game, and I'll not leave her to that fate. Help me. Now. Or I walk."

"I see," he repeated thoughtfully. I crossed my arms and waited as Storm considered me. "Not many people would have the gumption to bargain with me like this," he conceded.

"I'm not most people, Mr. Storm."

And then Nolan Storm, leader of the True Borns, slowly extended his hand to me. "No, indeed you're not, Miss Fox."

It was a desperate play, I muse now as Jared watches me from under a bank of curls. I'd never go back to the false prison that makes up the world of my childhood. But Nolan Storm need never know that. Jared, though—somehow I can't hide from him.

"I need to find her, Jared. I can't be apart from her." I'm not whole without my sister at my side. Margot is my everything, my sun and my moon since the day we first drew breath. My best friend. My constant companion. My true north.

I jump a little when Jared sighs and inches closer, the gap between us disappearing until he's so close I wonder if he can smell the weight of my sadness. "I'll do whatever it takes," I croak. "You know I'm telling the truth."

He nods. He's not pleased about it, but he knows. He understands what I need to do, accepts it as an integral piece of me—another layer to my complicated being. I've never seen a man look at me the way Jared looks at me now. It's far too intimate, as though he's seen beneath my skin. I can read it there, in his moody, unhappy eyes—the distance he's putting between us is making him crazy, too. But how much longer can I live with this hot and cold?

He nods again. "Yes." His mouth catches on the word. "But now you need to understand something, Lu. I've been assigned to protect you. I take that duty more seriously than anything. It's not just your body I need to protect. And—and this could *hurt* you, Lu." His hand goes to his chest, his expression naked and raw. How could I have ever thought this man was cavalier? "How do I protect you through this?"

"Well," I reason, "if I were to go back, you'd have no means to protect me. At least this way you get to do what you must."

His smile is small and sad in return. "Are you sure you won't reconsider?"

I hold out my hand and he grabs it, the touch so shocking that for a moment I lose track of my thoughts. "You work for him," I finally tell him, "but you can help me. Help me, Jared," I plead.

I am not above pleading, groveling, begging.

He keeps hold of my hand, reeling me gently forward. With his other, he cradles the back of my head before pressing a long, lingering kiss to my forehead. I want more, I realize as he moves away. *I want more.*

But as he slips out, silent and quick as he waltzed in, I realize that isn't my only regret.

Because Jared didn't answer me, either.

4

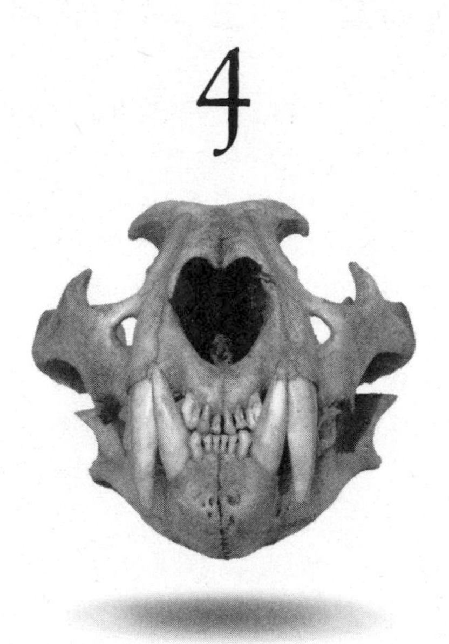

They say Splicers sometimes feel this way once a diseased limb or organ has been removed. Phantom pains, they call it. For me, that is my sister, a bright, terrible loss within me.

It used to be a living thing stretching between us. When the Protocols nurse sank her needle into Margot's flesh, the stinging pain invaded me and I reached for her hand. When she fell and scraped her knees, I bled. When they strapped her down on an examination table and plucked from her body the seeds of her future, my own guts writhed with sympathy.

There were times in our childhood that I detested that ghost flesh. When she kissed Robbie Deakins inside Grayguard's quad, I wanted to wash my mouth with bleach and hated with a passion the traitorous heat lighting up my body. Every month our cycles flowed at exactly the same moment, although my own was compounded with the aching echo of Margot's cramps.

Sometimes I wonder: Did our parents know? Did they suspect? Margot and I kept our secrets locked tight within us. But she is so far away now. And for the first time in our lives, I can't feel her. They could be doing any number of despicable things to her to get what they want. And what *do* they want?

Another question as mute and empty as Dominion's white skies.

I watch with a sigh as the streets flow past. The scavengers have been busy lining their nests with the debris of a ghost town. The rubble from the last insurgency took only a week to disappear. The bluc sneaker with the golden lighting bolt I'd seen lying on its side a few days before has gone, as has the red handkerchief that once lay on a concrete block, tumbled from the half-eaten building to the left. It may be easier to get around, now that the preachers have gone to ground, but Dominion is no easier to look at.

Storm barges into my train of thought. "There's a meeting tonight I'd like you to come to."

I don't want to talk about more parties. "What Colonel Deakins said last night," I say instead, gazing at the lifeless streets. "So it's true. They're all gone."

The moment I say it, I grasp what's been bothering me. We've been traveling to the tree at least twice a week for the past few weeks. But now there are no bodies in the streets. They're bare. Unless the Plague has diminished—unthinkable at the moment—Dominion has become a ghost town, and it has taken its ghosts to the grave.

Storm shakes his antlered head. His silver eyes regard

me with preternatural intensity, though the smile is sweet and kind.

"I think this is a tactical retreat. They're planning something. Which is why I need you to come with me tonight. We need to shake some trees."

It's not an expression I'm familiar with. People don't "shake" trees in Dominion. They tear them down for firewood. I'm unable to ask Storm what he means as we pull to a stop at Heaven Square. Mohawk, this morning's driver, jumps out and opens my door. Today she's pulled a necklace through the multiple holes in her ear, held open with weights. With her cut-off shirt and tight black crop shorts, strange against the stripy pattern of her skin, she looks like an exotic dancer from another dimension.

"Have fun, Ducky." She winks. "I'll be here, keeping an eye on you." She stabs two fingers to her eyes, then points them at me, startling a laugh out of me.

I follow Storm over to the Prayer Tree where Doc Raines looks up from a pile of wet earth. It rained last night and drizzles still.

"You've got to see this," she calls over to us with a wave.

The doctor is a throwback from another age. A tailored cream rain slick that screams Upper Circle covers up her khaki pants and crisp linen shirt, yet her frizzed curls bob everywhere. She scoops a handful of coppery corkscrews restlessly away from her face as she stares at us with sharp eyes.

"Hello, Doc." Storm stops in front of an excavation site bounded on four sides with planks of wood that the doc will pack up and take with her to keep from being stolen. Beside the hole, the doctor has set up a makeshift lab: a few beakers and vials of solution beside a field microscope.

Doc Raines rattles her curls impatiently. "Look," she says without preamble, pointing to her makeshift lab. Storm hitches up the leg of his monstrously expensive trousers and bends down beside her. We watch as she pours the contents of one beaker into another. She takes a pipette with a dirt-smudged tip and drops something into the beaker. She stirs once, twice. Something happens; the formerly clear liquid turns a cloudy red.

The doc turns to Storm with a sharp, expectant look.

"You're going to have to draw us a picture, Dorian," drawls Storm.

"I've been shipping the samples back to my lab and having the damnedest time getting a read on anything. With each sample test, the roots were inert. Like looking at rock. Which didn't make any sense, since they're *roots*. At the very least, there should be evidence of organic decomposition, if not some trace of chemicals or just—something."

The doctor grabs at Storm's hand, something I've never seen her do before. Doc Raines doesn't do touching, unless it's to heal. She turns to us with a beaker filled with clear liquid. She throws in a pipette of dirt. Even before she begins to stir it, the liquid turns stormy and red.

"I'm using a biosensor assay. In the presence of active nanoparticles, it changes color. The more active the nanoparticles, the faster and more complete the color change." She looks around, eyes lit with fear and wonder. "Do you understand what I'm saying? It's full of nanotech."

"Does it test for any particular kind of nano, Dorian?"

"The kind that targets biological agents. It must be loaded with some variation of a growth factor I've never seen before," the doctor replies with a wry smile. "My guess is, once the organic compounds begin to die, the nanotech is programmed to self-destruct, leaving no trace of its existence or the organic composition it was targeted to."

"Which is why you can't find it in your lab."

The doc nods at Storm like he's been a star pupil. "Which is why I can't find it in my lab."

I stare at the vial in her hand, the bright-red color fading as the technology kills its host. "What the hell made that?"

We stay at the Prayer Tree for hours, culling samples from different areas of the root system and the bark, and subjecting it to the same test. The results are always the same: The clear liquid turns a deep, rich red in an instant. At one point the doctor calls over Mohawk to help her jerry-rig a tent over her makeshift lab. Maybe it's the rain, zigzagging down in a wet blanket, that makes the streets so eerie. Or maybe it's that we don't see or hear a single soul. I keep half an eye out anyway, waiting for the urchins from the kid gangs to make an appearance, and especially the little girl I met the other day. I'd hoped she'd be looking for more food.

No one shows.

If it weren't for the new graffiti on the walls, now bleeding down in rich crimson streaks, and the jingling tokens newly left in the branches since our last visit to the tree, I'd have said the city was empty.

It must be ten minutes later that I catch a slight movement, quick and light as a bird, from the corner of my eye. I swivel my head, hoping to catch whatever it is, but it disappears. Feeling eyes on my back, I turn toward the tree and Doc Raines, who continues to school Storm on DNA-based nanotech. There—again. Just to my right, around the side of the building colored over with the largest set of circles.

"Just stretching my legs for a moment," I murmur to Mohawk, who busily chews on a stick with her sharp teeth.

Mohawk barely glances at me as she pulls up the collar on her trench coat. The rain has been relentless all morning, leaving us soaked. "Uh-huh."

I throw the strap of my bag over my shoulder and slowly pick my way across the rubble of the Square. Like a good merc, I scan the tops of the buildings. Nothing.

A brown head of dreadlocked hair flashes and disappears. I hurry my steps and turn the corner.

She's slinking away, her body tight against the building.

"Marta," I call softly, "wait."

The girl looks back over her shoulder, eyes wide and watchful. She's soaked through, her black wool sweater liberally dotted with gashes and holes where a dirty shirt peeks through. Her thumbs poke holes in the sleeves so that the rest of the cuffs dangle uselessly from her hands. She lifts one hand to her mouth and bites at her nail.

"Remember me?"

She doesn't say anything, but at least she's not running away. I approach slowly, cautiously, as I would a street dog. I reach into my bag and note her flinch. "No, no, just food." I pantomime biting into something. Her eyes spark with interest. "Want some?"

She nods. I come closer, the bag of food I've packed outstretched in my hand. She lunges at it and tears at the plastic, biting into the bread and meat as though it's her last meal. Little snorts of breath come from her too-thin body. "Slow down," I tell her gently. "You'll choke. Slow down, Marta. There's more here."

She chews and nods as I lean against the building and watch her.

"Not the nicest day," I say conversationally. "Do you have a warm place to stay?"

Marta doesn't answer. She hardly needs to, though. Her upstretched eyebrow says it all.

"I can't stay now. But I'll bring you more food. Tomorrow, right? Early morning. Meet me at the tree."

Marta stares back at me, her eyes dulling with the unexpected weight of food in her belly. She nods, a shy look stealing over her fine features.

"Good. Good." I throw out another apple from my bag. She raises her hands to catch it. And in another instant, I've disappeared.

The Square looks deserted. I know it's not. Cold rain drizzles down bullets, washing my face as I reach the Square. The tiny bells embroidered onto the branches of the giant tree jingle with the weight of the rain, as though the tree is alive and laughing at us all.

I look over my shoulder. The faint, creeping feeling of being watched itches my neck. I'd expected that, prepared for that. I'd made enough noise to wake the dead, after all. When I reach a wall with the scrawled red EVOLVE OR DIE, I slow to trace the letters with a finger. What would Margot think of what I'm doing? She'd not be happy. Then again, she'd probably do the same thing.

It's not that I don't trust Storm to help me get my sister, exactly. I expect he'll live up to his side of our bargain. Eventually. But there's other information I need, and the kid gangs are the only place I can think of to get it.

When I figure enough time has passed, I turn, putting my back to the hard stone behind me, and wait.

I linger for a few moments in the faint stink of death, that peculiar rot, wafting from nearby. The only thing the rain is good for is washing away the stench of the dead, unless the bodies are locked inside, as happens often enough. The tree can't be measured for growth any longer. I stare up at it anyway before kicking off the wall and heading to its trunk to make my rendezvous, and I wonder not for the first time who's behind the engineering feat of the magic bombs. Maybe it was the preacher man, Father Wes—that, at least, would explain how the Lasters got a hold of them. But something about that niggles at me.

Several months back, even before our Reveal, one of the preacher men had been arrested for sedition against Dominion. There had been rumors of technologically advanced weaponry.

When I mentioned it to our father, he'd scoffed.

"Don't believe everything you hear, girls," he'd said, eyes gleaming.

I'd asked, "What is the truth, Father?"

Our father turned his gaze first to Margot, then me, as though he wasn't sure which of us had spoken. "They don't have enough beans among them to light a match, let alone produce the destruction the Feed is talking about."

Margot said, "Why do you say that, Father?"

Our father stroked his chin thoughtfully. "Someone should really profit from their ignorance. But know this, girls. Preacher men are men of words, not action. Until they have generals behind them, real money to get their hands on some cannon fodder, they'll always be just—*phffft.*" His hands performed a vanishing trick. "Nothing but hot air."

It's a brightly tangled web in my mind. The bombs. The Splicer Clinic. The strange mutant men who tried to take Margot and me all those months ago. And then, finally, the preacher men. The preacher men who brought an army of Lasters to our door and lobbed the magic bombs. Why us? And if it wasn't them who'd made the bombs, *who was it?*

"Marta," I call. A brown head peeps up from beneath a heavy branch like a mushroom. I hold out a bag of food. "All for you," I tell her. "You just have to take me to your gang. Okay?"

Marta pops up and dashes toward my hand at full speed. Before I've even processed it, she has grabbed the bag out of my hands and set out at a dead run down the alley. "Slow down. Wait for me, Marta," I yell after her.

She's like a scared rabbit, loping ahead of me. After a block, she looks over her shoulder at me and slows but doesn't stop. I'm given the small luxury of looking at her. She's wearing some kind of short pants, ripped and frayed at the bottom, filthy sandals on her feet despite the chill, and a moth-eaten gray sweater that hangs over thin, brown-flecked hands.

It had seemed like such a good idea the afternoon before, and simple, too. Find one of the kid gangs. See if they know anything. See if they'll keep watch for the preacher men for me—for a price, of course.

Marta ignores me, hopping forward with her strange, silent, pigeon-toed gait. I'm falling behind. I reckon I should have thought through my plan a little more. "Marta," I call again as she turns a corner into an alleyway and for a moment disappears from view. I know I need to pay attention to where we are, where we're going, but somewhere in the last few turns, I've completely lost my bearings. And if I lose her, I, too, will be lost.

"Marta!" I yell. Only to see brown eyes peer impatiently at me from beneath a dirty brown strap of hair. "Stop," I say, "I can't keep up."

Something red flashes in the corner of my eye. Disappears. Marta beckons again, more insistently. A shiver works its way up my spine. Something isn't right.

I whisper, "I think someone's following us."

Marta grabs my hand and tugs me into the alleyway, then lets me go almost as quickly. It's a narrow passageway, banded on both sides with small, dark balconies, windows boarded up with cardboard under broken glass. The pavement is covered in debris: broken bedsprings, rusty nails, shards of dark and clear glass.

She disappears again.

I gape up at the windows and wait for her to reappear. A clatter breaks the silence behind me. I turn in time to see a second rock hit a dented Dumpster shoved in front of the building on the left, overflowing with refuse. I can't see who threw it. Then I see the stripe of red. Another kid, about twenty feet away. This one is a bit older than Marta, maybe fourteen. He's got the shifty look of a gang kid. But not doing that well, it seems. A gash sits below his right eye, oozing a bit of pus.

He doesn't seem to be up to much, but he is blocking the entrance to the alleyway. And I can tell from the bulges in his pockets, from the heavy weight in his hand, that he has a lot more rocks. Marta's head pops out from a balcony above. She makes an odd hook gesture to the boy with a finger and thumb. He nods, then holds his rocks steady as a sinking feeling rips through my belly.

It's a setup.

5

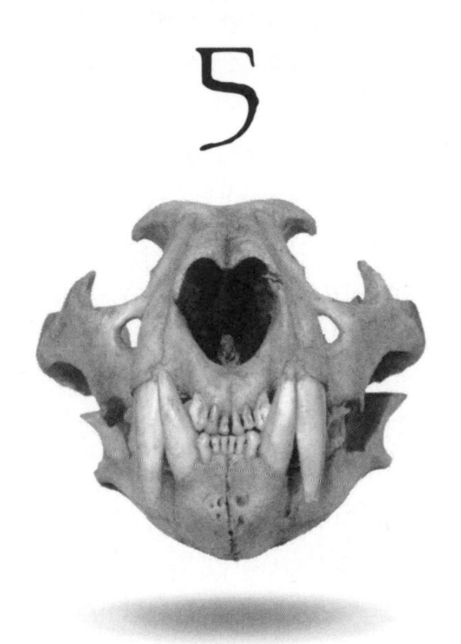

I stand there, stupid as the day I was born, and think through my options. I hadn't brought the phone that would connect me with Storm's keep. The last time I used it, I figured out it had a tracking device in it—absolutely the last thing I wanted for today's adventure. Only, getting myself gutted isn't exactly the other option I'd been hoping for.

"What do you want?" I say to the boy. "I haven't any money."

He tilts his head like he can't quite figure out what I'm doing. Maybe he can't hear? I sign a few words, but although he stares avidly at my hands, I can tell there's no comprehension.

"Don't bother," a twangy voice calls from above.

"I haven't any money," I repeat. The man who owns the voice leans casually over the balcony railing. He's got a shock of dark hair, striped white-blond like a dirty skunk. A green button-up opens down his chest. A smattering of chest hair. Beyond his shoulder bobs Marta's fuzzy locks. "Only five Dominion dollars."

"I know that." Even before I see his long grin, a mouth full of metal and rotted teeth, I know I'm in trouble. He pulls a crisp fiver taut between his hands.

"What do you want, then?"

The man nods to the boy behind me. I turn, wanting to keep an eye on him. But when I pivot my body around, I count four boys. Three of them look better fed than Rock Boy. I look back up to the balcony, but Skunk Man is gone.

The boys behind me spread out, their arms outstretched to form a net. They don't say anything more. A raindrop plops down on my face. It occurs to me, a little absurdly, that for a little while the rain had stopped. The drizzle changes to mist, making it hard to tell what the boys in front of me are doing. My heart hammers in my chest as my teeth start to chatter, a combination of terror and chill.

And then Skunk Man is standing before me on the broken asphalt. Marta cowers behind him like a dirty rag doll.

"What do you want me for, then? Since you've clearly already picked my pockets." I nod at Marta and pretend as best I can that I'm not afraid. My hair clings to my neck and face, but I take a small pleasure in seeing how unhappy the skunk man looks in the rain, his striped hair wilting around his face.

Skunk Man shrugs and looks me up and down like I'm a head of lettuce in a market stall. "Marta here is my apprentice, not some common thief. Thieves are thick in Dominion. Information is better. And interesting Splicers who hang about in Heaven Square are even better."

A chill works its way down my spine. I might be okay if he doesn't yet know who I am. Those hopes are dashed a second later.

He sucks his teeth. "You're that True Born's girl. People'd pay a lot of money for his girl."

They've been watching us, then. My chin goes up. "He'll rip you to shreds with his bare hands."

As though it's a signal, one of the boys, a thick, beefy boy in overalls, pulls out a length of painted black chain. Out of another pocket he pulls a rusty combination lock. He comes forward at Skunk Man's beckoning.

They're going to lock me up, it suddenly occurs to me. "Y-You don't want to do this," I stutter.

"Checkers," says Skunk Man to the beefy one. "Don't hurt her too badly. Just make her shut up."

The rain comes tumbling down from the sky, fat drops slapping like hands on my face. I stare at the beefy boy and wonder what making me shut up will feel like. I close my eyes as he comes toward me with outstretched hands. A thick crack rents the air like thunder. I open my eyes. Thick red ribbons of blood blossom from the beefy boy's chest. His face goes slack as he crumples to the ground.

The other boys seem as confused as I am. For a moment they look around, especially the lanky boy with the rocks. But then he hurls one. A bullet flies into the rock and it skips sideways, knocking into Marta. She falls, too, a streak of red oozing from her temple.

They scatter, leaving behind Marta and the lump of beefy boy at my feet, blood oozing onto the cracked pavement beneath him.

It takes me a moment longer to spot the gunman. He

wears a hat. The brim shadows his face so all I can see are wide, curving lips.

"Don't move," he calls out to me gaily. "I'll be right down."

He grabs at a cable attached to an old power pole and shimmies down, an automatic rifle strapped over his chest. I look about. There are no doors, only boarded-up windows and balconies too high to jump. A dead boy at my feet. And Marta, little Marta, crumpled and lifeless. There's a choice here. I can wait for the gunman. Or I can run out the alley, knowing the likelihood that I'll end up right back in the hands of the kid gang.

As I consider my options, the gunman looks up, and I get a glimpse of a handsome set of features. "I won't hurt you," he says in a wounded tone, as though he knows I was about to choose being a hostage over him.

"How do I know that?" I reckon my voice shakes as badly as my knees.

"You don't." He hits the ground with a *thud* and strides toward me with a strange loping gait. With one hand, he casually tosses up and catches what looks like a small reddish stone. "I'm a shade safer than a kid gang, mind." He looms over me, a tall, slender figure, though his shoulders are broader than I'd realized.

I choke out, "Who are you, then?"

"You can call me Alastair."

"What can other people call you?" I say, then kick myself mentally. Why am I being such a smart-mouth? This boy can kill me.

He regards me for a moment. When he tips his head back, I can see his eyes, a luminous brown flecked with green.

"You're a funny one, aren't you?"

"Some people think so."

The stone goes up in the air again, lands in the young man's palm as though magnetically drawn. Goes up again. "Is that what you're doing here? Making Fitz and his kids laugh?"

"I hadn't been properly introduced to him, either, so no."

"Touché. So what is your name, then, little girl?" His smile lengthens, a thin piece of rope.

"Are you always so rude?"

"Are you always so touchy?"

We stare at each other. His hands have gone to his hips. So have mine, I realize. *But he's the one with the gun strapped to his chest*, I remind myself.

"You can call me Lucy," I tell him grudgingly.

"Okay, Lucy." He eyes me like a salvager. "So what's a pretty Upper Circle girl like you doing in a dirty back alley like this?"

The puddle of Beefy Boy's blood has grown. The red fan is almost to my feet. "I wasn't being smart, I guess. I thought she'd help me," I grumble under my breath.

"That little ragabond? Help you what—become a slave?"

I don't know why I decide to tell the gunman the truth—maybe I'm in shock. "I need information, okay? I thought she'd be in a position to help me find it."

The gunman cocks his head and looks at me from beneath the dripping brim of his hat. He snorts. "She was in the perfect position to help herself. None too smart, you Upper Circle girls."

I decide to overlook the insult, since I'm not in much of a position to argue. "Well, then. Thank you for your assistance."

I don't meet his eyes. "I suppose I should be getting back. Can you point me in the direction of Heaven Square?" I cast about for the top of the tree, but all I can see are crumbling, ruined buildings.

A long silence falls between us as my champion looks me up and down. Then, "You look like a drowned rat." Alastair's eyes gleam like dark, polished wood. "You know, I just might be able to save you twice today," he says with a sly grin.

It's a long, wet walk back to Heaven Square—much longer than it had seemed when I'd been following Marta. Shoes drenched, my feet squish with each step. And I can't get away from the smell of wet wool.

I feel strangely inclined to trust Alastair, though that knowledge comes as little solace, given that I'd had no problem following Marta, either. Regardless, I need his direction, so I stay vigilant and allow him to lead me through the city.

"How much farther?" I inquire politely of my guide.

"Why, you bored of me already?" Alastair tosses back, casual as you please. I haven't a clue what to make of the strange young man who'd killed a boy to save me, so I decide to fish.

"Where are you from?"

"Around. Not from your block."

"You don't say," I tease back. "Talkative lot, your people?"

The young man scratches at his jaw. "Extremely." Then a beat later, "So Lucy, what information could a nice, rich girl like you be trying to dig up from a rotten kid gang?"

I give my rescuer a sidelong glance. "What would a

chivalrous young man like you need with a semi-automatic?" I ask, poking fun at his heroic escapades in a way that I'm surprised to note doesn't make me nervous.

It earns me a laugh. "I asked you first. And anyway, how do you know about weapons?"

"I'm a nice, rich girl from the Upper Circle, aren't I? You've got me pegged to rights. What do you think all us rich girls learn from our Personals?"

Alastair hitches his gun up on his chest. "And here I thought you were all busy studying dancing and knitting and such."

"You've a pretty poor opinion of us, don't you?"

He looks over at me, something strangely truthful in his eyes. "Not all of you." Alastair stops. The rain falls down like tiny hammers, cold and sharp on the skin. "We're almost there. So...are you going to let me help you?"

I shake my head. "I'm not sure what you're suggesting. Or why. Why would you?" I narrow my eyes suspiciously.

"Pretty tough for an Upper Circle girl," he says after a long minute, not looking at me. "I can't think of another one who would be brave enough, or silly enough, to seek out a kid gang." There's an insult in there, but I also hear a faint note of admiration in his voice. Still, that doesn't answer the basic question. What does he want from me?

He must read my silence as refusal. Face raised to the sky, Alastair pushes his hat back before giving me an annoyed look. "You need information, right?"

"I told you I do."

"It just so happens I'm having a sale on information." He grins, so much like a mischievous little boy that I can't help but laugh.

"So you're in it for the money, fine. But—how do I know I can trust you?" I put a hand to my hip and regard the stranger before me. Money, at least, is a motive I can understand. Money is power, both in the Upper Circle and on the streets of Old Dominion.

"How do you know you can't? I like to gamble, Miss Lucy. Do you?" Alastair stops to toss his little rock. "Besides," he continues, squinting at me. "I can't be worse than a kid gang, can I?"

He has a point there.

The reception line winds slowly around and down the elegant stone stairs of the mansion. I sneeze once, twice. Storm murmurs, "Are you coming down with something, Lucy?"

Surely being soaked in the freezing rain will leave its mark on me. I'll be far more marked, though, if Storm finds out I snuck out of his place. And even more marked should he discover I plan to do it again. "No, I'm fine." I sniffle.

"Glad to hear it. This will be our last outing for a few days. You'll have a chance to catch up on your rest."

I nod and smile vaguely at my guardian, sweeping my eyes over the understated opulence of Senator Josiah Gillis's home. This senator is a different breed than I'm used to. I'd crossed his path many times in my former life, of course. He was at our Reveal, Margot's and mine. He might have even been driving the car that mowed down a dozen or more Lasters at our gates as people panicked and spread like wildfire.

It's more than his opulent home that draws attention.

Gillis is huge—a towering man with the physique of a merc. Against his silver-black skin, the white of his tux gleams. He's clean-shaven, immaculate, his close-cropped hair kept military style. Unlike many of our father's other cronies, when Gillis looks around a room, you believe he really sees what's happening.

Two guests ahead of me in the reception line, Gillis engulfs the Asia Minor ambassador's hand within both his own. He adds a sharp military bow, shoes coming together with a *clack*, then crosses one arm behind his back and the other against his belly as he greets her with a few words in her language.

It has been more than two hundred years now since the various countries of the world were rolled up into continent-wide nation-states. At Grayguard they teach us that the continental blocks helped countries large and small deal with the creeping droughts and Flux storms that had flattened the world economy. Here in Nor-Am, for instance, there were once hundreds of vibrant cities across the continent. That all changed when the storms grew more frequent, more powerful, sweeping away the farmers' fields and, in some cases, leveling cities. My father always laughed at these history lessons, telling us girls to instead think like Foxes.

"Cause and effect is more complicated than a fairy tale. The harvest moved north," he boomed, "and when it did, the Upper Circle was ready to lead."

What our father meant was that Dominion was settled with an iron fist. They like to pretend differently now, but everyone knows that the powerful brought armies from the south of current-day Dominion. They expanded their empire, settling Nor-Am and its capital city through bloodshed—forging alliances along the way. All the country blocks owe their existence to Nor-Am and Dominion, the new world order's first and most powerful capital.

I eye the Asia Minor ambassador again. She's slender, with the dark-brown eyes and sweeping black hair common to her people. Asia Minor is now headed by a small country state whose name once meant "the land of the rising sun." I've heard the sun rarely rises there now, though. And while the chief diplomat for Asia Minor may be one of the most important visitors to our city, she's still just a pawn to those who rule Dominion's Upper Circle.

I mentally scroll through my facts on Senator Gillis: No one has ever mentioned military background, though it's clearly there in every nuance of his bearing. He's always glided below our father's radar, this one. Even his wife, a lovely and statuesque woman of mixed descent, has escaped our mother's claws. Marigold—that's her name—kept out of the spotlight and therefore out of trouble.

Tonight, the senator's wife shines. Her long dress, with its Grecian cut and folds, is printed with long dark-blue flowers. She's pinned one to her ear, holding her cascading curls at bay, the blue of her dress and the dusky hue of her skin accentuating the startling blue of her eyes. She doesn't look at her husband, but after a lifetime of speaking a silent language with Margot, I can read their cues. She gives the tiniest flick of her slender hand, tilts her chin, and Gillis is there to pull that guest forward. They're a team, these two.

When it's finally my turn, I grace them with my most respectful curtsy, head lowered to just the right degree.

"Senator Gillis, Mrs. Gillis. It's such a pleasure to be here this evening."

I don't think I imagine the frost in their eyes, and I reckon I can't blame them. Antonia and Lukas Fox likely represent everything these people detest: a plague of corruption they'd as soon tear down Dominion to get rid of than live with. And then, of course, there's the fact that I've brought a True Born as escort.

It's the senator's wife who greets me first. "It's Lucy, isn't it?" She tilts her head and stares at me quizzically, as if memorizing the uniqueness of my features. I'll admit, she's as good at this as any diplomat's daughter.

"Good guess." I laugh, crinkling my nose up in mock delight.

"I had heard your sister is on an extended vacation with your parents, so it was an easy game for me," she confesses. "And of course, I am in charge of the guest list." She smiles her welcome. There's that small flick of her wrist, and I'm passed on to her husband.

"And may I present Mr. Nolan Storm?" I indicate the hulking man at my side with a flourish of my hand. "Mr. Storm has been appointed my guardian while my parents seek their health."

Senator Gillis's eyes sharpen. "Mr. Storm." He greets Storm with the same two-handed shake, but he doesn't let go right away. "Your name has been coming up with increasing regularity," the senator says.

No subtlety with these two.

"I hope with complimentary and rosy tones," Storm replies. He shoots them both a charming smile that shows off his dimple.

The senator doesn't budge. "Some men's compliments are another man's complaint," he says thoughtfully. "Although I look forward to hearing your views on where Dominion should put its attention. I understand that the majority of the city's current contracts are your own."

"That's true, sir, and I look forward to sharing my plans with you." Storm steers me clear of the reception line and into a series of receiving rooms that ends in a giant ballroom. It isn't me Storm speaks to next. It could be any number of the True Borns on the other end of his ear bud, feeding Storm the intel he's looking for. Still, somehow I know it is Jared who's signed up for this assignment. He's been mysteriously absent for most of the day. "What have you got from all that?" My escort pauses, looks around with a sweep that speaks of years of ingrained intelligence work.

It's a sophisticated setup, subtle but effective. White light bounces into the room from an outside bulb. Discreet cameras rove at almost every cornice in the massive, airy room. Most don't bother with machine-based surveillance any longer, since there are men's lives to be had for cheaper. Then there are the Personals, security operatives everywhere murmuring to themselves, dressed in dark-blue tailored suits with telltale bulges. Not your ordinary mercs, I reckon, but true military.

Just where does Josiah Gillis get his backing?

"What do you make of all this?" my curiosity drives me to ask as I smile at an elegant couple nearby.

Storm stops a waiter bearing champagne flutes and hands one over to me. He takes the other, which I know he won't bother to finish. In his large grip it looks like a skinny toothpick. "What do you know about Senator Gillis?"

I sip delicately. A blush of bubbles and the faint aroma of flowers waft from the stemware. Real, then. None of that synth stuff for the newly crowned prince of the Upper Circle.

"He's got good taste in champagne," I offer Storm with a mock toast. When his flat silver eyes rake over me, I sigh and add, "Not much. He stayed out of our father's way… which means he's smart. Judging by this, though—" I look up from my drink to gaze around the opulent ballroom filled with the Upper Circle's most powerful players. "He seems to have done well in my father's absence."

The more I think of it, the odder I find it. Senator Gillis should have been a threat to Lukas Fox. Anything that our dear father can't control is something to be destroyed.

I blink up at Storm. "Do you reckon they're working together?" It's the only thing that makes sense. Our father must have had Gillis on the backdoor payroll. Maybe still does.

Storm's eyes glitter at me as he sets down his flute and takes my hand. "Good question. Let's go find out."

When I have danced with Colonel Deakins, a fat-cat banker named Hollister, and one of the lesser senators—with breath like the dead—Storm pulls me back into his orbit.

Since I went through this hell for him, I don't feel the least bit guilty as I wipe a greasy sweat trail the senator has left on my hands all over Storm's beautifully cut tux. He pulls me in for a dance.

"Well?" he murmurs into my ear.

"If you ever make me dance with him again," I say, indicating the stinky senator La Roche with a discreet dip of my head, "I will throw myself under a bus."

Storm chuckles. "Well, I don't think we'll need to worry about him much. Nielson just told me that the senator is about to be bounced for a financial indiscretion."

I pull back to stare at Storm. "You mean the mistress he's been keeping on House funds? Everyone's known about that for a decade at least."

Storm turns thoughtful. "Could Gillis be the real thing, then? They're calling him 'the Incorruptible.'"

I eye the decadent room meaningfully. "Is anything connected to the Upper Circle incorruptible?" I'm startled as the words leave my mouth. It feels like an oddly traitorous thing to say. After all, I was born and raised in this Circle. Half the people in the ballroom have been to my former home. All of them know my family.

Storm murmurs close to my ear, "You might have a point." He sweeps me across the dance floor masterfully. Couples turn to admire him. But I can't relax. A burning, prickling sensation picks at my back. Someone is watching me.

"Is Jared here?" I ask. But Storm doesn't have time to answer. One of Senator Gillis's aides silently walks up and taps Storm's elbow.

"Sir, a meeting is just now getting under way that you will want to attend. Please follow me."

Storm threads me through the audience of dancers and political pollywogs to a door set in paneled wood. The Personals swing their heads subtly as the cameras sway to catch our every movement.

We're ushered into a room at the back of the mansion, hushed and quiet and entirely paneled in dark wood squares, right up to the fifteen-foot carved plaster ceilings. Over these squares hang oil paintings of what I presume were once powerful men.

"Mr. Storm." Obscured behind the light of a glass-shaded desk lamp, Senator Gillis stands and gestures to a set of chairs ringing his desk. "Miss Fox," he adds as an afterthought, "please." One of the chairs holds the lumpy olive-uniformed shoulder of Colonel Deakins, who smiles sweetly at me.

Sitting in the chair opposite is a stranger to me. Wire-rim glasses pick up the light and obscure his eyes. He wears a fine suit, teal kerchief folded with precision into his lapel pocket. Bloodless, thin lips in a face drawn thin with pain, the bald sheen of someone who has recently been through hell and back and lived to tell the tale.

A Splicer, then. And recently, too.

Senator Gillis wants Storm to sit, but my escort insists I take the chair on the right. Storm perches solicitously behind me, one hand gently pressing into my shoulder. I get the message, but I'm not too big to admit I'm scared to Sunday. Whatever the purpose of this little meeting, I presume it will come at a price.

"Mr. Storm," Gillis begins. "The colonel here was just telling us that you and Miss Fox recently paid him a house call." *Ah, so that's what this is about.*

"Yes. Miss Fox and I are fortunate in our circle of friends," counters Storm breezily. The colonel blushes slightly and sits up straighter in his seat, the cigar in his hand all but forgotten. "How are you, Colonel?" Storm inclines his head ever so slightly, the fine cobweb of his antlers catching the light.

"Fine, fine," says the colonel, coughing into his hands.

Fox and henhouse, I think to myself, remembering the game Margot and I used to play. In the art and war of diplomacy, there are only two kinds of people: those who are eaten and those who don't go to bed hungry.

"I don't believe you know Senator Theodore Nash." The senator indicates the sweating man, who takes out his handkerchief and mops his forehead before folding it back into his pocket with elaborate care.

"I don't believe we've had the pleasure." The man smiles at Storm. His teeth are even and white, but there's still no mistaking the slight lilt to his words, the tinge to his teeth that marks all those outside Dominion's limits, no matter how carefully you dress it up.

"You're the new senator for the territories." It slips out before I realize what I've done. Stuck, I go on. "We've heard about your recent…victory…" I bite my lip and blush. "Over the NewsFeed, of course."

They say the territories are more of a wasteland than Dominion itself. With so few people to sustain the farmlands that keep the remainder of the city's populations fed, they've resorted to shipping lifers from the penitentiaries out into the fields. They barter for rum and a few less years on the line, and when their time is up, some of them even stay to make up their own merc franchises, take over lands where the family lines have bled to dust and bone. In the Upper Circle, these merc men of the territories are whispered of behind hands, accompanied by shivers of dread.

Our father used to say they were the problem Dominion

was going to have to stand against at some point—and the king of the territories would be key to it all. But even our father would have been shocked at the election victory proclaimed for Senator Nash a scant month ago. The NewsFeed hinted it was an unexpected landslide, when a third-rate senator no one had ever heard of came from behind to obliterate the competition…

No—our father likely would have thought the man a genius.

Rather than being offended at my social gaffe, the sweating Senator Nash gives me a great big NewsFeed smile. "Oh, you follow politics, do you?" he says politely. "How nice." The rest of us exchange an uncomfortable look.

He doesn't know who I am.

It's a first for me, the daughter of Dominion's unspoken king. I pick a spot behind his shoulder and smile. I would have been content to leave it there, but it's Gillis who won't let it die.

"Plague take you, man." Senator Gillis slashes at a paper on his desk. "Do they not have NewsFeeds in the patty fields?"

Nash dabs at his forehead and sits up a little straighter. His smile tightens like a vise. Gillis leans over the desk with a meaningful look. "Perhaps you've been so busy with your campaigning you haven't had a chance to meet some of our first families," the senator says with meaning. "Miss Lucy Fox is the daughter of one of Dominion's brightest stars."

The card has been played. I have no choice but to lay it down. "Perhaps you've heard of my father, Senator Nash. He works closely with the government. The Honorable Lukas Fox?"

The color drains from Nash's already pale face until I

think he's fainted dead-gone. I file this away for later: clearly our father has made an impression in the territories, too. Storm presses a finger down on my shoulder. He's paying attention, too.

"Now that we've gotten that out of the way, perhaps you can tell Senator Nash about your bid for the city's security contracts."

"I would be happy to, Senator Gillis, but perhaps another time? Forgive me, gentlemen," Storm breaks in. "It's getting late and I'd like to have Lucy home before the rats come out."

Nash stammers and wipes his head like it has been filled with a sudden, stabbing pain. I know the feeling. I'm tired, and we've gotten absolutely nowhere, and I'm wondering what the point was for this little meeting. I squeeze the hand on my shoulder briefly.

"Colonel," I say, addressing Robbie's father. He's almost as uncomfortable as Nash at this point "The other day you mentioned that you'd routed those bastards who burned down my home." I throw in a growl, making it clear where my loyalties lie. "I can— I mean, I trust that they won't be able to come back. Will they?" I give Colonel Deakins a wide-eyed look through strands of my hair, every inch of me praying that I'm a good enough actress to pull this off.

"Oh, sure, sure." The Colonel paws at the air and relaxes. "But Senator Gillis can speak more to that."

The good senator looks like he'd rather chew glass than admit anything to me. He rubs his ear as if he could rub out those last words. "Yes, the colonel is quite right. We believe that the preachers and a few of their more militant followers are contained. We'll make sure they stay that way."

The colonel clicks his tongue in approval. "Too right—and once we've routed the preachers, the rest of the population won't be so inclined to believe all that superstitious nonsense."

I wonder if the senator buys it when I force my eyes even wider, even more vapid. "But how? Surely there are too many to throw in the jails. And you wouldn't ship them out as lifers, would you?"

But it is the colonel who steps in this pile of bones. "Not at all." He chuckles, as though incarcerating thousands is a joke. "We won't need to throw them in jail. Just bury 'em, I say. Then we won't need True Borns— *Ahem*," he ends delicately. He thinks he's being coy, but by the way his eyes tilt toward the senator, it's clear Colonel Deakins expects a pat on the back for his rudeness.

I nearly choke on my tongue but am able to keep my face composed, and I studiously avoid looking over at Storm. "Oh, I see," I murmur, standing. "Thank you."

I wait for Storm to say his good-byes and let him lead me away. My gorge rises, and I fear I'll be sick before I'm out of the room. But it's not until I'm in the ballroom surrounded by a crowd of sequined and silked ladies, twirling around the perimeter on the arms of tuxedoed men, that the true horror hits me.

I grab at Storm's arm. "Wait. Did you…?" I begin.

But what do I really want to ask? Did the colonel just admit he and other factions of the government are against True Borns? *Did you know the government is planning on murdering a large portion of its remaining population? Are you in support of this? Will you stop it?*

I shake my head, as much to clear the seesaw of my thoughts as to think carefully about what I want to say next.

As usual, Storm is one step ahead of me. He sweeps me into a dance. Jaw rigid, his breath tickles my ear. "The answer is no. It's the reason we're here tonight." He turns me gracefully and I sink into the half curtsy the dance requires before I'm swept up again. "I thought we were going to have to abort. But you were marvelous."

I wasn't sure whether I was playing the part too well or not at all. This is the part of our bargain that troubles me, the odd blurring of lines between my old life and some fictional character I become for Storm. Which one is even real?

Storm smiles, but it doesn't reach his wintry eyes. The luminescent lines crackling around his head grow solid as flesh.

"What are you going to do?" I whisper.

Storm has the hearing of a forest god. He looks down at me, something gentling in his expression. His hands tighten around mine reassuringly. "Lucy, I won't let anything happen to you. You know that."

"That's not what I'm worried about. That's the *last* thing I'm worried about."

He considers me again for a long moment. We're barely swaying there on the floor. Then suddenly he swings me out before curling me back onto his rock-hard chest. I can feel eyes gathering to us. Not that we don't stand out anyhow. Nolan Storm has all the presence of a hurricane.

"You're not going to tell me, are you?"

"Not here," he murmurs with a charming, dimpled smile. I tamp down on my urge to stomp my foot and yell at him. Because he's right. This isn't the time or place. Not in this pit of Upper Circle vipers and vixens.

The dance ends and the floor erupts with polite applause. I turn to head off the floor when the sight of Jared arrests me. He watches us, still as a sculpture. Hands crossed at his waist, his back lines straight against a wall. He's decked out as a rich man's Personal in a perfectly cut black suit paired with a crisp white shirt, just a degree shy from a proper tux. Pale-pale face. Serious, so serious. The only life in his face throbs through his eyes.

I can't take my eyes off him.

For reasons I can't begin to fathom, I surge forward through the crowd, stepping past the broad shoulders of elegant men and their high-heeled ladies. My eyes stay riveted on Jared's handsome form, the flip of a blond lock on his forehead. Jared's awareness, the still attention of a hunting cat, remains trained on me. Maybe twenty feet away, I brush past a particularly large man only to be knocked by a waiter bearing a tray of drinks in cut crystal cups. The cups rattle against my bare arm. When I look up again, Jared hasn't moved but he looks ready to spring. His eyes brush back over me, making sure I'm all right.

I take another step or two, my skirt pulled behind me in the crush of bodies. "Jared," I call.

It's all I have time to murmur before I'm hit with a stab of panic so thick it chokes me. It lances through my head, my eyes burning hot with pain. My stomach drops as though I've been sucker punched. Something claws at my wrists. I drag my eyes away from Jared, who has lost the facade of a disinterested merc.

I hold up my wrists. Twin impressions of crescent moons appear on the delicate white skin, livid red and bloody.

"Margot," I breathe. Whatever hell my sister has been holding back from me tumbles through me like a broken dam.

And as I rush headlong into darkness, doing all I can to stifle a scream until I am out of earshot of the other revelers, I imagine I hear Jared calling my name. I sink into unconsciousness.

6

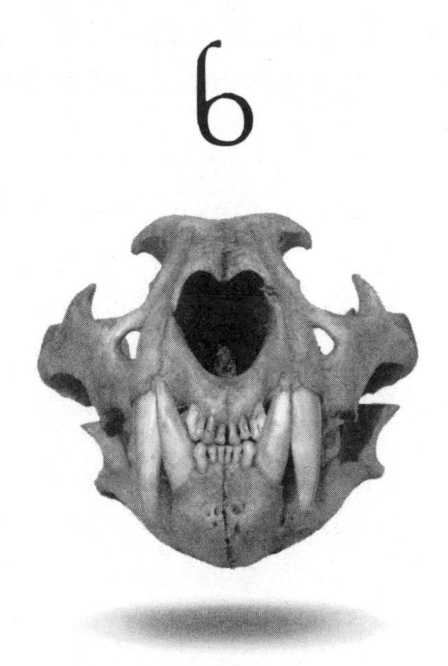

The voices arguing on either side of my bed don't help the splitting headache that threatens to pull me apart, stitch by perfect stitch.

"Calm down, Jared," Storm quietly warns. "She's fine."

"She's *not* fine. You need to cancel whatever the hell you're planning. Something's wrong."

"You're being dramatic."

"I *smell* it on her."

"She's tired. She'll be fine."

"You're not listening."

I crack open an eye. My attention snags on the giant watercolor opposite the window—huge red flowers, bright like fresh blood—and then watch as the magnificently untidy True Born above me grabs the bridge of his nose in frustration. It must hurt. The bones of his face have lengthened again, a sure sign he's feeling protective.

"I'm listening," I croak, deciding to sit up and take part in this interesting turn of conversation. "How do I smell again?" I sniff.

Storm smiles. "Good, you're up," he says, as though I've just had a nap instead of a strange narcoleptic fit brought on by…

"Margot." I almost yell the word as I try to pull off the sheets tangling me.

"Whoa. Hold on there." Storms blocks my path. "Where do you think you're going?"

I take one short breath and look the leader of the True Borns square in the eye. "We have a deal, Mr. Storm. You made me a promise. Your turn."

Storm crosses his arms and nods with gravity. "Yes, we do, Lucy. But you need to slow down and talk to me."

I take a moment to watch the window glass streak with rain. She's still there. Margot is a shadow self within me, an echo in my bones. With a squeak, I tell Jared and Storm about feeling my twin short-circuit me. And when I'm finished, when my so-called guardian doesn't seem any more ready to spring into action than before, I feel I have no choice but to push the point home.

"Well?" My voice rises in frustration. "When do we leave?"

Storm looks out the window. The crackling veins of energy pulse back a weak light. Somehow, when he glances at me, I know I've lost this round.

"Do you know where she is?" he finally asks.

"No, but I know we can find her."

"You said it felt like Margot was panicked about something. Overwhelmed. But no sensations of physical harm? Did you think she was hurt?"

I shake my head. "Not exactly, but my wrists..." I hold up the flesh of my wrists, swollen and red, as proof.

He leans in closer. "Can you tell who is with her?"

A stab of betrayal curls through me. "You know I can't do that," I say weakly. "That's not how it works."

His glance is so pity-filled I'd as soon he slapped me. "Lucinda," he says. Too soft. Like I'm a kitten he's kicked.

I slowly slide from the bed and walk over to the window. The rain calls to me, as wild and furious as I feel. I place my hand on the cool glass. It fogs up immediately from my touch, leaving an extra hand behind. The same size and shape as Margot's.

Storm comes to stand behind me. "Those idiot senators are going to try to pen the preachers. They haven't got a clue what they're dealing with. And if they continue on this path, there will be an all-out civil war. Which is bad for my plans. Worse for my people. In fact, it will be worse for everyone in Dominion."

Of course Storm is the True Borns' defender. So who defends Margot and me? *You do*, a small voice chimes in. *You're all she's got.*

I pull my fingers slowly from the glass, remember seeing Margot's hands pressed against our bedroom window, just so, so many months before. The last time I saw her. I shiver, but not from the cold.

"Our father always told us war was good for business and politicians. Shakes things up," I say, turning. "Turns bad situations into opportunities."

Across the room, on the other side of the bed, Jared slouches against the wall. Mouth drawn into a tight line, his already prominent cheekbones stand out sharply. His white dress shirt has come partway undone, I note with interest, revealing a spectacular expanse of hard, rippling muscle. He watches me from under a shag of blond bangs with an inscrutable expression.

"Did you ever have any intention of helping me get to Margot?" The question is for Storm, though I continue to look at Jared, who frowns.

Storm replies without hesitation. "Yes. And I still do." And though it's good to hear, I know he's not finished. "But Lucy," he says gently, "there are things that need to happen before I can commit resources to that."

"You're waiting for things to calm down?" I venture. "Here? In Dominion City?" When I see I'm right, I can't help but scoff. "And just when do you think that will happen? When the dead rise from their piles of dust?"

It feels as though the pieces finally fit together and I see where everything stands. Storm will try to save Dominion for the True Borns while my sister is lost somewhere out there—likely in Russia, and in the company of the coldest parents on earth. And if I don't act, she'll be stuck there. On her own. Suffering. And me along with her.

Storm walks over to the door, the curved bone over his head wreathing him like a bright crown. "What do you think would happen if I abandoned the city now, Lucy? Once they start purging the preachers—do you think it's likely they'll stop there? Next it will be the True Borns, just as your father and his cronies had intended. And beyond that, anyone who doesn't fit their political agenda of the month."

He's right—I know he's right. I heard the colonel myself. People are going to die, and Nolan Storm is probably the only one who can prevent it. That doesn't stop me from wanting to throw something at him.

I turn my back to him, freezing him out. As far as gestures go, it's childish. And stupidly ineffective. I can still see Storm's bright silhouette in the glass, still feel the magnetic pulse of his energy. But it's the only weapon I have to counter the helpless anger I feel, the sense that this betrayal is far worse than any I have encountered in the past.

Storm contemplates my back for a moment before quietly murmuring to Jared, "Lucy is wanted in the lab. See to it she gets there in the morning."

It's easier than I imagine to slip out from under watch and guard at Storm's headquarters. *Kept but not a prisoner*, I think to myself wryly as I punch the code into the elevator and it whisks me down without a sound. It's still early morning, though. Jared isn't expected to collect me for another couple of hours. Outside the glass of the tower, the sky is grainy, like sand, before which the buildings sit like dark bruises.

I tamp down a wave of guilt. In my former life I'd never contemplate setting up a secret rendezvous with a boy, let alone the strange boy I met in an alleyway while being attacked. I deliberately avoid thinking about Jared and what he'd say if he knew what I was up to. *This isn't my former life*, I remind myself. And Storm isn't my father. I can meet with whomever I choose. Besides, I reason defiantly, if Storm won't help me get what I need, maybe this person can. I step out of the building shaking my head. Something about Alastair makes me feel as though I can trust him. I pray I'm right.

My heart squeezes and relaxes as I spy a lone figure lounging against the glass and cement of the sky rise. *He showed*, I tell myself. At least there's that.

"What happened to you?" Alastair rakes me from head to toe, frowning. But if I look disreputable at this time in the morning—I'm clad in a pair of blue and white Grayguard gym pants and a sweater—he looks worse. Alastair appears to be one step from a kid gang himself. His brown leather jacket is ripped and torn here and there, the leather scuffed and old. The collar is turned up against the chill of the early morning air, catching on the strap of his canvas bag. His corded trousers look almost as beat up as Jared's, and beneath the frayed hems poke scuffed boots, though of a fine make.

I can only just make out his face beneath the broad brim of his hat, a collection of dark features and a pair of dark eyes that miss nothing.

"Not a thing," I toss out, though I'm a liar. My eyes are red and puffy from a night of crying myself to sleep, my hair a messy tangle.

"Riiiight," Alastair drawls.

I square my chin, putting on my best princess face, and stare down my nose at him. "I don't see what business it is of yours anyhow."

Alastair snorts a laugh. "Look, lady, I don't have to be here." He starts to turn away. My hand whips out and grabs his leather-clad arm.

"Wait. I just…got some bad news last night."

Alastair stares at me as though to read the truth in my face. Nodding, he jerks his head. "Follow me. We're too conspicuous here."

He leads me to the tiny courtyard beside Storm's building, mostly a snarl of dead hedge, not even good enough to start fires, though someone has hacked through a portion. There's a stone bench, though, and—wonder of wonders—no one sleeping on it.

He tilts his hat off and scratches at his head. The hair underneath is mussed and flattened in fat, thick whorls of black. "You know, I really don't get you Upper Circle folks." He squints at me.

"Oh?"

"Yeah. You have everything you could ever want. Food, nice place to live. And you can Splice. So why are you all so darned miserable?"

"I'm—w-we're not," I splutter, indignant. "You don't know anything about my life."

"Nope. Guess I don't." He grins, throwing me off balance.

"Look, did you come all the way here this morning to insult me?"

"Nope." He tilts his head back to study me. "I came to figure out if you really would meet me."

That catches me off guard. "What do you mean?"

"Why's a richy-rich girl living in a tower rather than one of the mansions on the hill? And why is this same girl meeting a strange guy like me when she can just buy off one of her Personals to get her intel? It's a question, don't you think?"

He's right. Any sane person would be suspect of me. "You think I'm setting you up."

"Not exactly." Alastair shakes his head at me. "You're just so…so *stupid*," he finally says.

We stare at each other, the dawning horror of his words

reaching his eyes. Alastair claps a hand over his mouth. And I begin to laugh. I laugh like it's the last funny thing in the world while he watches, a strange blend of fascination and something I reckon might be horror on his face. If Jared or Nolan or anyone else has said that to me, I would have been enraged. But I am long past that point today. I'm risking my life on the faint hope that a street urchin in Dominion may be able to find information on my sister's whereabouts in Russia. Alastair is absolutely right, I muse, letting another paroxysm of laughter take me. I'm an idiot—at the very least, a girl with no instinct for self-preservation.

When at last I can control myself, I swipe at my eyes and sniffle. "Sorry. It's just that I really can't argue with that. What was I thinking?"

I stand up to head inside. Alastair bolts up, holding his hands out as though to stop me.

"Whoa. Look—sorry. I'm not exactly one of your Upper Circle bucks. I'm not all suave and sophisticated. I say what's on my mind, even when sometimes I should just keep my damned mouth shut."

A drone flies overhead, low to the ground. It's just a surveillance drone, I recognize from the red-striped underbelly, though lower to the ground than usual. Alastair grabs me by the arm and pulls me closer to the wiry tangle of hedges.

"It's just a surveillance drone," I say.

The drones are meant to be helpful. We're taught the usefulness of these machines for sending out the Rovers to pick up the dying and the dead. *And maybe preacher men.* The thought strikes as Alastair keeps his eye on the meter-long flying robot. "What are you worried about?"

He pulls his hat lower, bathing his face in complete

shadows. But I can still see the glittering, playful darkness of his eyes. "Me? I don't worry about anything. Just the same, I'd rather not give Ole Dominion any more information on me than I have to."

"You think they're doing more than looking for Plague Struck." It's not a question. Nor does Alastair take it as one.

He grins. "Maybe you're not as stupid as I thought."

I ponder this. "Do you think they're keeping tabs on the preacher men?"

"How else do you think all those rich Upper Circlers control so many poor Lasters?"

"Ali," I say, grabbing his forearms.

Alastair pulls his head back with a frown. "Ali?"

I nod. "You found me in an alley, didn't you? Like a big, wet alley cat."

"And that's how you repay me for saving you? You just decide you can rename me…after a wet cat?"

He says it seriously, but the corners of his mouth curl up, barely suppressing a smile. We're strangely comfortable companions, this strange alley cat and me. As though we really can say anything to each other. "Well, you called me stupid. You'll get used to it. So listen, Ali, you seem to know a lot about these things."

"What things?" he asks warily.

"Politics. Surveillance."

"Sure," he says slowly. "Doesn't everybody?"

I shake my head. "I know dancing. Mercs. A different kind of politics."

Alastair squints at me and scratches his head. "What other kind of politics is there? It's people fighting over bones."

And it's just that, that one response, that settles everything into place for me. *He knows things I need to know*, a voice inside me insists. I decide to go with my gut, to take a leap.

"Have you ever traveled?"

"Sure. I've been to the territories. A few other places," he hedges.

"Ali."

"Are you Upper Circle girls always so weird?"

"You said you could get information for me."

"Uh-huh."

"Can you get me information on who's traveled out of Nor-Am in the last four months?"

7

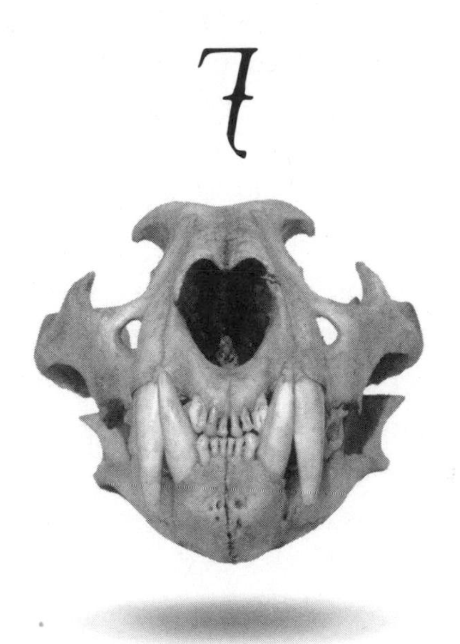

I let myself into the lab. Row upon row of stainless-steel lab benches with raised shelves. The watchful eye of a giant clock glares down at me from above the door. I now recognize a few of Doc Raines's tools of the trade. The large boxy machine, for instance, that allows her to separate genetic strands, then project them on a large flat-screen while she manipulates them. I imagine they have similar tech in the Splicer Clinics, where people go to have their blown genes ripped out of them and have fresh ones sewn in.

Unlike at the Splicer Clinics, here, amid the hand scanners for reading genetic strands and nano-manipulation gear for experimenting with DNA variants, I'm not overwhelmed by a terrible sense of wrongness.

In the Splicer Clinics, you're always at the mercy of a test result. Just one genetic switch, one protein expressed a bit more than another, and you'd never be the same. Eventually you'd grow ill. Be Spliced, if you were lucky. Be looked down upon in our little world devoted to the pretense that *the Upper Circle does not fall to the Plague.*

Here in Storm's lab, at least, I have a say. No one asks me about my body or how well it's functioning. Here, I am not illness waiting to happen. I'm still put through Protocols—but to get to the bottom of what I am, not what I will become.

Until the day Margot disappeared, it hadn't occurred to me to question our lives. It was only when I found her, stretched and clamped on a bed in our Splicer Clinic, a long and bloody pipette snaking from her body where they had been harvesting parts of her, that I realized things were not as they seemed.

I close my eyes and fight to lock up the image of my sister that day: white as a winding sheet, shaking, sunken into herself. I can't bear to think of what they might be doing to her now. Or what they've done with the tiny parts of her they managed to squire away.

A familiar voice breaks through my train of thought. "I get that you're mad at Storm. But are you going to speak to me again this century?"

Startled, I turn. Jared leans against the steel bench closest to the door, arms crossed. I note the lines of strain around his mouth, his eyes. The tired and bruised look, as though he hasn't slept well.

Good, I think. In my head I know it's not up to Jared what Storm does or doesn't do. But he didn't speak up. Didn't argue with Storm. Didn't offer to help me. And that's what my heart remembers.

Stay with me, Lu. Stay with me.

He'd asked me to stay. And with every day that passes I become more convinced that he didn't mean it.

Instead of answering, I let my hands fall on a pair of hyper-loops, for examining microscopic DNA samples. Doc Raines had shown me how to use them. They're the kind of gear even private schools like Grayguard can't afford. I pull them over my head and begin fiddling with the fit adjustments.

"Lucy." Jared sighs.

"I don't know yet," I finally answer. When I turn, he's too close. Always too close. His skin heats me from a foot away, and I tingle with awareness from head to foot. I inhale his dark-and-spice scent that somehow comforts me even when it's been dipped in someone else's blood. His eyes are blue now, like a deep sky you'd see in those OldenTimes films. Yet so intense it feels like he's pulling all the oxygen from the room.

"Why?"

"What do you mean, why?" I snap, earning a slight smile.

"This isn't my call."

"I know that," I say, looking down at my hands.

"So why are you freezing me out?"

But what else can I say that he doesn't already know? When I think of leaving my sister to her fate, I feel sick. I can't stay here if Storm won't help me. *If Jared won't.* I can't answer Jared. The words won't form. Ever so slowly, I turn my back to him. Feel his heat seep and comfort me there, though I want none. He doesn't touch me, though I can feel his hot breath on the top of my head, tickling my hair.

He says my name once more, so softly. Calls me by

Margot's nickname for me. "Lu." Tears prickle and burn my eyes and the back of my throat. He doesn't say anything more. And maybe I imagine that I can feel Jared raising a finger, ready to trace the fine skin on my neck. Without warning, he jumps back as though he's been torched. An icy-cold pocket fills the space between us. Back to normal, then.

"Good, you're here."

Dorian is geared up in what I call her Splicer gear. An earth-toned blouse covered by a white lab coat, a set of hyper-loops scooping the curls from her face like a jeweled hair band. When she smiles briefly at me, fine lines crinkle around her eyes. She could be my mother's age. She could be twenty years younger than that. Dorian Raines is not the sort of woman who leaves the Splicer Clinics augmented with more than a shiny new set of modified genes.

"Come over here, will you, Lucy? I have something to show you."

I follow the doctor as she pulls up the sleeves of her lab coat and strides over to the workbench. She motions to the loops around my neck. I pull them up and over my eyes. The world turns a deep, vibrant green, like being underwater. Dorian flicks a couple of switches. A machine hums. A screen blinks on like a bright eye.

"Look," she says. A white sleeve swims in front of my eyes, and I pull my attention to the small dish she indicates. Dirt. And trees. And maybe a leaf mixed in there. I touch the controls on the sides of the loops and instantly I'm looking at the specimens at a microscopic level. Fine lines, veins, and apartment-like blocks fill my sightline.

"What am I looking at here?" I ask.

Bright metallic particles swim like exotic goldfish close

to the cellulose bricks of the leaf. I watch as those goldfish nibble on the walls. The walls suddenly split in an act of mitosis so explosive I jump back. Jared's hand burns my skin where he's crept up beside me.

"What the hell is that?"

"Doc?" Jared asks from just behind me. But I can't wrest my eyes from the sight before me. The small, darting things eating, or maybe feeding, the cells. Blooming like time-lapsed flowers. My stomach sinks. I know what this is.

Nanotech. *Magic bombs.*

"How did you get it to work?"

The doc pulls off her loops and bobs forward. "Once I realized that the nanotech deactivated without the presence of organic matter, it was fairly simple. This phenotype of leaf can survive without nutrients for days."

"What's it doing, Doc?" Jared asks. I jump as his hand comes up and grazes my arm.

The doc expels a breath and her unruly lock tosses up. "What it was programmed to do, I fear. It accelerates growth exponentially."

My mind leaps to all sorts of horrible conclusions. "What if it hits a human?"

The doc just shakes her head. "I don't know. It could be that the nanotech is designed specifically to act on cellulose-based organic material. But we just don't know enough about this yet. We'll need to be extremely cautious with the experiments. It will take a few days before I can set up proper containment protocols."

Containment protocols. Meaning that there's a chance that whatever the nanotech in the dish touches could be dangerous. Ravenous nanotech, eating its way through organic matter with synthetic gold-coated teeth. When I think of it that way, it sounds far too close for comfort to that other monster, eating its way through the citizens of Dominion and the rest of the planet. I want to ask. It's there on the tip of my tongue.

"Do you think..." I start, but a lump rises up in my throat, too thick to speak through. Doesn't matter—the doc knows. She shrugs and looks away, appearing far more helpless than I have ever seen her.

Dominion used to be a bustling megacity of twenty million. Today there are just less than three million souls surviving.

"I haven't a clue," she answers. "We'll keep working on it. Just know for now that it's extremely unlikely that the Plague is anything but a natural evolution rather than something brought on by nano. I don't want this keeping you up at night."

We stand there for a moment in silence until I'm brought back to Jared's heat burning at my back. I want to step away, but if I move even an inch it will be proof that he bothers me. I remain still and try to unclench my fists. I am a Fox, I remind myself. I can handle one guy.

"There's something else you need to see, Lucy," the doc tells me. I don't miss the dark note threaded in her voice. "Come around here, please."

As I slowly follow Doc Raines around the counter to a second bench, Jared threads his arm over my back. I pretend not to notice, though my body hums at his nearness.

"Keep the loops on," the doc instructs, flipping on another screen. Little pink spinning globules fill the display. Blood cells.

"Now watch," the doc says.

She pulls a small wire pipette and zaps the molecules. "Magnify the right side to nano," the doc orders. I touch the sides of the loops. The image breaks into a series of three-dimensional geometric shapes, line drawings and dots you'd never imagine. DNA. The doc drops a molecule of blood next to the magnified DNA. I expect the two to shimmy about in their separate places—that's what should happen.

Instead, the blood molecules slide over to the lone DNA strand. I watch as a fat blood molecule transforms into a series of twisting ladders as it moves closer to the nano-magnified sample on the right. The blood ladder gloms onto the strand until it's completely hidden, completely overcome. I pull the loops up off my face.

"What is it doing? I've never seen anything like that." Beside me, Jared takes the loops from my hands and slips them on to get his own look. The doc switches her loops off. I don't like the look in her eyes, halfway between a revelation and something I know I'm not going to like. "Nanotech?" I point to the monstrosity on the screen. Because this is not normal. This is not human.

"No, not quite," Dorian Raines says, looking at me quiet-quiet. I glance back over at the action unfolding in the oval petri dish. "Notice how the stained DNA strands seems to magnetically attract the blood molecules? I've tried it again and again. It's only blood that it pulls. My hypothesis is that it's calling out to certain proteins in the blood."

Jared blinks owlishly through the magnified eyes of the loops. "Like a homing signal?"

"You could say that."

"But DNA doesn't do that. DNA switches things on and

off. What the hell have you got in there?"

"And this one does. Absolutely." She winces, answering only his first question.

"But it's active..." When she says nothing, I prod harder. "It acts like the nano in the bombs." I look up, bewildered, as another thought occurs to me. "What does it switch on and off?"

Feeling faint, my knees start to shake, as though I've just been waiting for the bad news I knew was on its way. Because I *do* know. Even before the doc says it.

"Lucy." She pulls up her loops to study me. "This DNA is yours. The blood—well, I've been using some of the samples we have of your sister's blood."

Feeling faint, my knees start to shake. Jared's hands grip me. Hard, harder, like he can keep me standing if he just holds me tight enough.

But it's too late to turn back the clock. Far too late to pretend I don't see.

I watch as my own sample pulls Margot's blood to it like it's a starving baby at a three-course dinner. A roaring sound fills my ears, and I reckon Jared has the right of it to hold on tight, because I consider sliding down to the floor in a puddle of limbs as the truth of what's just been revealed crashes over me.

My blood acts like nanotech? For what purpose? And how?

Amid the torrent of questions surfaces the mother of them all.

"Am I even human?"

•••

The image on the screen blurs around the edges, then goes hazy and flat.

"Wait a nano—you're cracking up, Deep," I say to the dark-haired wonder on the screen. Deepika Manda, another diplomat's daughter, was at Grayguard Academy with Margot and me until three years ago when her family moved back to Asia Major. Asia Major isn't falling apart as quickly as Dominion is. Then again, it was never that stable to begin with.

Deepika's form turns into a wave before going solid again, then blinks on and off. Her Feed tech tells the story of Asia Major better than I could. Developed in black market labs, most of Asia Major runs on tech pilfered and set up outside any regulated government channels, which, to hear Deepika speak of it, works so slowly they were still using dial-up while the rest of us had holographic systems. Still, Margot and I connect with her when we can.

Used to connect with her, I correct myself.

Deepika tosses a mass of shiny black hair over one shoulder. Smart, bright brown eyes fill the screen as she leans in closer to her face cam. "You really ought to speak with the Thorntons," she continues. "You know they are connected to everyone in the Upper Russian," she says, speaking in our society's short code.

Deepika's father works for the president of Upper Major—which means she's about as connected as a person can be on the other side of the ocean. And that's despite low-tech, faulty communications systems, and a population rapidly being wasted by Plague. If anyone would hear about the whereabouts of my parents, I'd reckoned it would be her. It seems I reckoned wrong.

It's not like our parents to stay out of touch so long. Then again, since the destruction of our house and Margot's kidnapping, I no longer have faith that I know our parents at all. *Are they even coming back?* A sharp pain jabs me in the chest as I realize I may actually have been abandoned. My parents may have made my life hard, but it would have been much worse without them. Family is family, and without them, I stand alone.

"Yes, good idea, thanks." I bite my lip, worrying the situation over. "But I can't call them myself. They'll know I'm fishing. I need to keep a low profile."

Maybe I need to keep my profile lower than low, given Doc Raines's discovery the other day. If the Upper Circle knew my blood acts more like nanotech than organic matter…? They have a saying among Dominion's elite. *The only thing worse than being Revealed a True Born is being dead.* So what would they say about me? I shiver in dread at the thought.

"You know," Deepika continues, "it's very strange the way it happened."

"What do you mean?"

"Why would such prolific figures disappear? Your parents have spent a lifetime building their position in society. Why have they let a bunch of rabble scare them away?"

Deepika's logic buzzes through me. *She's right.* Why have they? Why go underground?

Concern mars my friend's perfect, round face. I must look aghast. "I don't think you should be alone right now. I will get Father to—"

"No!" I shout before lowering my voice. "Thank you, Deep," I say with all the elegance I can muster. "I'm not alone. I'm safe where I am—safer than I would be anywhere else. Honestly, the last thing I would want is to drag your family into this mess. But..." I hesitate, biting my lip.

I don't like asking for things, let alone something that would put my friend in an awkward position. Still, I need the information. "I—I need to ask you to call the Thorntons for me. This needs to be discreet. Make up a story. Pretend like you haven't heard."

"Pfft!" Deepika blows out air in annoyance. "Who needs to pretend? This town is about as far from civilization as an outpost can get."

"Thank you." I sigh, sagging as relief floods my bones.

"I'll call you as soon as I have some news," she says, fading once again.

"Great—I'll be here," I tell her as we sign off.

I wish to Holy Plague fire that isn't true. I need to get out of here. I need to start searching for Margot.

I quickly erase the call history but wonder, not for the first time, whether Storm tracks my phone. According to Jared, the tides of information are at the heart of good security intel... Which leads me to question yet again how it is that a man like Nolan Storm can claim to have no idea where my parents have gone, dragging my sister with them.

Can I really trust Storm and his agenda?

A few moments later, I slide onto the soft, buttery leather of the couch in the den. Beside me, Kira lounges in an overstuffed easy chair, her hair a glorious red mop on her head. I can tell she's been working out from the fine sheen of sweat on her skin and a faint smudge of blood under her nostril.

"Penny kick your ass again?"

Kira sneers. "Funny. Especially coming from a girl I could smear under my heel like a bug."

I smile prettily at her. "Which is why I'm smart enough to hire you for security rather than fight you."

"You're not paying us any longer, though, are you?" she mutters.

It hurts, another icy jab of truth. I'm here, a ward of Nolan Storm, who insists on acting like my de facto guardian since my family home was blown to smithereens. Yet, despite Storm's claims that Margot and I are some different breed of True Born, after the "incident" in the lab, Dorian Raines insists that we're not—can't be. Something different, all right. Freaks within freaks. A category only my twin and I can occupy.

Something dark must have come across my face, because Kira kicks her legs over the side of the chair. "Hey, listen, I'm just messing with you. Relax."

She flicks on the NewsFeed. A pretty blonde with wide blue eyes blinks as she delivers a grim headline. "Mmm. Pretty," Kira says, sitting up a little straighter. "Listen, do you know her?" she asks.

I ignore her as the woman's image is quickly replaced by empty, rubble-lined streets filling the screen. The volume is off and yet, the grim city in ruins speaks as loud as thunder. I try not to watch the drone-fed images, but I can't seem to tear my eyes away.

The burned-out husk of my former home flickers onto the screen. It's raining. Even on the screen, I can make out the slanted hands of the rain slapping at the ruins of my former life. The front of the house has disintegrated. A forest grows straight out of the holes in the third floor. The gates are shut, locking in the destruction and waste. The wood could make fires for a dozen Laster families over the dark months. Doesn't matter, though. Even with no one shotgunning the gate, none will cross over to where magic bombs have fallen.

When I can finally speak, I ask, "Why is my house on the NewsFeed?"

Kira doesn't answer directly, muttering darkly instead. "You ask me, waste of a good mansion."

"Kira."

"They're going to tear it down. Apparently with the forest growing out of control on the second floor, they're worried about stability. Go figure."

I slump back on the couch, deflated. A pang of grief threatens to swamp me. I didn't love our life, but it was all I knew. Now my former home will become just another mess of things to mourn. I'm still coming to terms with the news as a pin-neat, dark-haired woman walks in the room and crosses over to me.

Alma is still a mystery to me: Part caretaker, part secretary, she stands outside the pecking order of the True Borns. I've often wondered whether she's somehow a relation of Nolan Storm's—not that I can trace a resemblance between this woman and my so-called guardian.

"There you are." Alma brushes a hand across her hair, pulled into a severe bun at the nape of her neck. "Thought you'd sprung free."

Kira lets out an unladylike snort. "We'd be so lucky."

Alma gives Kira a hard look. "Nolan has a job for you."

Putting two hands on either side of her head, Kira launches herself, catlike, into the air as she finds her feet.

Alma tidies for a moment before she pulls a beaten and worn letter from her pocket and hands it to me. She looks at me softly, maybe even a bit sad. "Thought you'd like to be alone when I gave this to you," she says.

And the second I see the rolling, looping slant of the handwriting, I understand why. Because I'm crying like a baby.

And I'm trying *not* to imagine what it took for Margot to get a letter to me.

8

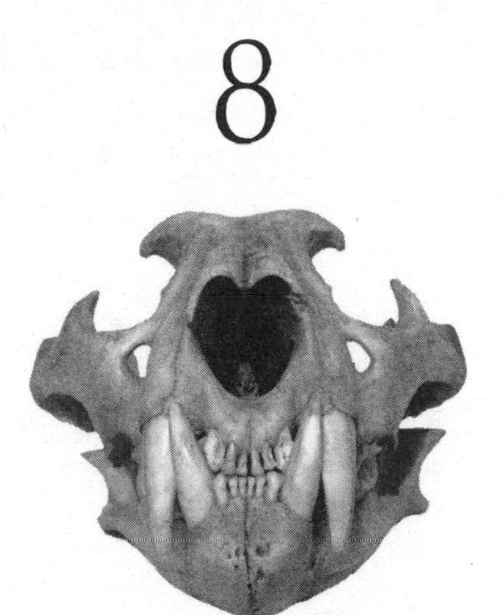

Dearest little sister.

I sink down on the rug, hands shaking. It's not so much the words she uses that tip me off—though calling me her little sister does it, since we were born scant minutes apart. It's her tone, as though she's living some idyllic high life.

For Margot and me, life without the other is a half life at best. Torture at worst.

The mere fact that she's sent a letter, and on paper no less, is by far the biggest tip-off. Real letters are the work of the rich, the Upper Circle—and not the kind who live here. Margot's letter is an Upper Circle post from another world. Somewhere where they haven't burned down all the trees and haven't enough tech to get everyone circuited. Set down on creased and crackled linen, I notice the telltale sign that someone had already carefully pulled away the glue from its lips before regluing it. Maybe more than one someone.

And the postmark? It's the red circle seal of the Russian subcontinent. *She's there. I can find her.*

I try to tamp down my excitement and concentrate on the letters, swimming and rearranging themselves before my eyes.

Dearest little sister,

Well, it's been a long time, hasn't it? I have been having so much fun that I have lost track of time and only just realized how long it has been since I've written. Honestly, it's so much fun here. Endless soirees, long afternoons of horseback riding, ending the afternoons with social teas on the porch.

Father and Mother send their love. They are very busy right now with work, but we get together whenever they can spare a moment. I hope you're not shutting yourself up in that big old house by yourself! Get out and mingle. I know you'll meet someone special who can help you get over your shyness.

Anyway, darling baby sister, I have to get ready for a big to-do, but I will write again when I have the chance. In the meantime, know that I am well and happy and having the time of my life here.

Love,

Margot

The tripping of the clock fills my ears like the metallic chop of an ax. My mind swirls and tries to unravel all the subtext and innuendo. Margot and I are the daughters of a politician—a true power broker. Our first lesson in life was to mask our feelings from everyone in the world except each other. I consider her words again. Go out and mingle. Get over your shyness.

Great, except for one thing: I may be *reserved*, but I've not been shy a day in my life.

What's she telling me? Where does she think I am? Surely if she's with our parents she's heard that our house is going to be reduced to a pile of rubble. But if not…the sudden thought occurs to me. *Is Margot telling me she's not even with our parents?* I press the heel of my hand to my eyes, hoping to shut down the looping, useless trains of thought. Margot has given me all the information I need to get to her; I just have to find it.

Thunk. Thunk. The second hands on the clock tick. I'm running out of time. She wouldn't have sent the letter otherwise. For a moment my flesh remembers the overwhelming panic I felt from my sister just a few days ago. How long does it take for a letter to arrive from Russian parts unknown, anyway?

From the relative anonymity of the backseat, shaded by tinted glass, I watch the drones hover above the buildings, keeping watch over Dominion's streets and occupants. Since my rendezvous with Ali, those empty eyes have seemed far more sinister, to the point where I had Torch hack into Dominion's security mainframe. He played back hour after hour of feed for me. Every once in a while, the drone's feed would zero in on a face and in immaculate, clean white letters, display everything about the person—from his job at the local tavern to his political leanings and life expectancy.

Since then I've been absorbed by the drones. If these little flying machines collect information for Dominion's government, why didn't they notice that an army of Lasters had crawled up to our gates and hurled magic bombs into our bedrooms? Why didn't our mercs use the footage to keep a better eye on things—why couldn't they stop the attacks on our school, for instance? *Who keeps watch over their feeds?*

I can't ask. Not yet.

"It only makes sense that Nash has a backer. The question is *who*. We'll stick close to him until we've figured it out. Are you listening?" Storm waves a hand before my face.

"He's going to die," I blurt out, turning my attention from Dominion's crumbling skyline to the giant man beside me.

I don't mean to be so blunt about it. But in a city where death creeps the streets, there's no point in tiptoeing. I feel Storm's gunmetal gaze on me, hot as coals. He leans back in his seat but says nothing.

"I know..." I start trying to put into words a lifetime of impressions that I've kept, like a locked box, between my sister and me. "I told you. I can usually tell. Not just intuition. It's part of my...special gifts," I end lamely. "Nash is a goner."

Storm continues to study me with restless, glittering eyes. The city seems abandoned, streets rolling out like a bone-strewn desert. Occasionally I glimpse a dog-size rat. They survive by eating through any dead left on the streets past dark. Sometimes before dark. Fewer bodies have been left on the streets as of late. *Owing to the fact that the preachers are hiding in the walls like mice*, Mohawk told me just this morning.

Maybe it's true, I think. I trace the outline of a pitch-black window through the glass. So many of the windows are empty and dark. It can't all be because the grid was destroyed.

I don't know when it became the tradition to ring the bodies with pebbles, but I know the street kid gangs still do it. You can hear them singing as they complete their enchantments, begging their gods to turn them into True Borns. As though that would magically wall away death.

"How soon?" Storm's question catches me off balance. I pull my eyes back in time to see Jared through the rearview, raking over me with a scowl.

"Pardon?"

"How soon?" he repeats gently.

They don't usually ask about time. They usually assume the worst—as they should.

Still, knowledge like this is not an exact science. I sift through my memories. "The longest stretch I've gone between a knowing and a dead man is about three months."

Storm nods. He's dressed in his finery for this evening's outing: black tux, crisp white shirt. His hair has grown longer these past few months and now falls over his collar. During the day he'll pull it into a short ponytail. Every woman at tonight's reception will be swooning over him and jealous of me, his escort. *But they won't know, will they?* I muse. They won't know that Nolan Storm keeps his heart for his tribe, not a lone Splicer woman. Any woman who would be swept into Storm's life will be a strategy, all mapped out in his campaign for the True Borns. Just like me.

"Does it matter? To your plans, I mean."

Storm considers the question carefully before answering. “Everything is a moving piece. You need to consider the movement of one before you can think of moving another.”

I nod. “You sound like my father.”

“Your father has a terrific head for strategy, I’ll grant him that.”

“And just what is your strategy, Storm? What do you hope to accomplish?”

Storm’s head drops. His spectral crown of bone illuminates the air before me as he chuffs a laugh. “I thought you knew.”

“I thought I did. I’m not as sure about anything any longer.”

My hands are clenched together tightly in my lap. Storm reaches over and pats them. If he’s aware of the electric jolt of his touch—so unlike Jared’s—he doesn’t show it.

“What would you like to know? Ask me anything.”

I’ve spent many a night thinking about Nolan Storm and his operations. The list of questions I have is as long as my arm, but I need to start somewhere.

“Do you know where they all are?”

“Who?”

“The True Borns.”

“No.” A small smile plays along his lips. “It’s not as though I have a homing device and can call them to me.”

“But surely they know about you?”

“Many do.”

“How?”

“I have people on the street. Some of those people are very visibly True Borns. Those people talk to other people. And then, of course, I’m Miss Lucy Fox’s escort to most Upper Circle events. Those events play on the NewsFeed.

As do my business dealings."

"They report on your business?" That Storm and I would appear in society NewsFeeds doesn't surprise me much. It didn't occur to me that Storm's business partnerships would also make headlines in Dominion. "I thought the Upper Circle would want to keep it quiet that they're working with you."

Storm inclines his head. "That might have been possible had I not secured a sizable portion of Dominion's interests."

"In what?"

"Oh—a bit of everything. Power, water, construction and building. Defense. Many, many security contracts. Loans."

"All the things that will keep Dominion going once the Lasters are too few to manage."

A cough sounds from the front seat. Jared turns from where he sits shotgun. "Another ten minutes, I think." His eyes catch on me as though I'm an inch shy of going too far. I keep my expression carefully blank. I'm not about to take social cues from one of the more untactful people I've met.

"And what will you do once you have them all right where you want them?" I ask, my sight still trained on the handsome True Born before me.

A low, rumbling chuckle accompanies Storm's response. "I'll turn the city over to the people, of course."

It's the most shocking thing he could say. *To the rabble*? *Lasters*, I mentally correct myself.

"Why?"

"Why what?"

"Why give it to the Lasters?"

Storm pats the back of my hand. "Oh, not just the Lasters. The True Borns, too. Especially the True Borns. As you say, soon the Lasters will be too few to manage things."

"So you get the city by default."

Storm looks at me gravely. "No, Lucy. We get the entire world." My head spins at the frank brutality of what Storm has said, though I can't argue. Still, it makes me feel sick. *All those people will be gone*, I think to myself. All the people we'll see tonight.

"Jared," Storm continues, not missing a beat. "Make sure you keep a close eye on Nash this evening. Kira, I want you to watch Gillis. Whoever they have their heads down with, I want to know about it."

Kira gives me a showy wink in the rearview before returning her attention to the road. Jared coughs into his hands once more, his eyes scanning for danger from under his crop of golden curls. *The perfect merc*, I think to myself once more. Except, I realize as he reluctantly turns to the front, Jared can't seem to keep his eyes off me anymore than I can him.

"Have you given any thought to Miss Fox's future?" the man before Storm asks. The man's light-green eyes flick over my Grecian-cut gown as though appraising my value before turning back to Storm.

I smile with my teeth, a smile so fierce my face hurts, and squeeze my clutch to my stomach.

I had never heard men speak of women this way before, so publically, so unabashedly. Our father might be a monster, but he kept at least some of this unpleasantness away from us girls. The man before us is the minister of finance, a lean, sleek greyhound of a man. His colorless hair lies flat against his head. A small scar notches his temple where I assume he has had some tumor removed. It's an old scar, though, speaking highly of his ability to survive more than the shark-infested political circles he swims in.

"How kind of you to take an interest in my future," I chime in.

It's not something he expects. Young women are meant to be silent at these functions. I've been working this circle with my family for enough years to know better. But I'm standing in a ballroom, white marble pillars stretching up a thirty-foot ceiling, walls covered in masterpieces. *And I'm not with my family any longer, am I?* I remind myself.

Storm touches my elbow and takes a sip of champagne before he answers the minister blandly. "Something for us to consider, certainly."

The minister takes Storm's noncommittal reply as he wants to. His watery eyes widen with interest, and I have no doubt that people will be making wagers on me before the night is out. We make polite motions and head toward the back of the ballroom, where the guest of honor is ringed by his cronies.

We pass through elegant crowds. Storm's spectral crown of bone gleams dully in the dim candlelight, heads and tails above the other guests. I want to keep it together, but I can't hold back another second. "You should have told him to go to hell," I say with venom.

"Relax," Storm soothes. "This works to our advantage."

"How is that?"

Storm leans down and murmurs his answer. "Yours is still a family of power. Your father is someone to be feared. They think I'm his partner." Somehow the thought doesn't comfort me. But then we're standing before the sweating, shiny mess that is Senator Theodore Nash of the outer territories, ringed by his entourage.

"Miss Fox, Mr. Nolan, so kind of you to join us this evening," Nash opens. The senator mops his forehead before shaking Storm's hand. He bows slightly to me. "We were just speaking of alliances."

Nash indicates a foppish man in an oversize gray suit, a delicate pink silk cravat at his neck. Beside him stands a woman in a gold lamé dress that hugs her generous curves. Her hair has been dyed a terrible yellow blond that shows her roots. But it's her face that I stare at. Once she must have had the skin of an angel. Now the telltale signs of ravage appear on her cheeks: the fine rash I've seen over and over again from the Splicer treatments. These people are sick.

I fight the urge to step away until I'm able to concentrate on their words.

"Our oldest is coming to that age," says the fop, whom I understand is named Charles Driscoll. "We're squiring her to all the parties. Just like you, *eh*, Mr. Storm?" The fop's elbow nudges Storm as though they share an inside joke. The inside of my cheek burns as I bite down hard to keep myself from speaking.

In a rush I realize that according to everyone here, Storm is searching for a suitable husband for me in my father's absence. Now it all makes sense: the parade of young men who've been presented to me at each and every reception. The private "cozy chats" Storm has enjoyed with keen-looking families at every single event we've been to in the past couple of months. *Why he's been allowed to enter their hallowed social ranks at all.*

At first I'm revolted. I scold myself for not noticing it sooner. I take a shallow breath. Fine—let them think what they want. Better to pretend I'm on the marriage market than reveal our true purpose. And I believe that for two seconds—until I realize that Nolan Storm has been playing this game with the Upper Circle all along. Pretending that he's interested in finding me a good match to help get his foot in the door.

"Excuse me for a moment, won't you?" I give them a bright smile and walk, shoulders back, to the refreshment table. The lemonade burns my throat but I force myself to drink it all. There, at the back of the room, Storm's antlers bloom like an idea above the heads of the crowd. I note the faintly blue luminescence that curls like sharpened knives over his handsome profile.

Dark thoughts make me shiver. With a murmured "thank-you," I hand the crystal cup back to the Laster who won't meet my eyes and for one brief moment let myself feel the horror of the truth.

Storm might not be pretending.

9

Overcome with dark and anxious thoughts, I make my way to the doors leading to the gardens out back. A prickle runs up my neck. I'm being watched. The shaven-head mercs guarding the doors survey me with dull eyes but they don't stop me, don't say a word. I race through watery moonlight, panting, and get lost in a landscaped garden lit with paper lanterns. At least I'm blessedly alone. I tug at the flowing drape of my dress over my right shoulder and wish beyond anything that I could snap my fingers and bring back my former life. The minute I think of Margot, the dam of tears I'd been holding back so carefully breaks. I sob my way deeper into the garden.

I haven't been there for more than a minute or two when a red handkerchief dotted with white polka dots appears before my blurry eyes. I halt mid-sob and hiccup. The arm attached to the hanky belongs to none other than Jared Price.

"Go away, Jared," I snarl. But I take the handkerchief and dab at my eyes anyway. Surprisingly, the cloth is perfectly clean and in good condition, if a little wrinkled.

"You're welcome," Jared replies as I blow.

"I said go away."

"Where my hanky goes, I go." He sounds so cheerful I want to throttle him.

He's painfully handsome by moonlight, his hair near silver. The planes of his face hollow out until he looks more like the sleek beast whose face he sometimes wears. Tonight he's opted for a faded tuxedo T-shirt, complete with a red bow tie at the neck. Before we left Storm's keep, he called it his "undercover Upper Circle" look, which had Torch laughing like a hyena.

It's so easy for Jared to mock, I realize. He's not trapped as I am. And at that, my anger explodes.

"Can you not follow me for five seconds?" I snap.

"'Fraid not. Kind of in the job description." He looks down at my strappy emerald shoes as though appraising their value. I make a strangled sound and stomp away. I hear nothing, not a squeak or a whisper, but I can feel him ghosting me as I slip deeper into the garden.

When I'm as fed up as I can be, I turn to confront him. And stare at an empty garden path.

"You think this is funny?" I call to thin air. But I know he can hear me. I know he'll not be far. "You enjoy watching girls cry?"

A few beats later, his voice floats out from the darkness and brushes my ears like a kiss. "Why are you crying, Lu?"

Even if I were inclined, I don't have enough breath in me to tell him all the reasons I'm crying. "Does Storm know that you're here?" I call out, surprising even myself.

There's silence from the darkness. Then, a soft, "No."

"I thought so. Does he know…?" I end with a dangling question, not even sure what I was going to say. *Does Storm know that you've kissed me? Does he know we can't seem to leave each other alone, even if we fight like cats and dogs?*

A beat, and then another soft "No" reaches my ears.

I march deeper into the garden, knowing he'll not be far. A small footbridge arches over a trickle of a stream and ends in a lovely, softly lit seating area. The evening is still fresh enough that the area remains undiscovered, so I sink down on one of the stone benches. It's hard, in moments like these, to remember that we're in Dominion. Less than a mile away, the drones record the lives of the rabble. People lay dying in their stacked cars, on the streets, in back alleys. Dying of the Plague or starvation or any number of the diseases that will kill you when you live hand-to-mouth with no help from anyone.

It makes me feel even sicker to think of the pettiness of my own problems, however cruel and large they seem.

A mosquito buzzes next to my ear. I swat at it and it flies away. Not a mosquito, I realize, but some type of miniature security drone. It circles back toward my ear with a high-pitched whirr when a small *snap* silences it forever. Jared's closed fist hovers next to my ear. He climbs over the bench and sits next to me, tossing the tiny metallic body he's crushed onto the ground.

"Leave me be," I say, refusing to look at him. I shiver, the cold seeping through me. Sending Jared away might not be the brightest thing. There are no mercs here, no one to call for help should something unimaginable happen. And

Jared has just crushed the security drone.

And lately—let's face it—the unimaginable seems to happen all the time.

His hands grip the stone as though it might buck him off. "I can't."

"Pretty please?"

I don't see his smile so much as hear it. "As much as it delights me when Your Majesty uses such fine language, I'm afraid I can't fulfill your request."

The tears threaten to spill again. "Why?" I finally face him. But though he shrugs in that deadbeat way of his, his face is as serious as I've ever seen it.

"I have an obligation," he starts.

I wave him off like just another mosquito. The panicky terror in my chest rolls over me in a wave, and all at once I've never been so miserable. And I can't bear him seeing me like this. Helpless. Weak. A pawn. "I absolve you. Go. Away." I push at him with one hand, hoping to shoo him. He grabs my fingers in return, threads them into his hands, warm and large and capable of doing any number of things, and pulls them into his lap.

"Let me finish. I have a job to do. I'm obliged to do the best job I can. Not just because I work for Storm but because that's who I am. That job is to protect you, Lu."

I turn my head, unable to bear even another second. I've had my fill of Jared's merc routine. Gentle fingers coax me back again until I'm just inches from Jared's glittering eyes. They look feral in the moonlight.

"But Lu." He breathes my name like it's a full sentence. "It's a good thing that's my job, because… Don't you know I can't even help myself?" He's so close it's as though the boundaries of our flesh have disappeared. And within one breath and the next, his lips are on mine. Soft, warm, molding me to his mouth. Then, hungrier, he pulls me closer, seeking more.

I'm dizzy with the taste of him on my lips, in my mouth. When my strength gives out, I slump onto his chest and he holds me tighter. I can barely react to the blazing warmth of his body full down the length of me, the scratchy feeling of his shirt decal under my fingers. There's a fire in me, too, and with his sudden nip to my lip, it ignites. I'm feverish for him. Jared's chest is molten rock under my hands. I'm struck with a desire to run kisses up his neck, to just behind his earlobe, just to hear the quick suck of his breath. I grab his hair and pull him tighter still. My lips sting from trying to get closer, closer, and rubbing too hard up against his teeth. Jared tries to hold them back but I can feel his incisors sharpen, the rumble in his throat deepen, his eyes flip to a luminescent green in the darkness of the garden as he drinks me in.

And just as suddenly as it started, he takes me by the shoulders and pulls me away. I sway on the patio bench like a rag doll, cold and dazed. The garden hums with some secret life, bugs and frogs, but it's just Jared and me here.

Touching a finger to my swollen lips, I watch him. He pants as though he's kicked the living tar out of someone, a glassy expression to his feline eyes. He doesn't take his hands off me, but he isn't going to bring me close again, either. And that's what makes me explode.

"What kind of game are you playing with me, anyhow?" I scream at him, thankful that the garden is empty for my tirade.

Jared shakes his head as though I've just launched into Russian. "What?"

I break away from him and step back a pace, hands on hips. "What is this for you, Jared? *I'm just your merc, Lucy. I can't stop myself, Lucy,*" I pantomime. Anger wells up inside me.

"Calm down, Lu. I don't under—"

"And here I thought the Upper Circle had the corner on mind games. Or is this part of the plan? Teach me a few of the basics so I can land a good catch? How much commission will you be taking for this, I wonder?"

This catches him off guard. A rare moment indeed. Jared cocks his head as though he's heard something strange. He puts his hands up as though to ward me off. "It would be helpful if you'd explain yourself so I know what the charges against me are."

Not a hint of a smile. He's dead serious. But so am I.

"I understand now." Feeling sick, I clutch my stomach. "I reckon taking any further liberties isn't part of the deal with you and Storm, is it? What if we lost our heads? Then what?" Sarcasm drips from me like venom. I rub at my chest, as if it can relieve the ache there, the throbbing emptiness in my chest.

Because it's true. In a flash, it all tumbles into place and I realize what a dupe I've been. Lasters are free with their bodies and their love. A Laster's life can be cut short in a moment. So they live each day for that day alone, taking pleasure and solace in each other's flesh as they can. These are lessons they drilled into us.

Life is cheap and Lasters are cheaper, the chant goes.

But with the Upper Circle, alliances form and fall over less. Upper Circle girls do not share their flesh for free. Upper Circle girls guard their maidenhead for the marriage bed:

This is the price of a good match with a man of fortune from a good family who can afford to buy a virgin bride.

Jared runs a hand through his tousled blond curls and stares at me as though I've grown a set of antlers to rival Nolan Storm's. "What in Holy Plague fire are you talking about, Princess?"

"Don't you dare call me that!" I try to ignore the ragged quality of my voice. "And stop pretending that you don't know what I'm talking about."

"Lu." Jared steps forward, genuine concern lining his face. "I honestly don't know what's just happened here…"

I take a step back. "Which suitor is at the top of the list? Teddy Nash, maybe, so Storm can get his hands on the outer territories? Please tell me it's not Robbie Deakins. I think I'd rather catch Plague."

Jared turns quiet. "Is that what's got you spooked? You think you're going to be married off?"

"It's true. Storm all but admitted it. They're brokering the deal in there." I nod to the ballroom. "And I'm the real estate." I give a jagged laugh, but there's no humor in this for me.

Jared turns his head and curses a wild blue streak under his breath. He runs his hands through his hair with a look one inch shy of tortured. "Lu, I swear. I haven't heard anything about this marriage business. There must be some misunderstanding. We…I would never do that to you."

There is such gravity in his expression. I give him the slightest of nods, showing I've heard him. But it's not enough. Not by far. Jared looks up at the sky. The clouds have swallowed the silvery moon.

"It's going to rain in a minute," he tells me. "We'll have

to go back inside."

I straighten my back and begin smoothing my hair and dress the best I can. I'm nothing if not poised.

"Lu." Jared stops me. He reaches out a hand as though to caress my cheek. But he pulls it back at the last minute. "Storm doesn't know about this. About—us."

With that, my red-hot anger fades to a dull, throbbing resentment. I wonder how he can be so dumb and blind. Of course Storm knows. Storm is likely using this, as with everything else, to his political advantage. Just because he hasn't tugged the strings doesn't mean they aren't there.

But all I say is, "I can see how you might think so," before sweeping back up the garden path, my head held high as royalty.

The minute we're back at Storm's keep, I say a quiet good night and make my way into my bedroom. It's as different from my former bedroom as something can get—and yet, curiously, the same. This is a room for an adult: no frilly canopy bed with gauzy drapes, as Margot and I both had at home. No girlish china dolls or dollhouses on exquisite display. And yet, just like the room of my childhood, this, too, is a room for display. Over the small fireplace hangs a portrait I've long wondered about. A figure kneels just outside the silver-treed woods. You can't see his face—all you see are the antlers rising up from his head like a crown.

And just like at home, you need to read into the subtle language of clues that spells out what everyone's agenda is. Storm's is clear enough: through alliances, threats, intimidation, and raw power, I reckon he will be the true ruler of Dominion before too long.

No wonder our father couldn't stand him.

I sink down on the bed in my finery, but other than taking off my sandals, I don't move to undress. There's too much going on, too many crosscurrents, for me to properly get my bearings. But if I believe Storm, soon we'll all be in trouble.

Father Wes and his followers are stockpiling weapons. Storm had mentioned this almost nonchalantly on our drive home. Expressionless, Jared had tracked my gaze through the rearview mirror. My stomach curled into a perfect knot. So much for the preacher men being safely tucked in bed, never to get up again.

"How do you know?"

"Senator Gillis has some resources on it. Our sources have corroborated this."

I thought very carefully about what I said next. "What does Senator Gillis think the preacher men will do with weapons?"

Storm looked at me, deadpan and dangerous. The cresting curls rising from his head flared briefly, reminding me why I couldn't afford to relax my guard around him. "Destroy everyone they can, I assume."

"Do you believe that?" I asked.

To his credit, Storm took a moment before lacing his fingers together over his knee, leaning closer to me. Raw power shone from his face, and for a moment, the outlandish thought ran through my head: *Behold, the power of a true god.*

"I believe my intel is correct. Father Wes is up to something. I've got resources tracking where those weapons came from, because they didn't come from here."

I blinked, surprised at the sudden turn of the conversation. "How would you know that?"

"I've had teams…let's just say, *liberating* Dominion's finest gangs of their weapons for the past several years."

My mouth gaped open.

"What on earth do you do with them?"

Storm smiled. "Bury them."

"Do you think…?"

But he shook his head. "No. They're secure."

"Where?" I didn't expect an answer. Storm's flat iron eyes raked over me, accusing me of asking the wrong question.

I stared out the window at the dark streets to gather my thoughts when Storm surprised me again.

"Back there, with the Driscolls… You don't have to worry." I arched a perfect eyebrow at my so-called guardian. Storm laughed. "I won't sell you to the highest bidder, Lucy, if that's what you're worried about."

Jared's eyes found mine again, locked. Some tacit understanding passed between us. *Jared isn't part of this, whatever it is*. The thought relieved me. Still, it didn't answer why he ran so hot and cold with me.

Storm continued, apparently not noticing the silent conversation taking place between Jared and me. "But this new situation with Father Wes and the Lasters… It has to take priority over everything else. If they're planning an offensive, we need to be ready. We need everyone on this."

I gazed over at the flat, hollow angles of my guardian's

face. That sinking burn in my stomach intensified. I prayed he couldn't read my thoughts. The bitter thought flashed through me like a knife: hadn't I known something would prevent Storm from helping me find my sister?

And so I sit on Storm's guest bed in my borrowed finery, clutching Margot's letter as though it's a Plague talisman. I've reread it more than a dozen times, so that now it's wrinkled and worn at the creases. All I am is a hollow shell with aching feet. *I need to do something. I need to do it now*. No more waiting. No more holding out for help.

A chopper buzzes by Storm's tower building, closer than I've heard in a while. I should check the streets to see if something has happened, but I can't muster the energy. There's a light knock on the door. I contemplate not answering. Then there's a second knock, a third. I utter a very soft, "Come in."

I know it's Jared even before the curl of his hair, glinting like gold, appears. He closes and locks the door behind him with a gentle *snick*. He walks over to the chair and slinks down like a jungle cat, eyes never leaving me.

"You're still awake."

"You knew I was," I accuse, heartsick and exhausted. My eyes sting with tears I refuse to shed. Beneath my hands, the bed feels like a rock.

Jared nods. "I could hear you."

This catches me by surprise. "I was just sitting here. I didn't move."

He tilts his head to regard me. That perfect mouth opens, revealing a row of white teeth and his long, graceful neck.

I'm reminded of the jungle cats I've seen in zoo archives. I watch him sink back in the chair and stretch out two lazy hands. *Don't be fooled by appearances*, my mind screams. Jared may look relaxed, but I can see the thin wire of tension running through his shoulders and arms.

Instead of answering my unspoken question, he drinks me in with eyes that begin to marble, indigo blue to bright jade green and back again. "You haven't even undressed," he murmurs.

"And you have." Jared has traded in his tuxedo shirt and dress trousers for a faded pair of pants that mold his legs like a perfectly broken-in shoe. He's thrown on a T-shirt from his collection with a picture of a schoolboy at a desk.

"Do you need help?" he purrs. Electric sparks flare painfully to life inside my body.

"Don't you dare," I whisper, staring down at my naked toes. Silence stretches between us as he stares at me, filled only by the tinny tick of the clock beside the bed.

"I'm sorry." He sighs, and suddenly he's out of the chair and beside me on the bed. Breathing in my hair. I am surrounded on all sides by his heat, his flesh, that peculiar smell of his that makes me feel instantly at peace. "I couldn't leave things like that. Too messy for sleep."

I grip the bedspread harder. "Maybe—maybe you were right about Storm. About the marriage thing. And he says Father Wes is gathering another army. Weapons, he said."

Jared nods into my hair. "I know."

"You believe this?" I look at him square so I'll know for sure he's telling me the truth.

Jared nods again reluctantly. "Storm has had Carl and Serena on it, Kira and Penny in shifts. They've seen some crates loaded with assault rifles and launchers, mostly. Some plastics for explosives."

"How are they getting away with it? How can they even?" I ask, and then find myself pressing my forehead against his chest as he breathes deeper and trails fingers down my back. But I know the answer. What do the dead have to answer for, after all? What wouldn't they do?

But the real question itching at the bottom of this pile is, *What do they hope to accomplish?*

I think about the tall, imposing figure of Nolan Storm. What does he really want from me? What is his endgame? I seem to know only one thing for certain. "He's not going to help me get Margot."

Jared winces, his fingers still on the sensitive skin at the nape of my neck. I shiver and realize that all those times I felt Margot's more amorous adventures, they were the palest ghost of this pleasure as his breath tickles the shell of my ear. "Not right now, at any rate. Not when there's a possibility of civil war. I'm sorry."

Jared's face pleads understanding. His fingernails curl up my forearm and I let slip a tiny breath of pleasure. His eyes are deep and heavy as they stare into me. It almost hurts, to be this close to him. But there's nothing in me with the power to resist. I gaze back at him, shuddering every few seconds until something inside me cracks. The tears start to fall, hot and wet and thick.

"Tell me what I can do." He holds my face close to his with the lightest of touches. It's a strange thing to know a man like him could be so tender when he could just as easily rip a man to bits. "I hate fighting with you, Lu. I hate feeling like we're clawing to get closer but just end up scratching each other."

I want to look away. I want to hide from the brilliant, glittering sheen of his eyes. They would follow me into the dark, I know. There is no place I can hide from this man.

And with a sudden jolt of pain, I realize what I'm going to do.

I take a few shallow breaths. "Everything is different now," I say quietly.

An unhappy crease mars his forehead. "What do you mean?"

I close my eyes against that fierce and protective *something* inside him when it comes to me. When I open my eyes again, he's still there, waiting for me. Always watching and waiting, the perfect guardian.

But is he my protector—or my jailer?

I stroke a hand through his curls, soft and fair in the dim light of the room. This might be our last night, if I manage to pull off what I must. I want to set the record straight.

"Sometimes I'm still terrified of you, you know. I've seen you do…remarkable things to people," I end diplomatically. And when he looks about to protest, I run a finger over his full lips, silencing him. "And then other times," I say softly, trying to memorize every line, every pore, every glint of light in his eyes, his smell, the thousand and one things that are him. Things I think I hate most times, and other times burn me to the quick. "I want to kick you in the shins quite a lot, you know. And then there are times like this, Jared Price. Sometimes I want to crawl out of my skin and into yours."

"Lu," he mumbles against my finger.

I stall him with a look. "You and I, we've had our ups and downs. And since I came here to live with Nolan, it seems like we've been stuck at a low point. Just like everything else in my life right now." He opens his mouth to object, but I shake my head. "Listen, I know you're just doing your job…and I wasn't ever safe until you… At least, that's how it feels." But how do I put into words the way he's turned everything upside down? I shake my head and try to clear the knot in my throat. "Sometimes it feels like a dream, do you understand? All electric and vivid in the way that real life isn't. Real life is people shaking and falling down dead on the streets. Real life is Upper Circle parties filled with sharks, and not of the True Born variety. Real life isn't *this*."

My hand fits across his chest. I can feel his heartbeat, a perfect clock against my fingers. I kiss his lips, the softest butterfly kiss, and my own skin ignites as his hands slide over the flesh of my collarbone. When I pull back, I can gather in the perfect symmetry of his face. The dark and light planes of his face. I hold a blond curl off his forehead so I can stare at him.

"I may hate you some days, but I'll never forget you, Jared. Not as long as I live."

I've rendered him speechless, I see as he stares down at me with a mixture of dread and something like amusement. "Why are you saying all this? Just what do you think is going to happen?"

I sit up, pushing my hair out of my eyes. "No reason. I—I just wanted you to know."

"Where do you think you're going, Princess?"

"Nowhere," I reply with false heat, hoping he can't smell lies, too.

"Good. Because if you did get any funny notions into that peculiar head of yours, know this." Jared stretches out beside me and gets comfortable. The relaxed position is a lie as he turns dark, intense eyes on me. "I'd come and find you."

10

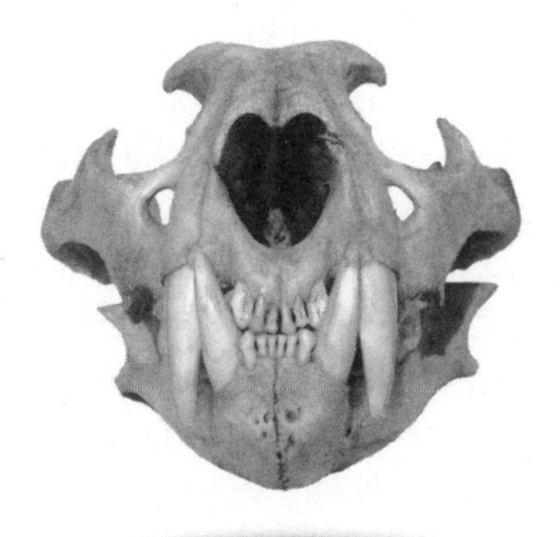

"You're joking," I tell the young man beside me. He pulls down his hat brim and hoists his bag higher on his shoulder, not taking his eyes from the ancient, peeling ship.

"Nope."

The name *S.S. Bostonian* is written in faded gold lettering on the side of the hulking cruise ship. I take in the shell-white hull, barnacles running up the front like scabs. Wide-eyed portholes line the side like a thousand dark eyes. From my vantage point on the jetty, I can see deckhands scrabbling around the deck. Cargo nets heavy with crates are loaded onto the ship by crane. Everything smells like an old sewer, ripe and thick. Tiny flies buzz around us in thick clouds.

"How old is that thing?"

Alastair shrugs. "Fifty? Maybe sixty years?"

"Oh."

"You having second thoughts?"

I resolutely square my shoulders. "You wish."

"Naw, not me." He grins and tosses up a pebble, snatching it out of the air. "This is going to be fun."

It had been a risk to meet up with Ali again so soon. My head had still been buzzing from the night before, my heart aching. *But I have to do something*, I'd reminded myself.

After Jared had left my room, I'd lain down on my bed to trace out my next steps. First, find Alastair. Get in touch with our family's lawyer, who could arrange some funds for me. And after that? No good-byes. I wasn't going to explain myself. I was just going to leave, to make a leap.

It would be more than a leap, though. It would take a miracle. Alastair hadn't been successful at finding info on Margot's passage to Russia. Then again, I realized belatedly, she and my parents would likely not have taken public transport. How had the good Russian aristocrat Leo Resnikov traveled to Dominion after all?

"We don't need to go first-class," I'd argued with Ali once I'd sold him on the idea.

He'd insisted. "Yes we do. I'm not going with you otherwise. Got it?"

I could hardly argue. It would seem odd if we ran into people who knew my family and I was staying in less than five-star accommodations. Though, as I take in the aging cruise liner, I'm no longer sure this was the best way to go.

I blow at the cloud of flies buzzing before my face. "Can't we try something else?"

Alastair throws me a dark look. "This is the last cruiser leaving for Europe for another month."

"Well then." I give him a crooked smile. "That settles that."

The ship would only get us as far as Port Alexandria. From there we'd need to make our own way across Europe and through the heart of Russia. And if my new friend thought it strange that a girl with Upper Circle resources would require his help, he kept his questions to himself. I told Alastair only what I thought he'd need to know. I was going to surprise my family—no lie there. Who would be very happy to see me…perhaps a slight exaggeration.

With a wink, Ali tucks his arm into mine and walks me up the gangplank. Over my other shoulder is thrown my small bag, filled with odds and ends: a couple changes of underwear, a few slippery dresses that take up almost no room. Three pairs of shoes and a sweater that'll do. I'll buy the rest, I reckon. Ships like this have floating stores for the rich and bored. It's not the typical way an Upper Circle heiress travels, however.

And I'm not the only one who notices. "Where's your baggage, then, Miss?" The purser tugs at his braid-rimmed hat. All around me, people stare. It's not the kind of attention I want to draw to myself.

I give a frosty pout. "Aren't the shops on board adequate?"

The purser looks uncertain. "And your parents are going to meet you at our final destination?"

I stare the poor man down, dismissing him with the wave of my hand. "I'm not in the habit of discussing my travel plans with employees." It's clearly a tone he's heard before. He steps a pace back and pulls at one side of his long mustache.

"Of course, Miss," he says, a hint of deference creeping into his tone.

I look over my shoulder, sparing one last troubled thought for the cool indigo eyes and messy blond mane of the man I was leaving behind. I rub at the invisible knot in my chest and hope it's he who first finds the scratchy note I'd left on the neatly made bed.

You know where I've gone. Don't try to find me. Thank you for everything. I'll never forget you. L.–

I cross over the threshold onto the boat. And as I do, Alastair and I are welcomed on board the largest five-star floating hotel to survive the Plague.

It could be any dining room in Dominion's Upper Circle if there weren't so many tables plentiful with people. Fine green and white linens, waiters in crisp serving suits, and row after row of gleaming serving tureens. The ceilings are swept with fans and chandeliers that twinkle and chime with the rocking motion of the ship. The synthetic flowers are a bit much—pink carnations and the odd red rose—but I suppose even floating luxury palaces have their limits.

My dinner companion, on the other hand, is a fake rose dipped in gold. We've been on the ship for mere hours and already I'm worried about him. He looks handsome enough in the tux I'm sure he's stolen from who knows where. He fills it out perfectly. And with his strong jaw and sweep of dark hair, the ladies can't help but stare.

On the other hand, I'm trying to figure out where a Laster like Ali got his hands on such a luxury item. I eye him with suspicion and lean forward over the white china.

"Where did you get that tux, again?"

Alastair tips his head back and laughs. "I told you. I brought it with me."

"In that little bag of yours? From where."

Alastair points to his sleeve. "Notice the wrinkles? From Dominion, silly," he teases.

I lean back in my chair and narrow my eyes at my travel companion. "You'd better not get us in trouble, Ali." He laughs again. I notice the envious looks of women around the dining room. I can't help but smile, and I realize what a long time it's been. My heart has been careening wildly between crippling sadness at leaving Jared behind and the overwhelming peace I feel now that I'm finally on the move for my sister. *I'm coming for you, Margot.*

But it's the relative stranger before me that I now need to understand. "Why are you helping me again?"

It's the first time I've asked so bluntly. I reckon I've asked in other ways—I've definitely considered the financial benefit to his attachment to me. But I haven't yet given the handsome young man any money. How can he trust I will? Unless he's a swindler looking for a fortune, I can't understand what he's doing here with me.

His smile stretches, showing off his dimples. "I like adventures."

"Come on, Ali," I say softly. "Truth."

"I don't know, Lucy. I guess I'm just a sucker for Upper Circle girls in distress."

I bark a short laugh and gaze out the glass walls of the dining room. The sea spreads out like a nubbly cobalt quilt. This is our first night at sea. I've become acquainted with the gentle rocking motion of the ship, feel less nauseous than when we'd first set off from shore. The sky is its usual leaden weight—just as it is over Dominion. But here, in the middle of nowhere on the ocean, I feel snug and safe. Every so often we crawl under a hole where a lighter patch of sky, almost blue, can be glimpsed. Every single time it feels like a miracle.

The ship is far more luxurious than I'd imagined from its rough and scabby exterior. Inside, the halls are stripped in dark, shiny wood and gleam with polished brass. The decks are long and filled with a surprising number of Upper Circle travelers, though luckily, no one on intimate terms with my family.

It makes a certain kind of sense. Too often there have been tales on the NewsFeed of planes dropping from the sky—captains taken sick in a locked cockpit and disappearing from radar with hundreds of Upper Circle families aboard. Still looking for luxurious modes of transport to the other nations, they've resorted to old-timey sea voyages where bodies can be buried at sea. And should one captain go down, another can instantly step into place with no harm done.

There are mercs here at sea, too. Men in crisp white uniforms stand guard strapped with semiautomatics at regular intervals in the hallways. Still, our father's man, Shane, would as soon call the ship's security lax, and I'm sure Storm would agree. Must spend a fortune transporting them everywhere. But they don't ask questions, don't frisk or point their guns at the frolicking members of the Upper Circle, many of whom have brought their own security aboard.

The higher decks are for the wealthiest of the set. Our cabins adjoin, Alastair's and mine, among these. I didn't ask whom the old gentleman was who sold his cabins to us at the last moment, nor how Alastair managed to find him. Some questions are better left unasked.

The first hours of the cruise I spent getting used to the two small but well-appointed rooms I'd be calling home for the next few weeks. My sitting room, all in light blue, has a chair and a writing desk across from a small couch. In the bedroom there is a double bed with cubbyholes to store books. But the cubbies are empty, as is the closet. I don't quite know what to do with myself when I am there save reread Margot's letter.

She might not be there—*they* might not be there—I remind myself. They could be anywhere. The place mark on Margot's letter is my only lead. And it seems to be roughly the area where Resnikov is from.

"It's more than mining, dear," our mother had said absently to Margot and me as she patted the perfect skin on her well-made-up face. "I think he's got some pharmaceuticals interests, some forestry. They still have trees over there," she'd mentioned with a wave of a contemptuous hand.

"Where?" Margot had asked this. I'd noted at the time how curious she felt.

"Oh, somewhere near the border, I think. Not too far from civilization," our mother replied with a delicate shiver.

But Russia was an even bigger subcontinent than Nor-Am. And all I had to go on was one tiny postmark. I stare down at my plate, trying not to hyperventilate. What the Holy Plague fire was I thinking?

"Lucy?"

I break free of my terrified train of thought. Alastair threads his hands together and stares at me with undisguised interest. He's been a perfect gentleman thus far. Not pressing attentions, not prying too far. If he's a conman, he's far better than most.

Still, his attention is unnerving. I find myself fixing him with a glassy-eyed stare.

"Is there a reason you're rudely staring at me?"

My plan doesn't work. Alastair doesn't turn his attention away. If anything, he grows keener. He sits forward until the shiny brush of his dark hair is only inches from me.

"Why are you trusting me like this? I'm a virtual stranger."

"You've got a point. Maybe I should leave," I mock, toying with the elegant silverware before me.

Alastair sweeps his brown hair to one side and leans on his hand, giving me a look so full of frank curiosity that I find myself blushing. "Seriously. Why have you decided to trust me?"

"Well, you did save my life." I shrug. "And"—I decide to dole out some truth—"it's not like I have a lot of options right now."

There's a long beat while Alastair absorbs this. "What I don't get is, why are you alone?"

I look around. "Am I alone?"

"I mean—a woman like you."

"A woman like me…"

"You're intelligent, beautiful. Obviously from the very top of the U. C. Witty…"

"Don't forget a major pain in the ass," drawls a voice from over my shoulder.

Awareness prickles up and down my spine. Alastair stares at a figure behind me in confusion. But I know who I'll find there.

I turn my head ever so slowly, only to find myself locked in to a pair of vivid indigo eyes.

11

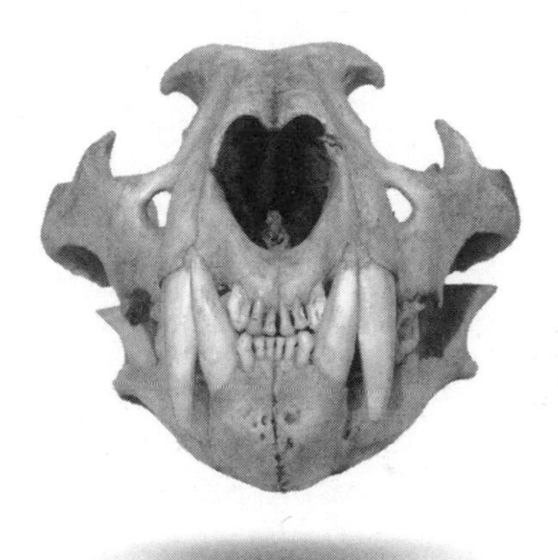

My voice is low and quiet. "What are you doing here?"

"What does it look like, Princess?" Jared says coolly. "I'm taking a cruise." A frayed nerve jumps at his temple. He pulls out a chair, swift as lightning, and plunks down between Alastair and me. Closer to me. I blanche. I'm not sure how to act. With each beat my heart lurches crazily from delight to terror. Jared's nose quivers as he scents the room. His eyes marble back and forth: blue, green, blue, green, until the pupils dilate like a cat's and he grins at Alastair.

"Nice of you to leave that note." He throws this out conversationally, as though we're at tea. Jared props his chin up on one elbow and gently brushes a thumb under my eye. "You doing all right?"

My mind stutters at the look of him. In an elegant black suit and a starched white shirt, it's so easy to forget he's not of our Circle. Except for the wild he wears in his eyes, that is. Where had he gotten the suit from—did he bring it with him or acquire it on board? And how is it that the two men I'd least expect to be wearing first-class evening wear are both dressed as formal as you come and sitting at a dinner table with me? But I quickly realize this is the least of my questions.

I tip my head in answer. Jared gives me a small, satisfied smile and turns to look at Alastair.

"Aren't you going to introduce me to your friend, Princess?" He enunciates each word, slowly and carefully.

My hand flips out almost automatically, the training second nature. I motion toward my companion. "Jared Price, allow me to introduce my travel companion, Alastair." I take a deep breath and decide to dive in. "A few weeks back, Alastair rescued me from a kid gang. They apparently had designs on selling me as a slave."

Jared yelps. "What? Why didn't you— Lucy!"

"Then Ali helped me get passage on this ship. So I can rescue Margot." I beam at Jared.

To his credit, Jared seems to take this in stride. He pulls in a few very deep breaths as he stares at me, a glint of something I'd as soon call sadness in his expression. His words, though, are for Alastair. "I owe you a debt of gratitude for saving Lucy. I appreciate your helping her out. I'm here now, though, so you don't need to feel obligated to stick around."

Alastair doesn't seem bothered as he leans back, casually mimicking Jared's relaxed stance.

"Oh, I don't feel obligated. And I guess it's up to Lucy if I stay, since she's the reason I'm currently floating across the ocean. And also, there's the little matter of my getting paid."

"I'll pay you." Jared flashes a row of shiny white teeth.

"Cut it out," I murmur under my breath. But he can hear me—of course he can.

"No need." Alastair nods in my direction. "She's good for it. Besides, I wouldn't miss this little adventure."

Jared looks down to pick invisible lint from his sleeve. "Do you know what I am?"

Ali looks Jared over with a shrewd look. "At first guess? Some kind of True Born."

Jared sits up a bit straighter. "Good guess."

"Not much of a gamble, really." Ali drapes an arm across the back of the empty chair beside him. "Your eyes are kind of going wild."

"Well then, this won't be too difficult for you to understand. I'm her Personal," he says, throwing out Dominion's word for the house mercs. It's strange to think that's what he is when he is so much more to me. "It's my job. And I'm damned good at what I do." A feral smile creeps out again.

"Jared," I warn.

"It's all right, Lucy." Alastair pinches a small red pebble between his fingers and sends me a blazing smile. "The more the merrier is what I say."

I roll my eyes as Jared pushes back his chair.

"Would you excuse us for a few minutes… It's Alastair, right? I think it's time we had a little reunion, Princess." Jared stands and holds out a hand like an Upper Circle gentlemen. All around us the other diners buzz and send us surreptitious glances. A waiter in a white suit approaches, then hesitates, finally coming to a stop five feet away. Jared waits patiently for my response.

But if I go…

"You don't have to go with him."

"No, it's fine," I tell Alastair with a brittle smile. "Jared is my…" I trail off, trying to rally a good description of him. *My other partner in crime? My professional confuser? My heartbreaker?*

"Kick-ass merc and professional dancer, among other things." Jared teases out another wolfish smile.

I roll my eyes again and take Jared's hand. His skin is hot, his touch electric, all but drowning out my awareness as we leave behind the admiring diners and one very amused Alastair.

There are more well-appointed passengers along the corridors. Women dripping with diamonds and men in dark tuxes, shiny shoes. As they pass by, they smile at us as though we're a perfect young Upper Circle couple. The older couples smiles indulgently at us. They're all fooled. I can feel it—the wild in the man beside me. But somewhere along the way I seem to have lost the sharp edge that has accompanied me since the day I realized what Jared Price was capable of. *Either that*, I reckon, *or he's a wolf who looks truly fine in sheep's clothing.*

I know he won't hurt me. Still, I find myself breathless when I realize he has walked me right to my cabin door. With deliberate movements, Jared takes my purse from my hands and fishes for the cabin door card.

"I don't want to know how you know which cabin I'm in."

The look he levels as he unlocks the door and holds it open for me could ruin a city. Jared casually tosses my handbag on the table by the door and locks us in.

The already snug cabin gets a lot smaller.

"Maybe I can open a porthole," I offer, moving over to the wall with its round fish-eye openings.

He beats me there. His hands cover mine and gently pull them away. With a deft yank, Jared has the window open. The sea blows in, smelling like a foreign land.

I don't understand the look he gives me. His eyes glitter as they meet mine, hypnotic and entrancing. I don't think I imagine the ghost of pain that passes over his perfect features. He pauses, as though he doesn't know whether to strangle me or kiss me. Then, taking me off guard, Jared gentles his fingers through my hair, pinning a lock behind my ear.

"Wh-What are you doing here?" I stammer nervously.

His eyes move over my skin as though they can read me inch by inch. "I told you I'd find you."

I give an unladylike snort. "I'm not sure you should admit to things like that, Jared."

He traces a finger down my upper arms and draws me closer. "Don't," he says. I can smell him, feel his exquisite heat wrap around me like a hug against the cold sea air. My senses and emotions are completely overwhelmed at seeing him again. "Don't. Don't ever disappear on me again," he rasps.

I stare at him, unable to comprehend the bleak look on his face.

"Jared." I gingerly place my fingers on his upper arms. He stares down at my hands.

The situation shifts in an instant. He pulls my chin into the *V* of his fingers. Angling my head, he brings his mouth down on mine. The kiss is heavy, drugging, as though he is memorizing my atoms. I cling to him, his blond curls tangling in my fingers. My senses reel so hard I barely notice when my feet no longer touch the ground. I feel his arms around me, hot ropes that coil and squeeze. And suddenly I find myself stretched out on the cabin bed. He pulls my hands above my head and holds them there while he traces the scents over my body. When he finally returns to my face, he looks drugged, his eyelids heavy with pleasure. An expression halfway between a snarl and a smile.

"Gods, I love your smell. Missed you. And that's an understatement."

He drags his teeth over my tingling lips. My spine dissolves. I lose all sense of myself for several long minutes as I reach for his lips with my own, feel the fierce heat between us build. But then, his hand trapped on my stomach, he pulls apart from me.

I gaze at him through half-closed lids, unable to think straight. All I know is I want more. More Jared, more of his gentle-fierce fingers on my back, my neck, his kisses on my collarbone—

"Lu, honey, look at me. Look at me," he insists with a little shake of my hip. I struggle to focus my eyes on his face. My stomach pools with how lucky I have been, accompanied by the dreadful knowledge that I might not have seen him ever again. Even though he's right here before me, even though I'm in his arms, I experience a dart of sadness so swift and merciless I gasp. *What if he hadn't come after me? What if he hadn't been able to find me?*

The thought is unfathomable.

"Lucy, we need to talk."

His words splash over me like icy-cold water. I struggle to sit. "I suppose."

He rolls off me and grabs a hunk of his hair as though I've pushed him beyond his sanity, which, come to think of it, I might have. "For starters, can you tell me what it is you're doing here with a stranger?" He tosses his head in the general direction of the door.

I grit my teeth. "I told you exactly who Ali is. And you know what I'm doing here."

"Do I?" He rubs his forehead like it pains him. "I know he hasn't hurt you. Your room is free of his scent. But that story you just told me..." Jared shakes his head. "I honestly don't know whether to throttle you or lock you up."

The ship rocks. I hold my gaze steady on him. True Born, I remind myself. Different. Alien. *Hunter*.

"How did you find me? What are you doing here?"

"What do you think I'm doing here? I'm your bodyguard, Princess. I'm here to look after you."

I swallow against the pain in my throat at his words. "Does Storm know where you are? Where I am?"

A cloud washes over his face. "I didn't have time to get in touch with him. I will soon."

"Were you sent to fetch me back?" I clench my fists, waiting for my heart to break as Jared examines me.

"No," he finally says. My breath comes out in a *whoosh*, and only then do I realize that I'd been holding it in.

My voice breaks. "Why, then?"

"You know why."

"No." I shake my head. "Why?"

"I can't."

"Can't what?"

Instead of answering, Jared crosses over to the porthole and looks out as though he could spy intruders in the ocean. "How did you get these digs, anyhow?"

"Alastair is resourceful."

Jared snorts and turns to me. "He's a crook."

"How do you know that?" The ship rocks again as he answers me with a look I'd as soon call snarky. Jared grumbles something under his breath. "Pardon?"

He glares at me again as the ship rocks harder and the room sways. "I said I hate water."

"Oh. Right." A True Born who shares genetic patterns with a panther? Of course he doesn't like water. He's a kitty cat. I chuckle, filing this away for later, and change the subject to something a little more neutral. "So where's your cabin?"

Apparently I'm not as clever as I think. Or I'm twice as funny. Through a chunk of his rumpled hair, Jared throws me a slightly condescending, very amused smile. He starts to strip off his suit jacket before setting to work unbuttoning his blindingly white shirt.

"Well?" I say again when I realize he's not going to answer me.

Jared flips off his shoes and throws himself on the bed, lacing his fingers under his head. "Oh, I'm staying right here. Where I can keep an eye on you and your new buddy."

"Pardon?" I say again stupidly.

"No need to get so excited, Lu," Jared says with a wide grin.

"No—no need? No!" I stomp my foot.

"Yes," he says contentedly. But his heavy-lidded eyes give him away.

Dark and delicious thoughts skitter through my brain.

I stuff them back into their box quick as I can. "I'd as soon sleep on the deck."

"Sure, we can sleep under the stars if you like."

"I said *me*." I stomp my foot again for emphasis.

"And I'm sure you meant it." Jared smiles sweetly.

My cheeks burn. But as I stare at the bare-chested True Born stretched out on my bed, I'll admit: It's hard to think of shivering under the stars when I've got Jared's warm body to curl up to.

The decks are busy with early rising Upper Circlers. I reckon a number of them believe that fresh sea air and stimulus ward off the Plague. Superstitions are ripe, even among the rich and educated. The faint buzz of anxiety still hovers over most of them, though they'll likely have been told repeatedly that stress brings it on faster. People spend most of their lives tying themselves up into pretzels to avoid catching sick, I muse.

A man in white trousers and a loose-fit pink shirt pushes past me, florid and sweating. He'll be one of the Upper Circle with a guru of some sort, a quack who'll have unearthed for him the dung of beetles or some other noxious cure the Egyptians had for earaches a million years ago. As though it would protect him. *Not so evolved*, I think to myself.

I stare around at the deck. The floating luxury ship is striking for its pristine white walls. No slogans written in jagged red paint to mar the facade of perfection. No kid gangs. No starving faces of the rabble or dead bodies. Not a single one of the Upper Circlers traveling on this ship will spare a passing thought for the hundreds of black-suited Lasters serving them flaming orange cocktails with fancy straws and bright-red cherries.

The deck fills with expensively clad passengers in what our mother would call "morning leisurewear." *Tacky*, my mother would proclaim. According to her, no one should be caught wearing exercise gear outside of one's closest circles. I'd heard those ladies once say there were only two reasons to get all hot and sweaty: the first is to land a rich husband. The second, and only to keep the rich husband, is to ward off the Plague.

"You certainly don't need to parade your Plague fears," she'd schooled Margot and me.

"There you are, Princess."

Jared has decided to play up the leisure role this morning. In his red T-shirt and sandals, his hair a nest of golden curls and his skin oozing vitality, he stands out from the other wan passengers on deck.

"As if you didn't know." I roll my eyes at him.

I'd come to the deck not just for the benefits of the sea air but because as Jared slept, arm draped over me all too comfortably, I'd had some time to think things through.

How had he managed to find me on a ship? How had he known where my cabin was, where I was?

"Where's the tracking device?" I say without preamble.

He cocks his head at me as though I've jumped into a foreign tongue.

"Well?" I push at his chest. "My arm?" I hold out the soft white flesh of my inner arm, then rotate it to produce my shoulder. "Here?"

Jared takes my arm in a gentle grip and examines the skin with rapt attention. I fight waves of pleasure. "Well, that's an interesting idea. I wish I'd thought of it. Save me a world of trouble," he murmurs. He runs his nose against the softness, darting his lips closed every few inches in a burning kiss that I feel to my toes.

"Stop it." I try to pull away, but I reckon I don't try very hard. My arm stays in his grip as his eyes burn into mine.

"You're telling me," he murmurs between kisses, "you think I tagged you?"

"You. Storm. No difference."

"I'm insulted by your lack of faith in my abilities, Princess."

It's not like him to lie even if it would suit him. Sensing my confusion, he taps his head. "Only made sense. Also I bribed a porter to tell me what cabin was yours. Told him I was your fiancé coming to surprise you."

"He bought it?'

"Apparently he's a bit of a sucker for romantic tales."

I look out at the sea, the irregular, choppy water somehow soothing. "I don't get you."

"Get what?"

"This." I indicate the arm he's currently running his fingers up and down.

"Oh. You mean this?" He traces his fingers up to my neck, threading deliciously through my hair.

"I can't handle this teasing, Jared."

His eyes, blue rimmed with green, bore into mine. His fingers still in my hair. "I'm not teasing."

"What about Storm?" I return with a stubborn tilt to my chin.

Jared looks over his shoulder. “What about him?”

“What are you planning to do with me now that you’ve tracked me here?”

For the first time since I’ve known him, Jared looks lost. He glances down at his hands as though he doesn’t understand why they don’t have a bloody limb in them. “I don’t know,” he tells me honestly.

It’s enough for now—this is truth enough.

“Be nice to Alastair.” I sniff. I take the time to gently untangle myself from Jared’s hands, though it causes me physical pain to do so, before heading to the dining room for the breakfast buffet.

Alastair is draped in the lounger to my left. I turn to my companion, shading my eyes from the bright white sea air. “Have you seen a Splicer clinic onboard?”

Alastair squints into the brightness as he watches the Upper Circle socialites stroll past. I’ve noticed that crinkles appear like outspread wings beside his eyes when he smiles or squints. They make him look older, more mysterious. I’ve also noticed that he looks at the women who shamelessly parade before my two companions—Alastair in the lounger to my left and Jared to my right—but he doesn’t really seem interested.

Except when he looks at me.

“You bet,” Alastair drawls. “A little more rudimentary than you’re used to, I’m guessing.”

“How can you know what I’m used to?” I argue.

Alastair just laughs and throws up his little pebble,

catches it. "Your family put the 'upper' in 'Upper Circle,' didn't they?"

Jared snorts on the other side of me but otherwise remains silent.

"So what kind of clinic is it, then?"

"The emergency kind." Alastair sobers.

"What does that mean?"

"It means," breaks in Jared, "when one of these fat cats falls down in a stupor, they can Splice some emergency DNA into 'im, but it's unlikely to be a good patch. The body likely won't take to it."

"Why? What's in it?"

Jared curls his hands behind his head and looks more relaxed than I've seen him in hours. "Synthetic DNA. It's like getting a blood transfusion. Only with synthetic DNA you never know if the host body will think it's the wrong 'type.'"

"They can't do tests?" I ask, but of course, I know the answer to that question. They will do tests, but Splicing is unpredictable at the best of times.

"Why are you so curious about this?"

I shrug and turn my attention back to the people going by. Alastair may not be able to guess why I would be interested, but I reckon Jared knows. I spy the man in white again, his hair falling to his shoulders in soft, dark folds, streaked with white. He's sweating profusely in his white chinos and dress shirt and is obviously uncomfortable. He gets closer, just ten feet away. I watch as he stumbles, rights himself. No one else seems to have noticed. Not even the merc in reflective sunglasses trailing him.

Jared has. He glances over at me, a question in his eyes, and I nod. This one will not last the voyage across the endless blue.

To take my mind off the man's impending doom, I glance up at the gauzy white folding overtop the dark-blue waters.

"It doesn't rain out here," I murmur.

"Pardon?" says Alastair, catching a pebble in his palm.

"Rain," I say again, lifting my voice to be heard over the ocean wind. "It's always raining in Dominion."

Alastair shoots me a funny look. "Aren't you Uppermost? Didn't your parents ever take you anywhere?"

How could I explain a life spent in our prisonlike existence? Grayguard Girls didn't just up and leave on the frequent missions our father was sent on. Grayguard Girls stayed at home and got good grades so they could land a husband befitting their rank.

Besides, thanks to the Plague, travel has become the kind of risk that needs to be weighed. And between mercs and Splicing, who was rich enough to bring their entire family on trips?

Although, to be fair, money was not our family's excuse.

The breeze picks up, and even as I take a deep breath of fresh sea air—the freshest I've ever drawn—my eyes bump against the sky. It's brighter out here on the endless ocean. Almost blue.

A funny strangled sound comes from nearby. I look over to where I'd last seen the man in white. Jared has already jumped up. I look around Jared's limb and see the familiar merc. He strips off his glasses, revealing the most piercing blue eyes against dark skin as he leans over the man in white.

"Can someone call the Splicer Clinic onboard?" the man says calmly.

None of the Upper Circle, gathering at a safe distance from the man like carrion birds, moves a muscle.

"How do I do it?" I say, pushing myself forward.

The merc nods toward a bright-red phone tucked discreetly in an alcove set in a wall. It has a receiver like a barbell, like something out of a museum. I fumble with its spiral cord and press down on the receiver until static comes on the line.

"Hello?" I call tentatively. "Hello—anyone there?" The man in white remains a motionless heap while his merc fumbles with the open collar of the white shirt.

"Yes, Miss," a crackling metallic voice finally answers. I sag in relief.

"There's a man here. Needs immediate medical attention. Splicing."

"Yes, Miss," the tinny voice says. "Stand by."

I replace the phone and stare into the icy eyes of the merc. "They're coming."

Jared cocks his head to the side as though hearing something approaching. Soon I hear them, too, the rapid clomp of boots on the wooden floors of the deck. The merc's forehead shifts up in furrows of flesh, giving him an oddly hopeful appearance. But we both know—his eyes tell me he knows already—that even with a good Splice, the man in white is likely doomed.

12

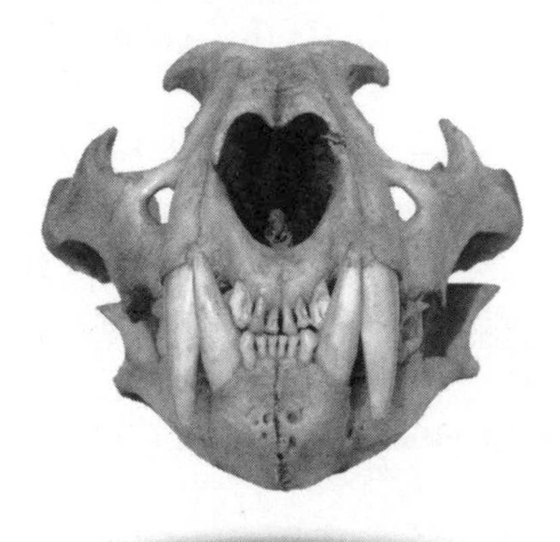

Christopher E.J. Turner is a man who doesn't forget debts. His is the presidential suite for the duration of the voyage—or his life, whichever comes to an end first. All around him is the kind of ornate luxury that I've grown up with. But here, surrounding the doomed man in white, the room's luxuries take on the character of an overstuffed mausoleum. There's a smallish bedside table edged in gilt. Its surface is cluttered with pretty junk: an antique clock, a vase of freshly cut flowers, a tissue-box cover made of gold. Small painted vases, which I recognize as some very expensive pieces, fine gold-edged china, priceless figurines. *My mother*, I think to myself without humor, *would love this.*

Turner is too sick to leave his bed, so we've come to him. His longish brown hair, streaked with gray, fans comfortably over his pillows on the oversize cabin bed, making his long, thick nose seem more prominent. He's sweating and gray, a faint sheen of whiskers settling over his hollowed cheeks. But with a pair of thick, impressive eyebrows framing eyes shining with intelligence, even sick Turner has the look of a scholar.

"Sit," he tells me, eyeing the two men behind me. "We meet again. Only this time I'm awake." He calls casually to the brutishly large merc with the piercing blue eyes who'd let us in. "Marcus, can you fetch everyone a drink?"

Something of my surprise must show, because Turner just laughs. "Marcus is more than just a merc to me. He's my right hand." He winks, and a flash of bright white teeth appears in the man's mouth.

He's still the man in white, though. This afternoon he's dressed in a white T-shirt with off-white lounge pants. His arms are covered in liver spots, though he's too young for those. Those arms seem oddly naked without long sleeves, too vulnerable. But it's his eyes I can't bear.

Even when he smiles, as he does now, Turner's dark-navy eyes look out at me with an odd hope that makes me itch.

I smile my most polite, most distant smile. "Your mer—Marcus," I correct myself swiftly, "mentioned you wanted to see us." Just then Marcus appears with a tray of lemonades in thick, frosty glasses fleshed out with green. He eyes the man in bed, one eyebrow arching up as if to say, *Are you behaving yourself?* Marcus doesn't say anything as he hands out the glasses to Ali, Jared, and me.

Not just your average Upper Circler, then. Christopher E.J. Turner is the real deal. Lemons and fresh herbs are worth their weight in gold. And onboard a ship? From some sort of personal stock? I can't imagine the astronomical fortune behind this man.

I take one of those glasses and breathe in the delicate

scents of lemons, sugar, mint. Taste the cold on my tongue, the bittersweet burn in my mouth. I don't realize I've closed my eyes until I open them again to see Christopher Turner watching me closely.

"Just a small thank-you," he tells me earnestly. "For your part in my rescue."

"It wasn't anything. All I did was pick up the phone. Anyone would have done the same."

"Not so. Not at all."

I clear my throat. Usually it's Margot who receives the inappropriate passes, and surely not in front of witnesses. What kind of man would do that?

"You like it," Turner says to me quietly, as though we're the only two in the room. It's a statement, not a question. But then, why ask? I follow Turner's eyes from my glass to the others. Alastair leans against a wall covered in delicate striped wallpaper edged with gold and stares around the room.

He whistles and fishes his lucky pebble from his pocket, jiggling it in his hand like a lucky di. "You must have some strings to pull," he says.

Turner's lean face takes on a fierce intensity. He leans forward, his arms crossed as comfortably as his legs. "Son, I *am* the strings," he says simply as a warning bell goes off in my mind.

There are giants in our world. Our father is one of them, though he prefers to keep the bulk of his affairs shrouded in secrecy. They call Lukas Fox a diplomat, though I reckon that's too simplistic to describe his dealings. "I put people into power," he liked to tell us, pulling on his signature black leather gloves, soft as butter. With a sweep of a black-clad hand, he'd say, "And I take power away."

But if our father is a power broker, the man before me is our world's emperor. Someone so far above the echelons my sister and I are used to circling in that they have a different name for it.

They say only a handful of people belong to the Gilt. They say that the Gilt is so rich, so powerful, they have their own kingdoms operating in secret behind our own.

But then, where are Turner's minions? Why is he on this floating death ship among what must seem like rabble to his elevated eyes? Something of my confusion must show, because Turner, watching me carefully, laughs.

"You think I should travel in greater style?" He winks.

I stare down at my hands, trying to find words that won't offend. "I think a man of your position may travel any way he chooses," I say carefully, noting Alastair's blank-faced confusion. "Still, I confess I am wondering, sir, why a man in your position would choose to travel this way."

His position is as precarious as it gets, of course. There are no powerful men in death.

The great man nods as though I've asked something wise. He sighs and beckons with a finger for his man, who leans down while Turner whispers something in his ear. Marcus stands, nods crisply. "Very good, sir."

"Of course," Turner says to me nonchalantly, "it's not very polite to ask a man about his health."

"I didn't m-mean," I bluster, blushing red.

"What I like about you, Lucinda Fox," he says, rolling my full name over his tongue. A full name I never supplied him with. I shift uncomfortably, aware of Jared's hackles rising beside me, Alastair coming to attention on the other side. "The thing I like best about you so far is your charming way of being both incredibly discreet and diplomatic while at the same time diving straight into the heart of things."

He laughs again, with genuine mirth this time, before breaking into a small coughing fit. When he recovers, he sips some water that Marcus produces from somewhere. And those eyes, intelligent and filled with something I'd describe as self-knowledge, rest heavy on me. "It's an unexpected pleasure to find such treasure at sea. Maybe that's why I'm on board, Lucinda. I'm a pirate hunting for treasure."

At that, Christopher E.J. Turner raises his water glass in salute and drinks to a new friendship I reckon I can't afford.

"You're not serious about going." Jared clenches his teeth at me.

Not surprisingly, he doesn't like it, the mysterious billionaire's interest in us. In me, specifically.

"He's a recent Splicer. What harm can he do me?"

"He looks at you like you're breakfast, lunch, and dinner," Jared mutters under his breath.

I look out the porthole at the waves cresting endlessly over the deep blue to hide my smile. I'm exhausted from two sleepless nights with the ship tossing me into Jared's solid brick wall of a back.

Still, I'll go to this party. If only to spite him.

"The party is in an hour." I roll my eyes at my so-called bodyguard. "It could be fun. And I might learn something interesting. You don't have to go. Alastair will join me.

Won't you, Ali?"

Ali throws his rock like a kid. Up and down. Up and down. He grins at me, humor tugging the lines around his eyes. He likes it when Jared and I "catfight," as he calls it. "Sure," he calls back.

Jared glowers some more. "You have a hearing problem, Princess?"

"No," I toss back, sweet as pie, meeting his eyes in the vanity table mirror as I clip a flower behind my ear. "I just don't care what you think."

Alastair chokes on a guffaw. "Know what? I was just thinking of going out to watch the storm for a while," he says with mock excitement. The door closes with a *snick* behind him. Jared and I are all alone.

He cocks his head slightly, lips parting as he continues to stare. "Why do you do that?"

"Do what?" I shrug. My hands are caught in my curls, trying to finish the pinning.

His fingers are suddenly there, tangling with mine. I drop my hands and let him do it. Jared's face becomes a study in concentration as he brushes one of my unruly curls away and slowly, methodically, tickles the pin in. When he's satisfied, he primps the curls at the back of my neck.

"Vex me," he says unexpectedly. "Ignore me when I'm trying to help you."

I have no answer for his questions. I know he'd lay down his life for me. The question I keep getting stuck at is, would he do it for me? *Or because Storm pays him to?*

"Do you know what this ship runs on?" I ask, turning to face him. It's a mistake. Up close I can't avoid his feral heat and musk, his blazing sensuality that appears in the blink of two absurdly beautiful, unearthly eyes.

"What?"

"The ship. Turner and Marcus took us on a tour this afternoon while you were"—I wave my hands at his chest—"doing whatever those other things are that you do. We went to the furnace room."

Where the air was hot and thick, a choking nightmare. The Laster crew was an army of workers in dirty blue and white striped sailor shirts. The bottoms of their navy pants were blackened as they shoveled coal and wood into the giant ovens that turn the giant pistons over and over. There were no dead when we toured, but they said the supervisors come down often, and the men rotate often. They said those who work the ovens last the shortest. One supervisor, a man named Mike who wore his cap down over one eye, told us sheepishly that the men received almost all their compensation for the voyage ahead of time.

"S'like an insurance policy, see." He'd nodded to the men. "They know the odds."

"But what is it?" I caught myself asking out loud. "What triggers it?"

But Mike only nodded again, this time toward the giant machines that carried the ship over an ocean. "Reckon it's the coal dust. Creeps into their lungs, Miss. We bring a'most four dozen extras just in case."

I coughed, something small and discreet. But it was enough to send terror into our guide, who hurried us topside so the brisk ocean wind could cleanse our lungs. Marcus took Turner to go lie down while I'd been left with Alastair and the black hole of my own thoughts.

"It's barbaric," I'd told Ali. His thin form had hunched

over the rail of the ship so it looked like a sail. He leaned over, touching his face to his hands thoughtfully.

"The rich ones travel across the oceans searching for their cures while the Lasters toil in darkness, just waiting to be struck down," he'd said, unusually sober. "It does strike one as unjust. Not all the richies are going to be good little Splicers," he drawled, motioning to Christopher. Even from here it was obvious he was struggling, leaning on Marcus as he ambled slowly down the hall. "Death takes us all."

The tour, and the conversation, was enough to jog my tired brain into thinking in straight lines. I manage not to look away from the overwhelming intensity in Jared's face.

"What's he doing here? Where's he going?" I whisper the words quiet-quiet, as though maybe I'm afraid to say them out loud.

"Who?"

"Turner. Where does a dead man walk?"

"He's not dead yet."

I shake my head. "Not yet. Soon. The Splice won't take. So where's he going? What's a man with that much money and power and no heir going to do?"

"I don't know. Enjoy a last holiday," Jared grumbled, but I could see his mind begin to whirl.

"Jared, you don't understand. Turner is the Gilt." I shove my hand over his mouth when he looks set to protest. "He's got more money than all of Dominion put together. What would you do if you had that much and faced a death sentence?" A flicker of blue glides over the green in Jared's eyes, but he doesn't pull away from me. "That's right," I continue as if he's spoken. "You buy your health. And wherever his cure is, it's not on board this ship. So where is Turner going? Where are all his friends headed to?"

Why is Turner on a public cruise?

I can tell the moment the final piece slides into place for him. He curls my fingers away from his lips. "You think you'll find Margot."

"I don't know. But he knows who I am, Jared. He knows my father."

"Could have been—" he starts. I cut him off again.

"No. You know that's not it. He knows my father and he wants to know me. It can't just be because I'm young and cute."

"Yes it can." Jared mock-bites the side of my hand, sending delicious tremors up my spine. "You look way too good to send you into that old goat's den."

I bark out a short laugh. "Did you just compliment me?"

"I'd rather just lock you up in here and bite anyone who gets too close."

"Bad kitty." I step closer to him, smelling the musky, sweet smell I'd know anywhere. I reach up to straighten Jared's collar. "A smart merc once told me that the best weapon a person had at hand was their brain."

Jared scowls. "And you believed that idiot?"

"Jared," I say. "If he knows something…"

Jared nods, though he's clearly not happy about it. "If he touches you, though, I'll kill him," he murmurs. I'm not even sure he knows he's said it out loud until I pinch him and he squirms.

"Ow."

"You can't follow the trail of a dead man," I observe.

...

It's a world as dark and mysterious as the preachers and their ilk. Darker still when you think they've existed with us, side by side, for years, and I've never even heard the whisper of their names.

This is not the Upper Circle, however much it looks like wealth. The Gilt don't play by the same rules. They're above rules, as Turner tells me moments before he introduces me to a pair of his Gilt friends, Matilda and Simon Mulholland.

It was so casual we almost missed the entrée to their world, as Turner greeted the couple and waved them over to where we enjoyed high tea on a private, sunny deck. They oozed charm, sophistication, genuine warmth. Immeasurable wealth.

As I stand at the door of the Mulhollands' suite later that evening, Alastair already mixing with the crowd and Jared's hand pressed warm against my back, I suddenly realize that the differences between the two worlds are more than skin deep.

"There you are." Matilda sweeps over in a simple black shift, her neck and arms free of adornments. A glossy mane of black hair trails over one bare shoulder. Like as not, Matilda is in her late thirties but could easily pass for someone younger. Smiling broadly, she holds out two champagne flutes and hands one to each of us. "We were wondering whether you were still coming."

"Sorry we're late," I apologize. Jared escorts me into a room brimming with some of the richest people in the world.

"Really my fault," he says urbanely. "We got caught up talking and the time just flew." He winks at me owlishly.

I blanch, but Matilda just laughs. "Ri-i-ight."

She moves aside, still laughing, and suddenly we're floating in a world of understated opulence. It's instinct, I reckon, that has me taking Jared's hand as we wade into the fray. Within moments I'm so overwhelmed I want to cry. Freshly cut flowers adorn every spare surface. Flowers I've never seen before, with wide, dark red petals and mysterious yellow pistils. Drinks made from the husks of pineapples—what black market sells those?—and crystal stemware overflowing with bubbly served by men and women in severe white uniforms.

And the people: no glittering dresses here. But the relaxed, casual dress of people who have it all. I catch sight of Turner in his signature white pants and shirt, open at the neck. He waves, looking happy and well. I wave back, choking down tears.

What is the Gilt? A year ago I might have answered: It's a group of people richer than all of Dominion's Upper Circle put together. I reckon I know differently now.

The Gilt can remake the world to a time before the Plague.

Jared grabs me and presses me into a white-walled corner. "What's wrong?" he blazes, looking anxiously over his shoulder.

"It's nothing," I lie. The tears fall fast and hard down my cheeks and I brush them bitterly away.

"What is it, Lu?" he pleads.

"Can't you see?" I say, as though it explains everything. "Can't you *feel* it?" I grab weakly at his shirt. It's a departure for him: an orange Hawaiian with a sunset print riding in large bands all around it.

"Lucy," he whispers, soft and sad and on the verge of wild. And my heart breaks a little more. I shut my eyes and take a deep, shuddering breath. And try not to imagine that *this* is what life might have been like if there was no such thing as the Plague.

"Sometimes I just wish," I tell him under my breath, knowing he can hear me anyway. "And sometimes there's this wonderful illusion, like it isn't even happening. And then I just—" I choke on the words. Begin again. "How can I feel so sad for a world I've never known?"

Jared presses in close to me. His heat traps and surrounds me, blasting the sadness away. He runs his hands down over my hair, smoothing the glossy waves over the soft petals of the flower tucked behind my ear. His fingers trail gently down my face. The ship rocks under our feet like a lullaby.

"But if there had never been the Plague, I might never have been. Or I'd have died. And then I wouldn't have met you. And that would be..." He looks up at the ceiling, flummoxed. "Completely unacceptable," he finally concludes. "Unbearable."

His lips come down on mine, the gentlest of brushes. I barely kiss him back, but my body ignites. He kisses my eyebrows, my chin, my wet cheeks. And when I finally look up at him again, I don't have the words to describe it. He stares at me a long, long moment, as though coming to a hard decision. Then he laces his fingers through mine and leads me over to our new friends.

•••

I say good night to Alastair, who grins and waves from his place at a table filled with card players. He rolls his pet rock between his fingers, a poker chip between the others. I don't even know if he has any money to gamble with. But I'm sure as anything he doesn't have the kind of funds these other men have. A wave of heat touches my side. I look up and Jared is there, a deep, dark promise blooming in his luminous eyes.

Something shifted between us over the course of the evening. I'd expected Jared to short-circuit all night. For him, social affairs are more to be endured than enjoyed—a test of security and wills. But he'd laughed at jokes, casually leaning against the wall and chatting with those who came near. He'd been friendly, open, gregarious, even when Turner had gotten tipsy and brushed my arm and hair. Jared had simply made an excuse to move me, his body coming between the weak but determined Turner and me. At one point I caught Marcus and Jared with their heads bent low together, but when I asked what was happening, Jared just laughed and tipped his head to the muscular man who was always just a few feet away from Turner.

He pulled me into a dance. In the middle of the room, and blocked by two women who stroked each other's hair as they waltzed, we were safe from interruption. But Turner's gaze kept looking for me. And Marcus, though rolling his eyes, was on us, too.

Jared just smiled and tucked me tighter against him as we spun and the ship spun with us. "He was thanking me for not killing his boss, which would have obligated him to fight me. He's glad he doesn't have to."

•••

When Jared leads me out into the corridor, I don't protest. I say nothing as he leans me back against the railing. He tips my chin back, examining my cheeks, my neck. He's in shadows, his face dark with some fathomless expression. A couple walks by, interrupting us. Jared grabs my hand and tugs me back to the cabin like an impatient boy. Picks me up and tosses me on the bed. I'm still bouncing as he turns around and locks the door.

The dangerous predator once more, Jared saunters over to the bed. His eyes burn into me, tracing the curves of my dress, my legs, my feet. He slips off my shoes and plants tiny kisses on my toes, the soles of my feet. He runs his hands up my legs, casually running under my floral skirt. He brushes the soft skin of my thighs with the lightest of touches.

He kisses a path up my body to my neck. Hot breath stumbles across my skin, stutters in my ear. My heart knocks so loudly I can't hear anything else. And then his mouth slants over mine and I'm lost. I pin my arms around Jared's neck and let him press me gently down, where he runs his hands softly up and down my body.

I'd never been one of those girls. I'd never been like one of the Lasters who gave herself away. Still, I know better than to think I'll live the life my parents constructed for us: the carefully planned political marriage, the safe and passionless life that the Upper Circle girls are saved for.

It's too late for that life. Our parents are gone, my sister vanished. The world is being chewed up and twisted in the insatiable iron teeth of the Plague. But more: *I want more.* I want the man of my choosing, the one who lights me up and makes me feel whole even while the Plague gobbles everything. *This man.*

These thoughts swirl and swim through my head as Jared wreaks havoc on my senses until I'm as wild as a True Born. Jared sits up, instantly alert, watching me with sleepy cat eyes. I reach behind my neck and pull the ends of the string of my halter dress until the knot gives. The halter falls down and away from my neck. Jared looks at my skin as though I've grown alien. Even though he's slept against it night after night on this ship.

Understanding heats his eyes. He murmurs, as though he's forgotten how, "We can't, Lu."

But I'm already running my hands up his shirt, unbuttoning each sunset on his orange shirt, pulling it away from his chest slowly, slowly, so I can run my fingers across the smoothness of his skin.

Jared traps my hands against his flesh where it flares like the sun. "Lucy." His eyes grow dark and serious. "You need to stop. I can't." He swallows and opens his mouth to try again.

I shush him with a kiss, a deep, wild kiss. As wild as the Plague is terrifying, as deep as my sorrow for my missing sister.

Which makes it hurt all the more when he pins my hands and pulls away from me. He's breathing hard, his perfect, sculpted chest rising and falling.

"Stop, gods, please stop, Lu." I wince at the pleading in his voice. "We can't."

"Oh," I say, tugging my dress back up. My face flames with embarrassment. I sit up on the bed and think about flinging myself into the ocean. Jared lets out a frustrated noise and turns me to face him.

"You don't understand, Lu. I said I *can't*. I didn't say I didn't want to."

Though I'm about three seconds from tears, I take a deep, shivery breath and screw up my courage to look at him.

He's gone wild. His eyes are that bright green, his face tight and twisting. "You're killing me," he grumbles. "Don't look at me like that."

"Like what?"

Jared groans and flips off the bed so fast I'm reeling. "Like that. Hurt and innocent and so beautiful you make me ache." He rubs at his chest as though I've caused him physical injury.

My mind trips over his words. Did Jared Price just call me beautiful?

"Why are you doing this? Why are you playing games with me?"

Jared barks out an unholy laugh. "You think this is fun for me? You think I enjoy this?"

I let out a yowl. "Then why did you?"

Jared tips his head in confusion. "Do what?"

"Kiss me. Touch me. If it's so distasteful to you, *why do you*?"

"Oh, gods, Lu, is that what you think?" Jared kneels before me, pulling my face into his hands. "Don't ever think that." He shakes his head. "That's not what I'm doing. That's never, ever what I'm thinking."

The tears start to fall then, traitorous tears that I can't hold back. "Why, then?" I sniffle.

"Because… For a million reasons. Because I need to keep you safe. Because you're so young and beautiful, with this bright future ahead of you. Because—"

"Stop it. Just stop." I try to pull my face from his fingers. "It's better if you just shut up now, I think."

"Come on now, Prin—"

The anger bubbles up and spills. "I get to decide my future, Jared. I make the choice. Not you." Yanking myself from his reach, I stalk off to the bathroom. "And don't call me Princess!" I shout over my shoulder.

13

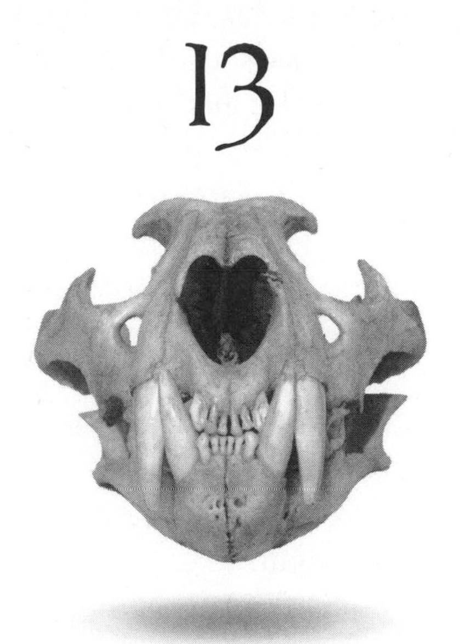

I wake folded in a pool of warm sunlight. The sun sputters under a wisp of cloud but reappears to bathe my bare arms in the first sunlight I've seen in what seems like years.

Jared nuzzles the back of my neck, his arms tight bands around my body. I can feel him breathing me in. His lips trace a path across my neck to my ear until he pulls back, remembering.

I'm surprised to see him at all.

I'd stayed in the bathroom for a long time after our fight, as long as it took to steel myself for round two. But by the time I was ready to face him, Jared had gone. So I'd lain down and cried myself to sleep.

This morning my throat feels raw, my eyes puffy and swollen. And Jared is beside me. Pulling back. It causes me indescribable pain. Under the sunlight, his hair glows a brilliant orange and white, his skin turning to marble.

"You all right?" He's so beautiful it hurts my throat. I nod. I'm not, of course. Not all right. Not by a long mile. I don't trust myself to speak, so I hold out my hand. Sunshine pools in my palm, instantly warming my skin. Regardless of what is happening with Jared, this presence of blue sky and sun is the kind of miracle I can't ignore.

I clear my throat. "When's the last time you saw sun like this?"

When Jared doesn't answer, I drag my eyes away from the warm blue sky to him. There's a stillness to him, a quiet I've never seen before. For a moment the sun falls on my face, bleaching my eyesight.

"Just now," he replies, so quiet I almost don't hear him. He's not looking at the sky. He's looking at me.

I squeeze my eyes shut, not letting the tears come again. When I open them the sun has slipped back under the endless gauze of cloud. I heave a sigh and try to ignore the overwhelming sense of betrayal I feel.

It doesn't work.

"What are you going to tell Storm, then?" I say, wrecking the beauty of the day as sure as a Flux storm.

Jared stares at me like he doesn't hear me before rolling over with a sigh. "I suppose I should have expected that."

"What are you going to tell him?" I repeat.

"Don't know yet."

"Are you going to let me keep going?"

"Stop it, Lucy."

"Are you? I can't let you stop me, Jared. Margot is out there somewhere. She needs me."

My bodyguard brushes a curl from his face. "Stop picking

fights with me, Lu. Cut it out," he growls.

His reply—*because he's right*, that little voice tells me, I am picking fights—only causes my own frustration to grow. "I reckon you have a choice to make, Jared. Are you going to make me your prisoner?"

"Storm would never ask that of me."

"Are you sure? Because Storm lies, Jared. He lied to me. He said he'd help me but he didn't. He used me."

"You know there's more to it than that. Why do you have to go and twist it up like that?"

I take Jared's palm and press it to my heart. "It never lies, Jared. Our connection—when I feel Margot? It never lies. Not like people. Never like people."

All his annoyance leaks away as he stares at me. "I've never lied to you, Lu."

"Maybe so," I rasp, fighting tears. "But when you let Storm lie? When you let him use me, when you aid him in it? That's as good as, if not worse."

Jared stares at me, slack-faced. "I don't know how you can say that."

"Because it's the truth."

"No," he says gently, brushing a strand of hair from my eyes. "The truth is, you're hurt and scared witless, so you're pushing me away. I don't blame you." Jared lets out a huff of a laugh, but there's little humor in it. "I haven't exactly been handling this very well myself."

I'm about to roll away, unsure I want to hear any more. But Jared closes his fingers around my hand, stilling me. Those indigo eyes shutter and close as I watch his Adam's apple bob with a swallow. And then he's right there, watching me with inhuman intensity. I could drown in his eyes.

"Lu, I'm scared, too."

This shocks me to my core. "What are you scared of?"

A crooked, terrible grin takes over his face. "Of holding your lifeless body. Of—of never seeing you again. Worst is the thought that you'll wake up one day and look at me and realize I'm nothing."

I gasp. "How can you say that?"

"I'm a merc, Lucinda Fox. And a True Born."

I think I see where this is going. I take a deep breath and steel myself against the wave of disappointment. "And you have a job to do."

Jared nods, very slowly. "And I have a job to do."

And you always will, I think to myself.

Turner's Splice won't do him for long. They say some just aren't good Splicers, no matter how many times they go under. This is not something we talk about as I sit across from him, sipping a cocktail layered with orange and yellow and red and topped with a fake cherry.

Marcus stands behind his boss, hovering. A faint crease of worry lines his light blue eyes. He's strapped today. A shiny semiautomatic hangs from a special holster, and he stands guard from a few short paces away while the ship's servants come and go all around our private rooftop sitting room.

"Is there something I should be worrying about?" I nod briefly Marcus's way. For his part, Marcus turns and smiles faintly as he folds his hands together. Perfectly charming, for a killing machine. Earlier that week I'd been told that Marcus had served in Dominion's black ops. *There's no better man you want in a war*, I'd heard Shane tell our father many times, *than black ops.* Trained to kill doesn't begin to cover it.

But here he is, a former black ops guarding the back of a single rich man. I'd wondered why a man of Turner's standing didn't have more mercs. Maybe, I speculate, that's just a mark of how good Marcus is.

Turner slumps over crossed knees and waves a finger at the merc behind him. "Marcus here likes to be ready for the unexpected. He's always armed. You just might not see it."

As though hearing his name, Marcus turns and glowers at me. I sink back a little in the sofa cushion. A servant in a sailor suit pops his head in from behind a glass door and nods at Marcus. Marcus waves a hand, dismissing the man, and goes back to pretending he's one of the exotic potted plants ringing the room. It's glass walled on three sides, the fourth holding an oil painting of a ship tossing in a storm. *Not the best of choices.*

"You think there might be preachers onboard?"

"No." Turner laughs, showing two rows of perfect white teeth. He sits up straighter on the wicker couch. "Too many rich people onboard who pay their bills and tip well. Besides." Turner leans over conspiratorially. "Where would they go if their rabble turned against them, eh?"

It was funny to hear that word in Turner's mouth. *Rabble.* How many times had our parents said it, too? How many times had it passed our lips?

I don't say it any longer.

"Did you see what the Lasters are painting all over Dominion?"

"Evolve or die," Turner says drolly. He leans back and sips a tiny cup of espresso. No alcohol for him, he's told me.

Doctor's orders. The new Splices need to be clean to take.

Turner's salt-and-pepper hair fans across the white collar of his shirt as he stares out over the endless vista of blank sky and choppy seas. "Such a funny phrase." I wait, certain he'll go on if I'm patient. Finally he does, taking another delicate sip of coffee.

"On the one hand, it sounds like a threat. 'Do it or else.' One the other hand..." Turner continues. "Did you know that only two percent of the species survived the purge that killed the dinosaurs? Just two tiny percent."

"Maybe it's a warning that change is always happening." I shrug. "None can force evolution, can they?"

Christopher E.J. Turner raises an eyebrow and regards me seriously. "Can't they?"

I swallow, uncertain where the conversation has gone. "Do you know who's behind it?" It can't hurt to ask. Besides, there must be a few things the Gilt knows that maybe Storm, with all his intelligence networks, won't have gathered.

"No," he says playfully, "do you?" I shake my head, unsure how to deal with a man twice my age flirting with me. Lightning-fast, he changes the subject. "You're going to meet up with your family, I understand."

"Yes," I say, truthfully enough.

"Where are they?"

I pause, deliberating on the question. It will seem strange that I don't know. As though sensing my unease, Turner says, "You've been staying with Nolan Storm."

I set down my glass, startled. "Yes."

"True Borns. I wouldn't have expected it."

"Why?" But I stop in my tracks as I realize Turner has just given me an opening. "Oh. You know my father."

Turner nods. The wind whips up. He hands up his tiny cup, over his shoulder, where Marcus takes it and passes it off to a waiting servant. "Some interesting politics, your father's."

"Yes, sir."

Turner's eyes grow sharp and daggered. "Don't play nice with me, Lucinda Fox." He smiles then, showing too many teeth, in an effort to take the sting from his sharpness. It's too late, of course. And such a reversal from the standard request to keep quiet that I don't know what to say. "Your father also has some interesting business interests."

But this is one area where I'm in the dark as much as anyone. Probably more so. Letting us girls in on the goings-on would create a vulnerability, according to our father. *What if you were kidnapped*, he'd said on more than one occasion as he made us leave the room.

Then again, Margot *was* kidnapped. Only it wasn't for what our father knew, as far as I can tell. She was kidnapped for the information growing inside her. Secrets blooming upon secrets.

Blooming inside me.

I shrug again and look him squarely in the eye. "Our father didn't trust us with his secrets."

Draping an arm across the long black sofa, Turner leans back and laughs. "Well, this is an interesting turn of events. Tell me, Lucinda, have you ever been to Russia?" There's that gleam in his eyes again, the one that speaks of hope sprung anew. "No."

"There's talk among the Gilt that a new, experimental cure is being developed in Russia."

I try to contain my shock. Heart tripping madly, I stutter, "Th-there's always someone yapping about a cure. Sure as not it's more snake oil. And anyway, what does the Gilt know?"

"Maybe you're right." Turner cocks his head. Marcus leans over and whispers something in Turner's ear before discreetly backing away. "But as I hear it—and I hear a lot of things, Lucinda—there's more to this cure than snake oil. And one of the men behind it, they say, is a well-known power from Dominion."

I start to shake. Shoving my hands under my thighs, I swallow hard before I answer. "You think this man is my father."

"I do." He nods solemnly.

"And that's where you're heading. To where you've heard he is."

"That's right. And where are you headed, Lucinda?" Turner puts his hand on my knee. Marcus comes forward, a troubled *V* creasing his forehead.

"Time for Miss Fox to go, sir. You're not to overextend yourself. Doctor's orders."

Turner gives his Personal a foul look but pulls his hand back. Marcus stays where he is, looming over me with his wide shoulders.

I stand and smile wide. Turner blinks as though he's been blinded. "Where am I going? Same place as you, I reckon. Thanks for the drink."

I look my travel companion over: his mottled green trousers and dark button-up shirt. His hair flaps in the breeze like wings. I wonder if that's what's bothering him until he points to the sky. A line of thick green clouds settles over the horizon like a fist.

"Flux storm," I murmur. "Is it heading our way?" I feel my stomach churn with fear. What would happen if the storm were to hit us while at sea? If a Flux storm can level half a city, what can it do to one little boat?

Alastair pulls out his little rock. Holds it tightly in his fist. "Don't think so. It will skate by us, I bet, though the ride will get choppy."

We're just two days from shore, or so says the crew. Two days for me to figure out the logistics of an entire voyage. *And who is coming with me*, a little voice says, drilling the point home. I'm still not certain what Jared will do. And while I now have a much better idea of where to head once the ship docks, thanks to Christopher E.J. Turner and the bread crumbs of the Gilt, I still don't know *where* exactly Margot is.

Will that special sense of Margot flicker on again? Will I just know—will she *feel* closer? Margot and I have never been so far apart before. Everything about this situation is new and strange—a living, breathing experiment.

All I do know for certain is that I'll get much farther, faster, with help.

"Are you coming with me?" And only when I've said it out loud do I realize I'm frightened he'll say no.

Alastair nods and leans on the rusted iron railing. "I'm coming. Though I'll probably regret it." He grins ruefully at me and glances over his shoulder as a crewman with a machine gun perched on his shoulder saunters by.

I stare after the figure, perplexed. "Are we expecting company?"

Alastair looks out over the sea at the growing mass of clouds. "Desperate times, Lucy Fox," he says mysteriously.

"And we're nearing shore."

"What does that mean?"

But Alastair doesn't answer. He comes to stand in front of me. He takes my shoulders in his and squeezes slightly. Then he tips my chin up until I'm staring into his fathomless brown eyes. "It's time you told me what's really going on."

I pull my chin from his fingers but stand my ground. "I told you. I'm going to meet up with my family."

Alastair studies me with a look of profound impatience. "Tell me something I don't know."

But what can I tell him? That I think we've got to follow the Gilt to wherever they're going, certain as I can be that they'll lead us to Margot? "My sister and I," I tell him, swallowing deeply, "we're different."

"Different how."

"Different. We can't seem to catch Plague," I say. "At least, that's the theory."

"So you're True Born, like Jared." Alastair shrugs as if to say, *So what?*

"No."

"No?"

"I don't think so. We don't know for sure."

"You don't. *Know.*" Ali's eyes practically cross with annoyance. "You're Upper Circle. How can you not know?"

"I told you. Different," I say, irritated. A seagull weaves overhead like a carrion bird. Close to the shore, then. Very close. Anxiety pinches at me at the thought. I need to start making plans.

"Have you seen Turner today?" I ask.

"No, he slept in, I think."

"I need to see him."

"Wait just a minute." Alastair grabs my hand. "Dammit, Lucy, I've gone out of my way to help you and then some. Least you can do is talk to me. Tell me what we're going to face."

"Can't do that," I tell Alastair truthfully. Because I don't have a clue.

"So what *can* you tell me?"

"We need to follow the miracle seekers." I spare a glance down at the heads of the Splicers taking their constitutionals on the deck below us. "Then I think we'll find mine."

Alastair lifts an eyebrow. "Your sister."

"Of course. That's what all this is about. I've been telling you the truth, Ali."

"Is she with your parents?"

"She might be," I say carefully.

"Might she also be with someone else?"

"Might be."

"Might this person have guns?" As my face falls, Ali barks a laugh, his dimples winking. "Oh, you're fun. Is she anything like you?"

"She's exactly like me," I tell him, not bothering to explain.

Alastair chucks me under the chin with a grin. "Then she'll be okay. And what about you and Cat Boy?" He nods in the general vicinity of below.

I shrug. "What about us?"

We're barely speaking, Jared and me. Almost crawling out of our skins. We revolve around each other like the sun and the moon, strange and untouching objects in the same orbit. Yet he still crawls into the softly rocking bed and goes to sleep by my side every night. Sometimes, instead of getting in, he sits in the chair across from the bed for a long time before lying down beside me. I wonder what he's thinking. I want to ask, but I can't.

And I still want him. That gnawing, hungry need for him doesn't seem to go away. When I wake up and his arms are curled around me, I sometimes just lean back and pretend I'm still sleeping so I don't have to pull away. I've wondered more than once if he's pretending, too.

The wind from the Flux storm picks up so I almost miss Ali's next words. "Just waiting…pick up…pieces." I hear him in chunks.

"What? Ali, the storm," I say, pointing to the gigantic funnel cloud that swoops out of the sky unexpectedly.

"Do…worry!" Ali yells in my ear and drags me down the stairs.

At the bottom, we spy Jared, one ear plugged with a finger. And with the other, he talks into his mobile.

"Maybe another thirty-six hours. No. *No*, that's the wrong way to play it," we overhear.

Ali tugs on the sleeve of my sweater, trying to lead me away, but when I refuse to budge, he just sighs and lets me eavesdrop.

"Listen. You can't ask her to turn back now. She'll just run away again… Well, next time, I might not be able to track her." Then, after a pause, "No, that's not a threat. Listen."

But the storm takes over and sets upon the world with howling claws that slash through our clothing like tiny knives. Jared turns. And freezes. His face is a granite mask, giving away nothing. And I do the only thing I can do.

I turn and flee.

14

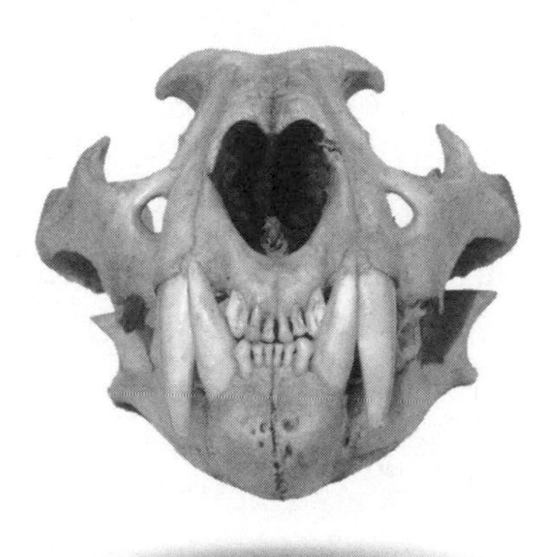

Three hours later, I'm packing my clothes. I've been unable to think straight with the wind howling and Jared's face in my mind. The old-timey cabin phone shrills, startling me. I pick it up.

"Yes?"

"Miss Fox." Marcus's gruff baritone fills the line. "Chris is asking for you. He's taken a turn."

"Oh. Do you—er—want me to come?"

"Please. I wouldn't ask, but…"

There's no need to say it. We all become both colder and kinder with the approach of death. "I'm on my way."

The cabin is dark when I arrive, curtains drawn. Turner is in his bed, curled up on his side. His sickness tugs at me the way it sometimes does with a fresh corpse. Like a nagging toothache or shattered nerves, nails on a chalkboard.

"Christopher," I say, moving slowly over to the bed. The

closer I get, the more I feel it, as though something in the malignant cells is tuned to me.

Marcus stands on the other side of the bed. His hands are empty, clenching and unclenching as though unsure what to do.

"Pull the curtains, please, Marcus," I tell him gently. "We need some light in here."

Turner winces as the frosty light flickers through the room. He rolls over to avoid the light, bringing me face-to-face with him. A pink rash leaves blotches across his wan features. He dozes on.

"Did you call Alastair or Jared?"

Marcus shakes his head. But it's Turner who places thin, cool fingers over mine. "Not them. Only you."

"There you are," I say as cheerfully as I can muster. "I reckon we're almost to shore." I'm overwhelmed by the desire to pull my fingers from Turner's. But it's the least I can do for a dead man. He'll not be able to hurt me now.

He gives me something between a cackle and a cough. Marcus helps him sit up as I hand him a glass of water with a straw. He's lost so much weight since just yesterday.

"What's the matter, Lucy?" he asks once he's sipped.

Deep lines of exhaustion have sunken his face. The navy blue of his eyes seems shrouded in the mist of pre-death. "I don't like to see you like this," I tell him honestly.

"Nor me. So close," he says almost under his breath. "I was so close." Then, he glances over at Marcus.

"You might still make it," Marcus lies.

Turner sits up a little higher. He's not even dressed today. Just lounges in a pristine white undershirt that shows the bony nubs of his ribs, arms covered in a loose white robe.

With a chuckle, he says, "Don't let anybody tell you it doesn't hurt."

There are new threads of gray and white in his shoulder-length hair, in his eyebrows, thick and wiry. They say the hair continues to grow, even after. It's the one thing the Plague doesn't put a halt to.

"Remember what we were talking about, Lucy?" I'm shaken from my thoughts. *"Evolve or die."* His free hand twirls in the air, punctuating the absurdity of the phrase.

"Yes." My fingers curl.

"You asked me if I knew who's behind it." I nod. "I don't," he tells me quietly. I suck in a pained breath, hating myself for being disappointed. Turner squeezes my knuckles. "It's odd that I don't. My set deals in information as much as money. But I have some theories I thought you might like to hear."

"You probably shouldn't be talking so much," I say, wanting to pull back. But Turner just laughs and grips me tighter.

"Save my breath for what—death? What's the point? Listen here, Miss Fox. Let's say for the sake of argument that this new catchphrase, all the rage in Dominion, is the works of Lasters. Many of whom are under the sway of the preachers. Tracking me so far?"

"Yes." I nod, picturing Father Wes, gone underground, and all the tiny ribbons and things sewn onto the tree in Heaven Square. "I think so."

"Evolve. Or die. What do you think happens when we're Spliced, Lucy?"

I sit up straighter, unsure where this is going. "The patch genes are hardwired to our DNA. Genes without their Plague switches thrown."

"Good girl." He pats my hand again, though I can tell he's growing weaker. "Someone has been paying attention in Genomics class."

Little does he know. Girls who have been put through as many Protocols as Margot and I have can't afford to be ignorant. Girls who have secrets locked away in their bodies, bodies like a lock and its key.

"So why would a Splice fail, then?" he asks.

"When the native genes resist and overcome the newly introduced genes. It's like a hyperimmune response."

Turner nods weakly. "Did you know? A bunch of the people you met at the Mulhollands'—they're all going to seek the new cure. Word around the Gilt has it that this is a special new kind of cure. Overcomes even the most resistant strains of Plague. And best still…you don't need to be Spliced."

What? My mind swims with all that Turner is suggesting. "And you think our—*my*"—I catch myself—"father is behind it."

"I am aware your father has a business partner in Russia. Bit of a dark horse. But certainly someone to pay attention to."

Turner coughs, which turns into a long hack. Marcus leans down and pats his back while Turner tries to get himself under control. The dying man takes a sip of water from the cup in my hands before continuing. "Lucinda Fox," he says with a sweet smile. He brings his hand to my face, and I struggle to suppress the chills crawling down my spine. Brushing my cheek with papery fingers, he continues. "You'd make a good nurse. If things weren't turning out this way, I'd want to take the time to get to know you better. I'd make you mine."

The hand falls, heavy and limp. I stare at it, the skin almost the same shade as the white sheets. I look back into Turner's face. His navy eyes are still open. Open but unseeing. A small smile still lingers on his lips. But I can see even now the skin around his jaw relaxing, the pallor of death as it crawls over him.

I scramble off the bed. "Marcus," I call. I press myself against the wall, feeling nauseated, but I can't figure out if it's from a man dying in front of me, the way he touched me, or the sudden pitch of the boat. *Flux storm coming*, I remind myself.

Marcus leans over his former employer. He gently pulls the lids down over those navy eyes and sighs. "For what it's worth, I'm sorry. I did what I could to keep him from you."

I'm shocked by Marcus's matter-of-fact explanation. And then suddenly the enormity of death stuffs the room. Everything, from the china figurines down to the gold boxes, looks as it should: a proper mausoleum. The relentless tug of illness that I feel around the catching-sick halts abruptly. I breathe deeper, as though the room has suddenly flooded with oxygen. When something wet falls on my arms, folded across my middle, I reach up and realize it's my own tears.

"I'm sorry." They're the only words I have. I'm not sure they're for the man or the merc he leaves behind. I stumble over to the door and am out into the eerie brightness of the deck before I hear Marcus call me back.

"Wait. Miss Fox—Lucy." I stop and let him catch up to me. "We'll be docking soon. I know he wasn't the best of men." Marcus looks up at the heaving sky. He hands me a crisp white envelope with my name scrawled on the front.

I look at the merc. His shoulders are hunched. I wonder

what his life will be like now that his employer is gone. "What will you do?"

Marcus smiles, but it doesn't reach the ice of his eyes. "I'll take him home. He left me everything, you know. Everything save what I'm giving you, in there." He nods to the envelope. "Go ahead, take a peek."

I fold the envelope open. Inside are three printed billets for a first-class train, along with a map. Europe is stitched in red where it joins with Russia. A large red bull's-eye marks a town just across the border.

"What is this?" I ask.

Marcus nods. "Your inheritance."

I meet Marcus's uncanny gaze. His lips twitch with something I'd as soon not call humor. "Thank you," I finally manage to say.

Marcus nods and flips his shades down over his eyes. "You're welcome." The words come out frosty, but his next are softer. "I hope you find what you're looking for."

"You're Gilt now, huh?" Somehow it seems fitting that what must be one of the largest fortunes in the world is going to a caregiving merc. "You going to buy shares in this miracle cure?" I almost don't recognize the cynical edge in my voice.

But if Marcus is offended by my question, he doesn't show it. He squares his shoulders, hunching them against the howling wind. "I'm going back to Dominion. And I'm going to build a hospice for mercs."

It makes me feel better that I believe him.

15

The train car sways violently as it hits a bump. I come off the seat a fraction, sitting down hard enough to feel my teeth clamp. It's an old train. The beige leather seats are cracked and blistering. The car smells of mildew and dust, and the windowpanes are streaked with dirt. Down the aisles run carpets that in places have kept their diamond patterns. In others, they've become frayed and gummy with age. I shiver with a cold that hasn't left my bones since the ship docked at the small port town in the area formerly known as Greece.

Ghost yards. That's what they call them. Places where the dead pile so high there's little more to be done but to bury the town. Though I could smell nothing but sea air, everywhere we walked I spied the black dresses of old fishwives standing in doorways, eyes rheumy and tired of weeping. There were no children, none that I saw. But I heard the braying of dogs, probably wild packs, a hungry sound that set the hair on my neck on edge. Around the small, dilapidated town ran barbed-wire fences. Probably to keep the dogs at bay.

Once they start eating flesh they don't stop, they say.

Then we were on the train, courtesy of the late Christopher E.J. Turner. We sat in a berth reserved for funerals, though the place where the coffin would ride was empty. Not another soul rides in this car. The conductor has assured us, in his stumbling English, that we'll reach the border by nightfall. Add another day's journey and we'll be mid-distance to the small town printed on Turner's faded tickets.

"You need to eat something." Ali nudges me and holds out a sandwich. He bought it off an old woman weaving through the cars with a straw basket of goods. It smells like moldy socks, bad enough for me to lose my already nonexistent appetite.

"No, thank you," I say in my best socialite voice. "I'm not hungry."

"What's the matter—you Upper Circle girls too good for train fare? I don't think it's dog or anything." Ali gives me a lopsided grin and unfolds a corner of the sandwich to sniff at his mystery meat. He takes a bite. "Mmm. Tastes like chicken," he says cheerfully.

I smile, but it doesn't reach my eyes. "Maybe later."

I turn my head and pretend to watch the darkling view zoom by, avoiding looking at Jared as much as possible. *He's here*, I remind myself. *Isn't that enough for now?* I try to be happy about it, but the words from Jared's shipboard call endlessly loop through my brain. *That's the wrong way to play it.*

I assume the person on the other end was Nolan Storm. Jared was fighting not to turn me back to Dominion. I want to be grateful. But the words are stuck in my head. Am I something to be played?

"Why would they be in this place again?" Alastair mumbles through a mouthful of bread and meat I'm certain can't be very good.

I shrug. "Turner knew things."

"Yeah, but he went to his grave with those things." Ali munches.

I briefly meet Jared's eyes. We've not passed a single word since leaving the ship. My legs wobbled on the dry dock, and he grabbed my arm, helping me walk until I could get my land legs under me. Other than that, he's not laid a finger on me.

Nor said why he's defying Storm to help Margot and me.

"The ticket ends in…" I read the stiff cardboard ticket again. "Starry Oskol. That's where she'll be."

"You're sure." Alastair lets out a whiff of disbelief.

"Sure as coffins," I toss back.

Jared's eyes rake over me, making me doubt myself. Was it true? Could Turner's sources be trusted? And what did we really know about the man? Along with the rest of the Gilt, Turner might just been following shadowy hunches and bad rumors.

In the end, what did we really know other than it's the end of the line? The trains don't run past Starry Oskol anymore, we're told.

They say Russia has been in lockdown for the past three years. Under quarantine. The main rail line was shut down, the highways cordoned with barbed wire and sentries riding tanks.

•••

“They still believe in superstitious nonsense,” our father had scoffed at the time. “Those peasants,” he’d spat, “still think the Plague is airborne.”

“Don’t they have genomicists, Father?” Margot answered meekly, tucking a strand of hair behind her ear. “How can they not know?”

Our father beat his black leather gloves against his open palm. “You know who runs Russia, girls? Those who know how to exploit the rabble to their advantage.”

It wasn’t until later that we wondered whether our father had been telling us that the scientists and NewsFeed had been bought off—the way we suspected was happening in Dominion.

Jared’s phone buzzes unexpectedly. A washed-out lemon-yellow decal flashes across Jared’s chest as he leaps up to answer it. *Life sucks. And then you make lemonade!* runs beside a crude drawing of a glass and some lemons. His indigo eyes flicker over me—not cold, exactly, but distant—as he gets up to speak to someone back home. Only after he’s left do I realize I’d been staring.

Alastair tosses his rock. I half-heartedly watch from the corner of my eye as the rock bounces slowly back into his outstretched palm, as though attached by a spring, before hovering slowly down in a highly unnatural fashion. I turn my head hard. He’s watching me, a sly smile dressing his handsome face.

Did I just see what I thought I did?

Before I can ask, Ali finds a way to distract me. “Tell me

something about Margot."

"What would you like to know?"

"You've said you're the same." Ali cocks an eyebrow and shoves his rock back into his pocket. "What do you mean by that?"

But I don't have words to describe the person I have shared my soul with since before we drew breath. Margot and I aren't just sisters. We'd shared flesh and blood. *Lock and key*, like the strange birthmarks on our toes where they had separated us.

"Everyone always says that. So how are you different?"

We're different now, I want to say. Disconnected these past four months, I've been steadily gaining an independence that leaves me as sad as it does uncomfortable.

The pinch of the soft skin on her thighs, the hot pressure of a kiss at her neck—I'm not sure we'll ever know why I've had this eerie extra sense of her. Up until now it's always been enough to know it exists. There has always just been a "her" and a "me," never quite separate, never quite the same. A coin with two faces.

And now? Jared stalks up and down the length of the car, his face a mask as he listens to someone half a world away. He meets my eye, spins, and heads back to the other end of the car. The muscles in his back bunch beneath the pale lemon of his shirt.

Now, under the spell of the clacking train, there is only the silence of me.

"In the Upper Circle, the ladies say people fall in love so they don't have to be alone," I say, surprising both Alastair and myself. I run my finger over the grime-coated window. Making the letters of a name I know as well as my own.

"Margot and me, we've never been apart. Never been 'alone' until now. We used to switch places, you know. It felt like putting on a fancy party dress. No one knew. Not even our parents could tell when we were determined." I grin at a memory of me donning one of my sister's party dresses before pinning up my hair. The hair was the key. Margot always wore her hair slightly longer and straighter than my own shorter curls. Margot's eyes, with the faint shots of gray streaking through the hazel. Her skin like cream. "She's so beautiful. When she walks in the room, people can't peel their eyes from her." I can feel the wistful smile tug at my lips. I miss those days.

A funny expression steals over Alastair's features. Brown eyes marble black with some emotion I can't name. His fists clench in his lap as his long, thick eyelashes hood his eyes, and he tells me, so slowly I can't help but blush, "So you are both the same, then."

I stare back out the window at the endless darkening vista and pretend I don't understand his meaning. "I guess so."

Ten minutes before we reach the border, a man in uniform tells us to prepare our papers for the blockade. It's fallen full dark by the time we arrive under the canopied station. Lines of men and the occasional woman in drab green khakis and machine guns halt the train. All along the tracks, men enter the cars with guns drawn and scream at the remaining passengers in Russian, French, Greek, then English, to get off, to pull out their papers.

Our car is boarded by a man kitted up in a blue hazmat

suit. His face purples with rage under the clear film of his visor. He screams as another suit behind him trains a machine gun on us.

"I was feeling so welcome," mutters Jared, who stands and flares his eyes at the duo. They visibly shrink back, guns lowering like withered flowers.

"It's for Plague, then," I say.

Jared ignores me. "Stay behind me, Lucy. Alastair, you take point," he tells Alastair, hints of steel in his voice. "Keep Lucy between us at all times. Do you hear me?"

Ali smiles, putting a hand on my lower back that Jared doesn't miss, if his frown is anything to go by. Ali's dimples deepen. "Hearing has never been one of my issues."

The hazmat team tags us and leads us off the train. We're in a station of some sort. Concrete walls are lit by fluorescent lights, flickering and garish, that track the length of the industrial ceiling. Everything the light falls on looks sick and spoiled. Everything else is pooled in shadows. At our feet, pools of grime-filled water pock concrete walkways, as though we've landed at a sewer instead of a border crossing. The air is fetid and ripe with fear.

We're not alone. The train has disgorged a least a hundred poor souls. They now shuffle in well-behaved lines through a maze of partitions, over to a bank of tall desks shut off from the crowds by what looks like bulletproof glass.

"What are they afraid of?"

Jared's eyes rove restlessly, cataloguing each gun, each man. A tired-looking woman at the window of one of the closest booths breaks down and weeps before she's dragged away by four hazmat suits. My stomach drops. Alastair asks under his breath, "How do they know if they're sick?"

The woman howls, kicking her legs and flailing. The hazmat team grabs her firmly and hauls her out of sight. Jared's nose crinkles, the bones in his jaws longer than before as his instincts flare. Not more than a minute later, four shots ring out. Half the line ducks. The other half closes their eyes and stifles sobs.

Instinctively, I grab for Jared. He swivels his head toward me, and I'm not surprised to see he's going feral. The outer rims of his eyes lighten to a deep, vivid green. Claws extend on his hands, a hunch in his shoulders starting somewhere near his neck. He snarls. The room goes silent. And though I know it's not intended for me, some part of me shivers with it. His nose quivers as he scents the room.

It's then that I clue in to what kind of trouble we're in. If soldiers come at me, he'll not be able to control himself. Jared will rend them limb from limb. Then they'll kill him. It might take an army, but they'll kill him. I close my eyes and lean into his clothes, tightening with his transformation across his ripped chest. His flesh is hot and smells peppery. He's ready for a fight.

"Stay with me," I murmur, using the same words he gave me all those months ago. "Stay with me, Jared. Don't leave me alone here."

Jared looks down at me. His lips twist in confusion. I place my hand above his heart. Its steady pulse calms me. "I can't do this without you. Don't take any unnecessary risks. Please."

We're interrupted as a hazmat team approaches. One of the men steps too close to me. Jared's snarl turns into a roar that echoes through the cavernous space of the depot. The hazmats and everyone else freeze. Moments later, two uniforms step forward, machine guns trained on us. A dark-haired one lets go a violent stream of Russian and motions for us to step out of line. We comply, while the second uniform pulls up the rear as they lead us to a room tucked off behind the processing counters.

The door opens and we're dumped in a brightly lit office. Behind me, Ali sings, "If the Plague don't kill you, we got bullets." It's the refrain of a song that was popular in Dominion a few years ago, during the bread riots.

An examination table sits to one side of the room, the desk across from it. Over the windows are steel bars and metal slat blinds. A square industrial clock with Cyrillic numerals hangs over the desk. No personal touches. No filing cabinets. Just a small sink for washing. A bare white cupboard, I assume for supplies. A small fridge.

Protocols, I reckon. Seconds later, a man in a white coat and wire-framed glasses strides briskly into the room. A second man with a gun, glassy-eyed and looking trigger-happy, stands sentry.

Jared's chest puffs out, his hands clenching automatically as he steps in front of me. I lay a hand on his shoulder to let him know I'm there, safe and whole. I feel his shuddering breath, the restraint it's taking for him not to rip the room to shreds.

"Let's just ask them what they want," I whisper into the heat of his back.

But I know he won't. He's busy sussing out the armed sentry. Even I, with my untrained eye, can tell we won't get out of this unscathed. Face red and still covered in spots, our young guard has got his machine gun aimed at us, twitchy finger on the safety. I can practically see Shane shaking his head. *Hold a gun like that and someone ends up with scrambled brains, sure as rain.*

The Protocols doctor steps forward, eyes black pits beneath the glass of his wire-framed glasses. He throws out something in a language like slippery ice cubes. Jared shakes his head. The doctor repeats it, in another language this time. It's too fast for me to catch. We stare blankly back.

Ali steps out from behind me. He raises his long, thin fingers, the hands of a pianist, and utters a few slippery vowels. In there I hear Ali throw the odd word I understand. "Visitor," "girl," "English." He speaks slowly, so obviously he's not a native speaker, but has enough to get by.

The cold-eyed doctor stares at us meanly. Then says, in stilted English, "State your business here."

"Family," Ali pipes up again, this time in English. "This one is our charge. We're her men. Her mercs, see?" Ali thumbs in Jared's direction. "True Born merc. We reunite this one with her family. Not safe traveling alone, is it?" he finishes.

I choke down a bubble of hysterical laughter. Who would believe Alastair is a merc? You can practically see his skin and bones under his dirty brown leather jacket. One of the pockets ripped and dangling. And what kind of merc doesn't have a gun?

The cold-eyed doctor just regards us carefully. "We will see."

My chest knots. They can't take Protocols from me. Not here. If they draw my blood, they'll know I'm not the normal sort of Splicer. They could kill Jared and Alastair just to get their paws on me, keep me locked up here for years.

"You can check," Ali calls as the doctor pulls out two

plastic-wrapped Protocols kits from the cupboard. "Perhaps you know her host. We're traveling to Starry Oskol?"

It's not something you'd notice if you weren't looking for it—the doctor pausing for just a second too long.

"A lot of people are traveling to Starry Oskol these days," scoffs the doctor as he unwraps the trays.

"Why?" I ask before I can think of what comes out of my mouth. Jared growls again. I shrug in apology.

The doctor, though, seems to like this game. "Starry Oskol is the place where the foreigners think they'll find their cure." His black eyes flash a glare as he comes forward, clearly amused at the stupid foreigners. "They arrive by the trainload, and we end up with a trail of corpses all over Russia. But you already know this, I think."

"We're not them," Ali says firmly. "We didn't know."

The doctor nods, his mouth a blank and colorless line. "Perhaps her family is already there, seeking their cure."

Resnikov. He was a big enough fish to make our mother sit up and take notice. Maybe he's a big enough name to drop here. I clear my throat and shrug again. "It's an engagement party. My sister is getting married to a man from around here...maybe you've heard of him? Leo Aleksandrovich Resnikov." I scrunch up my nose and tilt the vowels on the name like I'm unsure of it. As though I've barely heard it before.

It's enough. The doctor stops, syringe upturned in one gloved hand. He stares hard at me.

"Who?" the doctor asks. But he's lying. I know he's lying. He knows.

"Our father and he are very good friends. Business partners, too, I'm told. Do you know him?"

The syringe drops to the doctor's side. He barks out a command in rapid Russian to the sentry, whose gun dips up and down in the chaos. The sentry barks at us, his mouth angled and hinged wrong when it opens and closes. With the tip of the gun, he waves us, red-faced, to the door. The doctor puts down the syringe and wipes his glasses carefully.

Under his breath, the doctor mutters unhappily, "Why didn't you say so?"

"If this is first-class I want my money back." Alastair clamps down on the pebble in his hand, fist turned down, and complains. "Seriously? This is supposed to be a good thing?"

We've been relocated to a "special guest" car, according to the doctor. He'd watched us board the train while a squadron of olive-clad uniforms stood behind him. Their guns weren't trained on us, but they weren't relaxed, either. And now we sit in a garishly lit car. Like our last car, this one is empty save us. It smells better, though, and the seats aren't cracked. Still, the conductor doesn't come by as the dark train speeds through the night. We're all three on edge.

Jared, who's been more a mountain than a man the past hour, stretches and nods to the top corner of the car. "Cams every four feet. Whatever tripped them up," he says, his voice muted so it doesn't carry beyond us, "they're not just letting us go." A shiver of fear travels up my spine as I spy the small box with its round, dark eye, aimed at us.

I let out a disappointed huff. I had hoped Resnikov's name held more weight than that. Maybe he has enemies among his countrymen.

"Do you think it helped at all?" I murmur close to Jared's ear. Close enough that his smell invades me, swamps me with longing.

He reaches out to touch my hair, almost as though he's forgotten we're barely speaking. Lightning-fast, he pulls his fingers away. Something shifted between us at the border crossing—we've reached a tacit truce, though we're still unsure of each other.

"Yes," he says, his voice hoarse. "I think they would have taken our blood and killed us all."

I shiver again and turn, suddenly aware of Alastair's dark, thoughtful gaze on me.

"No guards, though," I say, pretending cheerfulness. "Good sign?" Jared barely moves his head. The news must be bad. "What is it?"

Jared slowly turns and looks me full in the eyes. "Lucy." He shakes his head.

I can't sit still. Too close to Margot. Too far away from Jared. "Well." I put on the well-worn act of an Upper Circle matron. "I'm ripe for a new set of clothes. I'll move to the next car to change."

Jared nods at Alastair, who jumps up. "I'll come with you." Ali follows me through the overly lit car to the dark juncture. It's still unlocked—a good sign, I reckon. He pulls open the heavy door. We step inside a car flooded with people.

I jump into the queue for the bathroom at the long end of the car. Blank, horrified faces stare at us. Dark, smudged eyes, crying children. Something smells dead in the car, though no one says a word. They are crammed in here, sometimes three or four to a seat rather than the two it holds. And the children: babies sitting on the floor in dirty diapers, crying for their mamas. There are a lot of orphaned kids in this car.

I've heard it said that Laster women get hit hardest. Something to do with the rigors of having children. A hand reaches out, grabs my wrist. I look down into the exhausted face of a young woman. *Sick.* The other sense of mine prods me gently, sending gooseflesh up the back of my neck. Thin, haggard, her hair is covered in a bright scarf tied behind her neck. A baby rides in her lap, quiet and watchful in the way no baby should ever be, its face sucked dry of fat. Slumped into the woman's side is a little girl no more than seven. Her hair is neat enough, falling around her face in long, honey-brown tresses. Every so often her eyes flicker open and I see the glaze of swiftly approaching death.

The woman's voice floats up, thin and reedy. "*Pozhaluysta.*" *Please.*

"My Russian is...poor," I tell her haltingly in her native tongue. We speak many languages, Margot and me. Mostly just a smattering, though, enough to get us through cocktail parties with politicians and their wives.

It's enough that her grip tightens. Her hands are full of false hope. "Help. Please."

Behind me, Ali tenses and tries to break her grip. "Now wait a minute, sister," he tells the woman. She doesn't spare him a glance.

I stop Ali with a small shake of my head. Turning back to the woman, I glance again at her two children. "How?" I ask, blinking against the stinging of my eyes.

But we both know. Her baby with the watchful eyes will likely be orphaned and alone by dawn.

"Take...Sigil." The mother holds up the thin wrist of the baby.

"I can't." I shake my head. My stomach roils with upset. "Can't," I say again when she spends too much energy gripping me harder. "I'm very sorry."

"Will need...healthy mother." The voice thins, grows weaker.

"Yes," I rasp. "I know. I'm so sorry."

She shakes her head as though it pains her and finally looks about. All around her the hordes stir restlessly. My own eyes occasionally light on a woman, eyes averted to our little scene, desperately tending to her own brood. The woman before me swallows painfully. "Help," she commands.

The Upper Circle says Lasters don't feel for their children. Too close to the shiny bright teeth of the Plague for love, they tell us. But I see a different tale in the feverish eyes of this mother. How old is she? Hard to say, as she's taken by the ravages of Plague.

I kneel down before her, squeezing her hand tight between my two. I'd do just about anything to take her baby in my arms and keep it safe. But there is no safety with me. I may not even survive this train ride. I keep my eyes on hers, willing her to see I speak the truth.

"Trouble...follows me." The Russian tongue fits in my mouth like marbles. "No good...baby." Her head nods down, defeated. I squeeze again, tilt her chin up with gentle fingers. "Hello?"

It's defiance I see glittering in her eyes. She'll fight for breath. I admire her suddenly. As much as I've ever admired anyone.

"Mother," I say softly, just loud enough for her ears. "I go now. I look and return. Look for good mother."

She nods, sinks deeper into her skin.

"Fight," I tell her fiercely.

A shadow hulks over me then as Ali leans over the woman and whispers something—a blessing, a promise maybe—into her far ear. It's only because I'm watching intently that I see he's palmed his little pet rock in one hand, presses it to the woman's cheek as he talks.

But as his words die, I feel something hot and electric course through the woman's fingers, heating her skin. I drop the woman's hand as though she's electrocuted me, which in a way I guess she has. Ali straightens, all evidence of his little rock disappeared as the woman sighs and smiles and shifts her body so it's more comfortable.

But she wears a peaceful smile on her face. Her baby relaxes into those thin arms and closes its eyes.

"What did you do?" I ask under my breath as Alastair hauls me up and points me toward the bathroom at the end of the car.

"Nothing," he tells me.

But he won't look at me. *Who is this boy?*

An old man holds on to the doorframe ahead of me, his eyes rheumy. Coated with cataracts, blind and milky. Like Serena's eyes. The eyes of a Salvager. I try not to stare and instead send Ali a question with my gaze. Leaning into an arm against the wall, Ali stares down at me with his own question.

"What the hell was that, Lucy?"

The door opens and a young girl darts out. The old man shuffles past her into the small stall and closes the door with a harsh rasp. I compose my face, the careful mask of the diplomat's daughter. "What was what?"

"You're about as jumpy as a flea. What the hell kind of

deep game have you and Jared pushed me into?"

I blink hard, clear my eyes. "You don't know everything, Alastair. This isn't a game."

"I have two eyes, don't I? I'll ask again. What kind of storm are we heading into?"

I look around. Curious eyes light on us from all corners. "Not here."

I turn, but Ali grabs my arm so I have to meet his eyes. "Who are you running from? Do I need a gun?" He bites his lip in frustration. "What does he suspect, Lucy?"

"Trouble," is all I can say.

The lock to the door trembles and finally opens. I dart past Ali into the foul-smelling stall and hang my bag on the door peg. The lights, dark and tinged with green fluorescence, flicker on and off. There's a square of a mirror over the little pump sink, spackled here and there with dark spots that could be anything from mold to dried blood. I stare at my reflection and shove my fingers through the wild tangles of my hair. Stare at the wan, still face in the mirror. Her likeness so close to Margot's it's like having my sister back. But then the differences give way: the way she holds her head, stiff and square. Her eyes more gray than Margot's. And what the eyes hold: Margot has always looked more innocent, no matter what's happened. Even after her time as a captive.

When my eyes finally light on it, I don't know how I could have missed it. My stomach plummets as my breath hitches in my chest, coming out in shallow gasps. Faint red lettering angles out behind my head. I turn. It's smeared in places, like lipstick after kissing. As though someone was in a hurry to remove it.

I pull on a change of clothes quickly and rush out the

door, surprising an older woman who supports her weight with a cane. I push past her, tugging a bewildered Ali along with me.

And I'm looking. Everywhere. Eyes roving to the seats, the crevices above the luggage racks. When we hit the front of the car, I see it again. This time more elegantly scrawled, high above the sliding door that will let us into the "special guest" car. Two conjoined circles in red. And beside it, lettering.

EVOLVE OR DIE.

They're here.

16

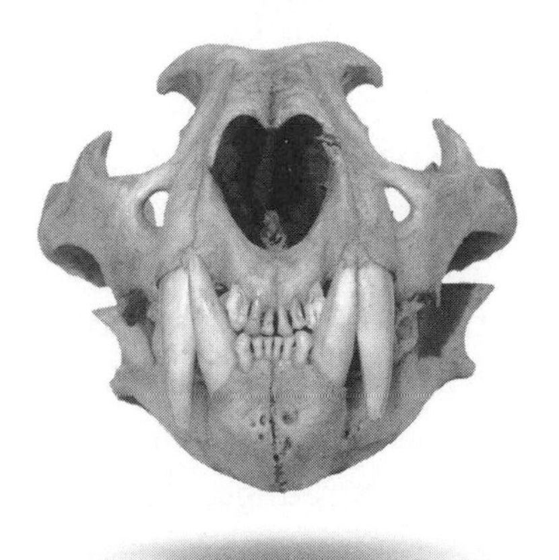

Once we return to our seats and I mumble my secret into Jared's ear, he jumps into action. He pulls out a tiny notebook I'd not seen before and starts scribbling letters in it. He tips the letters toward us, one by one, then crosses them out, all the while making sure the cameras can't see what he's doing.

"Giggle every so often," he murmurs to me, his breath a hot tickle against my ear. "A game." The giggle sounds forced even to my ears, earning me a sharp look.

Across from us, Alastair stays silent, watchful. An outsider to our secret language.

"Your turn, Ali," Jared says loudly, plastering a big smile to his face. Alastair blinks and sits up straighter. "Hang on." Jared scribbles something in small, neat capital lettering. He rips it from his notebook and hands it to Ali.

KNOW THE PREACHERS?

"Ha-ha!" Ali chuckles and shakes his head like Jared has passed him a dirty note. "Yes, I know this one."

He hands the paper back to Jared. "That doesn't belong in this game." He smiles, but his eyes stay inky black and hard.

"Well put!" Jared thumps him on the arm. "How about this one?"

Jared scribbles something else. I catch only a word or two as he hands it over to Ali. PREPARE FOR ANYTHING, I think it says. But it's gone in a blink, crumpled up and tossed into the heap of other scraps.

"Well." Ali leans over and drapes an arm across his knee. His fingers reveal his little orange rock that he pinches between his thumb and forefinger. "If we're bored with this game, there's always Hangman." He shrugs.

"I was a merc once, you know," Jared says suddenly. He's a charming loafer again as he leans back and regards Alastair from beneath heavy lids.

"No kidding." Ali smiles.

"Yeah. We'd do these exercises. Little jogs, we called them. We'd set up these human alarm systems to help protect our clients. Gives the guys who stay put a chance to figure out what the enemy would do if the targets split up, how closely they're being tailed."

"How many of you went at a time?" Alastair's voice stays devil-may-care, but he sits up straighter and shoves his little pebble into his pants pocket.

"Oh, sometimes we'd be a whole team. Sometimes just one or two of us as a time."

Alastair tilts his head as though confused. "Why one or two?"

Jared blinks. "Recon, but protected."

I can smell the change in the atmosphere. Feel the tension rippling through Jared's body, just this side of transformation. I'm amazed that the room doesn't suddenly erupt in flames. *"Pfft,"* I start. "All our father's mercs ever did was ride the gate…present company excluded, of course."

Ali glances sharply at me, a question in his eyes. Jared tap-taps two fingers on the armrest. A code, a command spoken in a language Margot and I know so well. I yawn and stretch, big and messy, before shaking my head.

"Jared, we've been on this train for days," I whine, putting on a production of yawning and stretching out. "I need to move my legs," I say, not looking at either man.

Jared bobs his blond locks at me. "Take Ali with you. Don't want you alone on this train full of Lasters." He curls scorn into his voice, like he can't think of anything worse.

"Fine," I huff, crossing arms against my chest. "Just—keep your distance, Alastair. None of your breathing down my neck this time."

Alastair stands and bows, extending one arm into the aisle. "Your wish is my command." I roll my eyes and step past him, putting on my best princess routine.

The lights have gone dim in the other car, though by accident or design I can't say. Keening fills the dim, soft and low, keeping the rhythm of the train. I smell death. A baby draws in and wails in loud, hiccupping cries.

"Leave it." Behind me, Ali plucks at my sleeve. "Don't even go there. You guys going to tell me?"

I round on him, putting a finger to my lips. "Shhh," I admonish in our mother's frostiest tone. "People are sleeping." I turn quickly and walk faster, putting a bit of distance between us the way a princess with attitude would, and then hurry toward the back of the car where the sounds of crying grow louder.

EVOLVE OR DIE. Copycats out with their red markers? Travelers all the way from Dominion, like us, only searching for a miracle? Possibly. It's the Watchers' bywords, though, sure as death. But what it means…

My tired brain shuffles through the possibilities. Either Jerry Westfall has escaped Dominion and is tracking Margot, just as I am—the thought sends shivers down my spine—or… or something worse.

If the Watchers are here, halfway around the world, I can't help but think that maybe Jerry Westfall isn't the only one leading a passel of crazy Lasters. There would have to be other men, men slick enough to cause a stir over here, where it's harder for news to travel. Which means—

The train lurches and I stumble as blank terror overtakes me. A *crack* and *thud*. The crying grows louder at the back of the train. Ali clutches me from behind, holds me up.

"We should get back." His voice pitches anxiously.

I shake my head, not trusting myself to speak. My legs are too shaky still.

"Ali." Ali's dark eyes are framed by almost girlishly long lashes. Now those eyes pool with anxiety. "The baby."

The train jumps and stutters to a sudden, grinding halt. The air screeches, all of us in the car holding our ears as the train comes to a full stop. A hiss of air. Seconds later the doors at the far end are ripped open, revealing a drab shoulder, another rapidly filling the space behind him.

I hear myself whimper. We'll be cut off from Jared in

less than a minute.

The other passengers crane their heads but don't move. No one says a word. And neither do the soldiers, who search their faces and move on. *They're not the target*, I realize quickly. Not the dead, nor their survivors.

Us.

As the car fills with soldiers, the penny finally drops. If the Watchers are in Russia, it can mean only one thing. The preacher men aren't the ones pulling the strings. Someone else would have to be. Someone more powerful—and that someone must also hold sway in Russia. Enough sway, at least, to lead the Protocols doctor to stop the train before it reaches Starry Oskol. *For what reason?* The feverish thoughts fire through my head. For ransom? Money? Power?

There's just one more thing I figure out as rifle scopes turn to bright-red flares around the now-dark car. They're coming for me.

Ali grabs my arm and spins me round so I'm facing the way we came in, leaving Ali's back exposed to bullets. My hope that they won't shoot, worried they'll hit their target, proves false a moment later when a bullet rips into the wall beside our heads. We race back the way we came but stop at the door. Shouts fill the air. A loud *crack* echoes through the car. The cries of the baby disappear.

"Don't stop," Alastair hisses and pushes me to the doors between the cars. Just as he pulls the heavy steel open, another bullet goes wide and ricochets off its metal frame. The screams of children cover the tromping of boots down the rubber-lined floor. Shoving me through and tugging the door closed, Ali struggles with something until I hear a loud *twang* as he pulls free an iron bolt, locking the door behind us.

The tiny space between the cars smells like cold metal and oil and rotten food. The air is burned and unhealthy here, and I shiver with more than cold. We stare at each other, mute with horror. I don't say the words, but I think them. Over and over, like an alarm bell. The baby. That poor baby.

Hands on hips, Ali regards me. "They'll be on the other side, too."

"Jared."

And as though I've conjured him, a massive *thud* slams behind us, where our backs rest against the door. The slim rectangle of glass in the middle of the door smears with flesh and blood.

It isn't Jared's. I reckon it's that of a soldier dumb enough to jump him.

I tug on the handle but Alastair covers my hand. "I don't think you should go in there."

"I think you should leave me be." His hand tightens over mine for a moment, but I pull anyhow. The door sticks. I pull harder. A bloody limb wrapped in olive-green is caught in the rails. I kick at the sleeve and step over the body.

The car's lights have been blown out. The air is already tinged with blood and thick with Jared's peculiar form of violence. A harsh cry toward the back of the car tells me where he is and I follow it, ducking low in case there are more guns. A touch on my back tells me Alastair has decided to join me. We creep forward through the mess.

And it is a mess. The rubber runners are slick with something, but I'd as soon say it isn't blood. Bits of things—

chunks of olive-green fabric, a large black button, a boot—litter the floor. They must have really annoyed Jared, I think hysterically, for him to tear them to pieces like this. I don't have time to feel disgusted by the flippant way I think about death. I am not that person anymore.

I reach him at the other end of the long car. He's partly changed, more animal than man. Sleek-boned face, feral eyes and teeth, and a chest of rippling lean muscle, he lets a body slump to the floor. Two? No, I realize, spying another by the back entrance. Three. I know the moment he's smelled me. With a slight twitch of his nose and a subtle toss of his head, he begins to visibly relax—his animal side recognizing that I'm close, safe.

"Jared," I call out quietly. Relief floods my voice and I get a good look at him. "You're all right." There might have been a time when this animal side would unnerve me. But as I stare at Jared's inhuman form, I realize his shifts don't faze me. We've been through far too much for that.

He shapes his words awkwardly around a panther's teeth. "More coming. Time to go."

I nod my understanding. "Do we jump?"

"Hell yeah," Alastair says fervently. He surveys the gore with a practiced eye. No surprise, no fear. I haven't time to think it through, though, as another uniform bangs on the door Ali locked behind us.

"Jared?"

Two unearthly eyes travel over my body, each bone, each scent traveling through his inventory. "Need to keep you safe."

The words come out dripping sass, though I don't mean them to: "So catch me, then."

17

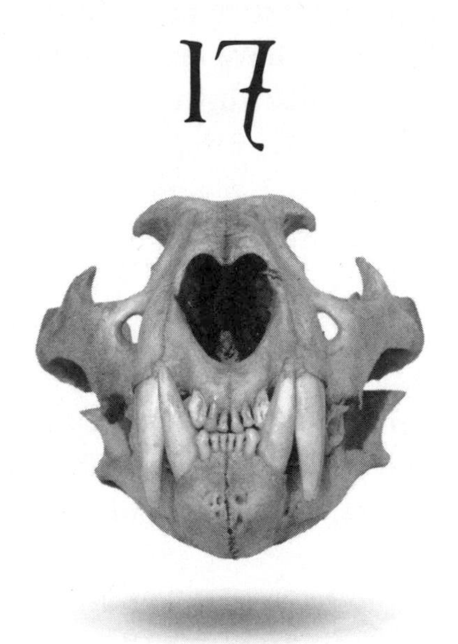

The eleventh farmhouse we break into turns out to be the lucky one. The floors are a rich, painted tile with intricate design work, the walls a creamy stucco plaster. Here and there Oriental rugs cover the tile, lending the simple dark wood furniture a regal air. In a place like this, no one will notice a little missing food.

"Why is there no one home?" Ali whispers in my ear.

It's a good question. I smell no death. Nothing seems to worry Jared.

But there are no portraits of a family on the walls or side tables. No children's rooms upstairs. It's like a perfect, empty hotel.

Perfect, except when the wrong guests come to stay.

"We don't camp here," Jared mutters. "We bunk out in the barn."

Careful not to leave footprints, we quickly raid the

larder—stocked for an apocalypse, apparently—and tramp out to the barn. Jared pulls two bottles of water and one of wine from his bag. Ali sets a blanket down in the hayloft where we make camp.

I watch as Jared turns, muscles rippling through his back. He hauls up the ladder and rests it against a wall. He comes and sits down between Ali and me.

"Open the beans and the soup," Jared orders with a grunt.

"Yes, Your Highness," I grumble. But it's Ali who takes the rustic can opener and does the honors, pouring the cold contents into three oversize mugs and handing them to us.

We're quiet for a moment, gulping down our first meal in what feels like an eternity. The air grows cool, the sky outside the hayloft beginning to marble despite the heavy cloud cover. I sneeze, the hay tickling my nose and throat, and settle my back against a bale. Real hay is so much different than the synthetic stuff we've sat on during class trips.

Occasionally Jared flips out his phone and tries to get a signal. It's been as blank as a dead Feed in every one of the farmhouses we've tried. At first I thought we'd been moving on so we could find a signal, so Jared could check in with Storm.

It wasn't until the third house, at least ten miles from the one we've camped at, that I finally understood. The farmhouse was small, with a quaint red-tile roof sagging down over the door like a bushy eyebrow. There'd been a woman outside, dressed in a simple cotton work dress. Her hair hung in a limp braid under a kerchief. She hummed to herself as she hung laundry on a line. I'd been about to get up from our hiding spot, wave at her, beg her for running water and food and maybe even a bed, when Jared clamped one large hand around my arm and the other across my mouth.

"Don't even think about it, Princess," he warned in a small hiss while I glared at him from beneath my bangs. Something in his face changed as he looked at me. Then he leaned close to my ear, his breath buzzing the short hairs there, stirring dangerous thoughts that were doused in the next instance. "If they're looking for us, they'll kill her, Lu. Don't do that to her."

Fight knocked out of me, I nodded into his hand. His fingers still smelled of blood and gore and the sticky sap of grass. It wasn't until they were slowly pulled away, one after the other, his eyes locked on mine and looking as lost as I felt, that it hit me. Jared wasn't truly worried about the woman. He was worried about what it would do to me if I got her killed.

Ali poked at my shoulder. I swayed. Jared bared his teeth, but Alastair ignored him. Then we were off once more, tramping through the small copse of woods we'd been following to get from farm to farm. Eventually we arrived at the tall grasses of a farmer's fields, tall enough to swallow us whole. Jared's heated gaze burned into my back. It was hot enough to make me feel empty and full of longing for some ending I could never have.

There, in the twilight barn, we chew the cold stuff in silence. The wind kicks up. The air is layered with the smell of hay and fire and smoke, darker than a campfire.

"What do you think it is?" I ask, sniffing. "That smell? You think there's a fire nearby?" I don't miss the dark and brooding looks Jared and Ali exchange. "What?" I ask, mystified.

Jared's growl nearly drowns out Alastair's answer. "The soldiers were setting fire to the train cars as they went through."

My stomach jerks violently. I barely have time to stagger to my feet before I get sick on a pile of hay in the corner. Ali wisely stays put, though Jared comes up behind me. He throws one arm around my back, and with the other wipes my hair from my face. Breathing heavily and leaning my weight against an old wooden beam, still smelling of nice things—trees and dirt and earth—I try and fail to put sense to the attack on the train.

"Does anyone understand what happened back there?" I finally rasp through a scratchy throat.

Unlike in Dominion, there are no clocks here. There's nothing to mark the gaps between moments. Instead there's just the silence of the grave until Jared scrapes his foot along the wooden floor.

His eyes glow green against the darkness of the hayloft as I turn to him. "Things have changed."

"You think I don't know that? Stop trying to protect me. I'm not a baby."

Those eyes deepen, the muscles in his neck tense. But then he shifts his hands behind him, and the loafer is back. Unconcerned, untouched by the chaos and death and violence all around him.

"All I'm saying, Princess—"

"Do *not* call me that," I bark. And oddly enough, it works.

Jared nods, his eyes snapping back to indigo. "All I'm saying is, things changed the moment we figured out there are Watchers here."

I don't feel myself moving, just feel the moment of impact

as I flop down in front of him. "I know it. I feel it. I just don't understand what it means."

There's a question behind the question if he's smart enough to find it.

"You already know the answer to that, Lucy," he says solemnly.

"Do I?" I eye him, wondering if I have enough of the pieces to puzzle it out.

"I think we should abort."

"No!" My hand shoots out to Jared's chest. "No, we can't. We've come all this way."

"Jared's right, Lucy," Ali chimes in. "This is a whole bag of awful. Going back to Dominion is about the only sensible thing we can do."

I dart a glare at Ali and turn to plead with Jared. "We can figure this out, Jared. I know we can." My fingers curl and tighten around his wrist.

Jared flexes his fingers, and my own hand flares out in response. He stares down at his cuticles, still rust-colored, as though surprised by them. "What do you think it means that there were Watcher signs on the train?"

"That there are Watchers here, obviously."

A ghost of a smile tips onto his lips, disappears. "What else? Other than the obvious."

Think like Foxes. The familiar refrain jogs through my head. What *does* it mean that soldiers tried to abduct us on board a train marked by Watchers? "I suppose… I guess it means there's a preacher here somewhere, or someone who is connected to Dominion."

"Right. And what do the preachers in Dominion want?"

"Me." My heart sags as I struggle with the words. "Margot

and me." Admitting all that violence is because of us, because of my sister and me, is worse than living through it.

Jared gives me a look so full of tenderness and understanding I think I'll crack in two. "Lu, this isn't your fault, honey." He stretches his other hand over mine, the heat seeping into my cold bones. "Let's think about this. The Watchers want you. The Watchers are here. But here's what I'm thinking. There's no way that Father Wes is organized enough or, hell, rich enough to stretch his sticky fingers across the big pond."

Of course. What's my father's cardinal rule? *Follow the money*.

Light blooms in my mind as the idea takes root. "So the Watchers have a backer. And that backer wants the Fox sisters."

"I think so. Badly enough that he or she is willing to invest in resources all the way over here."

"Wow." It's all I can manage for a moment while I contemplate the staggering amount of money that would be necessary to pull the strings of a group like the Watchers—and on two continents nonetheless. Only one of the Upper Circle's most elite could afford that kind of clout. The niggling thought claws at the back of my mind.

"So the Watchers clearly know that Margot is here, too… As did, I suspect, our buddies back there on the train." Jared scratches at his jaw.

"What do you suppose the soldiers wanted? I don't think they know where Margot is, either."

"Well, they sure as hell weren't throwing you a Reveal party. My best theory is that they were hoping you'd tell them where Margot is and they'd nab you both. Not a bad idea, really. Whoever was in charge of that little operation, they had at least a few brain cells rubbing together."

"That doctor..." My stomach shrinks again. "And I was stupid enough to mention her."

"Aw, c'mon. Stop making her feel bad," Alastair drawls from nearby, his soup cup abandoned.

Jared cuts him with his eyes. "Stay out of this."

"I'm as *in* this as a body can get," Ali grumbles, and busies his hands with his rock.

Jared fixes on me. Every line and juncture of his body is tense and ready to spring, despite his best laid-back act. "It was either that or we were going to be lab rats, poked and prodded until we were in even more hot water. You did what you had to, Lu. You got us out of there, and without bloodshed."

"But what if—"

"No," he cracks out. I don't think he intends to sound as harsh as he does. "Never think about the 'what-ifs,' Lu. They'll eat you alive. This is survival. This is war." His finger jabs the floorboards as he talks, punctuating his words like bullets.

But the question behind the question remains hidden, unanswered. As quiet-quiet and deep as the riddle of my blood.

Who pulls the Watchers' strings?

I don't know what wakes me. A slight tension in Jared's back, maybe, nestled so close to mine his heat is like a blanket. I can feel his wakefulness moments before headlights cut the darkness around our heads, lighting up the shadows of the barn like search beacons. Jared soundlessly jumps to a crouch and presses himself to the side of the small open window like a perfectly trained merc.

I'd been dreaming of the baby. Bald, its anemic face drawn and purpling in death. When I went to hold it, my fingers turned a mottled blueberry, infected by the baby's last sharp, stabbing cries. I dropped it and it fell with a *thud*, and I knew it had been lost. Its family gone. Then, in the darkness of my dream, I heard Margot. Just her voice, my sister's words echoing through my head like a summer's breeze.

"It's too late, you know. The babies have already come and gone."

And just before the dream ended, I saw a bank of metal monsters—huge, glistening metal machines that pushed skyward in a vast space, skyscrapers growing like metal flowers under a roof. A wall of cribs fell under the shadow of the metal monsters, teeth polished and bared. And then the world erupted into flame.

When I open my eyes, I'm sure the warmth I feel is coming from the flames of the fire that had consumed me, stripping the flesh from my bones and leaving me nothing. My mouth full of ashes. Wet tracks soaking my face. I press the heel of my hand across my mouth to stop my whimpers.

Alastair's still-sleeping breath fills the small hayloft. I touch Jared's shoulder, his flesh scalding me through his light-blue cotton T-shirt. He turns his head slightly, a wry look to his lips that tells me we're on the same page. There's no way Alastair is from Dominion's mean streets if he can sleep like that. Lasters in Dominion sleep with one eye open and a hand on the trigger, if they're lucky enough to have one.

For one long second, his eyes linger over my face, my neck. He crosses one spectacular arm over his shoulder to touch the hand I've left there, capturing me for a moment. I lean harder into his back. His flesh hard and muscular, a jungle cat. I inhale the unique him-smells, now mixed with sweat and hay and dirt. His back heaves, as though he hasn't breathed deeply in a year or more. I feel us both relax despite the dangers below.

We have visitors. The car that drives up is olden-times, a Rolls. I'd seen them often enough at the homes of Dominion's most elite, chauffeured by mercs in drivers' uniforms and strapped with semis. It parks with a final loud purr in front of the farmhouse. The sudden silence is deafening. All four doors open, spilling out men in uniform.

Jared presses himself tighter against the window frame, pulling my body with him, huddling me close at his back. I can see nothing now but the cloudy outline of a bright yellow moon. A cat's eye, as Margot liked to call it. Rapid-fire Russian drifts up from below. I catch about every word in three. "Woman." "Guns." "General."

"Jared," I whisper, grabbing a fistful of his T-shirt. He tenses and shifts, leaning his ear down to hear me. My lips meet his flesh as I make the words. "They are on the hunt, too."

For hunters, they're doing a lousy job, I think to myself as the sounds of merriment waft up to us where we hide like mice in the corners of the hayloft. The night has deepened from gray-black to gray-blue, a sure sign dawn is coming.

One of the soldiers sings a bawdy song, loudly and off-key, on the farmhouse porch. A moment later there's a telltale sound of a zipper being pulled, a stream of water hitting the dirt off the porch. The glug of a bottle as the soldier drinks and sings another verse.

Then the shuffling of boots on the wooden beams of the porch. The door bangs open again and the festive sounds of a party spill out over the hum of cicadas before it's muffled by another *bang*. Jared still stands sentinel at the window frame, keeping an eye on the one lousy guard posted at the perimeter of the farmhouse.

Jared whispers in my ear. "They should have been smart enough to search the grounds. And if they were smart," he tells me with a wicked, feral grin, "they would have posted at least four sentries. Would have kept the odds a little even."

We wait some more. In the early dawn light, the yard is washed out, everything turning the soft color of bone. Ali's rock skips over his fingers soundlessly. He hasn't said much since we woke him with a hush. But it's become clear that with these so-called hunters on the loose, the only thing they'll manage to shoot is one another. Someone named Sergei is being shouted at—something about his mother. In another few moments they stumble out again into the yard, all of them staggering as they weave over to the Rolls.

It's Sergei, the one who looks like a barrel-chested bear, who says in a thick, slow baritone, slow enough that I can understand him, "Russia is big and she—she is small." His grin is sloppy as he holds up for his friends a grainy black-and-white surveillance image blown up on a Feed page.

Another one—I heard someone call him Aleksei—tries to grab the image with fat white fingers. "That bounty is mine, Sergei. I'll get her." His words slur and he trips, falling flat on his back in the dirt.

The other two laugh, knee-slapping laughs. And Sergei holds up his prize again, this time high enough for me to see.

A pale face, pointed chin. Hair falling in loose curls just past the shoulders, a color I'd as soon say was reddish brown if the NewsFeed image were in color. I can't see the eye color but it doesn't matter—I know her face as well as I know my twin's.

18

I see rather than hear Jared's snick of breath as he gets a good glimpse of the NewsFeed image. Feel his primal rage building, hot lava under a still surface. His muscles twitch with the effort of staying calm, of not turning into a murderous machine. His eyes flash bright. I reach out my hand. He takes it in his, the sharpening nails grazing my skin.

Another loud *crack* fills the air. I wince, and we turn our attention to the scene outside. Sergei's pistol is drawn. He holds a corner of the Feed screen, now torn and smoking, while the rest lies in shards on the ground. The men are laughing again. It sounds like the barking of hyenas. On the ground, the one called Aleksei rolls, tears falling over his reddened face. A dark patch mushrooms across the front of his uniform. The third man says something and points to Aleksei's crotch and the men rooster with laughter again.

They are laughing so loud I almost miss the quiet-quiet,

merc-like return of the sentry. He bends and says something in low tones to the hysterical Sergei. Sergei listens and nods but doesn't seem to take the sentry very seriously.

Still, he's the one to watch. Tall, skinny to the point of being see-through, even in his uniform. And scariest of all—sober. He's seen something, heard something, I reckon as his eyes track the semidarkness. The sentry looks toward the barn as though he could peel back the dark and see through wood.

Skinny casually slings his Uzi from its resting place across his back to his hands and starts toward the barn. It's like watching an accident. I can't pry my eyes away from the scene below, so I miss most of a silent exchange between Jared and Ali. I catch the tail end, though, which involves Ali dragging me, hand over my mouth, to the hay bale nearest our hidden ladder. He shoves me down behind the hay as the first steps scrape and echo on the stone floor below.

Skinny methodically paces the long barn. The occasional clatter or bang tells me he's opening the doors to the stalls, about ten of them. They are all empty, cleaned of hay, but there is still moldering feed filling the bins, harnesses and equipment I couldn't name on long nails across the walls like hunting trophies.

He wanders back below the hayloft, his boots slow and steady. Pauses. Sniffs. Here, near the lip of the hayloft, I can smell it, too, and curse myself. Because here, over the scent of the hay, is the smell of my own sick, rubbed clean by hay but not gone.

A sudden *thud*. I imagine it's the barrel of the Russian assault rifle Skinny is carrying, smacking against the wooden slats of the hayloft. Once, twice more. Then he moves rapidly to the barn door and calls harshly for his companions to come.

The hay muffles most of the exchange, but I can almost make out Sergei's lazy, drunken drawl telling Skinny to get out of the barn and drive them somewhere. Skinny argues, moving rapidly toward the other soldiers.

Sparks dance before my eyes. I hadn't realized I'd been holding my breath until the soldier has left the barn. I don't have time to recover before familiar strong hands clamp around my arms, hauling me out of the hay, Alastair popping up beside me. A crazed look has crept into Jared's face. It's an expression I've never seen before, something I'd as soon call panic. I don't have a chance to ponder it long before Ali has jumped down. Jared lifts me effortlessly. A scant second later, I'm flying through the air, down into Ali's waiting arms. Jared follows, his own landing making a soft *thud* I'm sure will bring Skinny running. There's no space for me to protest, so instead I fix Jared with a glare that he promptly ignores.

We slip out the door into the fields not ten feet away, tall and thick enough to block a truck. The stalks slap my face and hands and legs, holding me back. A pressure at my back is Jared's hand, propelling me forward. Ali takes the lead, forging a zigzagging path.

Shots ring out. A bullet zings past my right ear. Jared flattens me out on the muddy ground as several more whip over his head. The world goes mute. Winded, I try to catch my breath. Jared blazes me with a look that promises death as he cradles my head like an egg.

"You're all right," he whispers, his lips thickening as he partially shifts into beast. It's not a question. His nose riffles gently through my hair. Beneath the scent of my fear, he knows I'm safe. I nod anyway as Jared hauls me up and pantomimes running in a crouch. Bullets keep flying, but with

Ali's zigzagging flight, it seems they keep missing the mark.

Now I can hear them: the crackle of a radio, Sergei shouting loud, crude obscenities at the intruders in the grass as the drunken hunters call in reinforcements. What I don't hear is our silent stalker.

Where is Skinny?

I reach back, and Jared's hand is there. It covers mine, stilling the panic in my chest. He puts a finger to his distorted lips that open to a snarl. Underneath his shirt, his muscles ripple, build mass. A True Born about to fly loose. But the grass is blind. They can't see us, but we can't see them, either. And already I can hear the sound of distant drones.

They're coming.

We wade deeper into the ocean of grass and stumble into Ali. He's bent down over something, I can't tell what, until I see him writing on a small pad of paper. His pen and paper seem absurdly antique, like the OldenTimes car in the yard.

He spares us the shortest of glances before bending back down to his task and scribbling furiously. He finishes with a snap of a button on the tip of his pen before folding it into some hidden pocket inside his brown duster, then folds the small rectangle of paper into squares.

"Here." He hands the folded mass to Jared. "You know the best chance here is to split up." Teeth sharp and long, Jared snarls a silent answer. Ali nods. "I say we meet up in Starry Oskol. On that paper"—he points to the square, locked in Jared's inch-long claws—"is an address. Friends, Jared. Don't kill them or maim them or scare them to death. Got it?"

"How is it you have friends there, Alastair?" Jared's voice rumbles from his chest, deeper than normal.

Alastair levels a long, hard look at Jared. "They're my friends. Just as I am your friend. That's all you need to know."

Alastair is not the simple Laster from Dominion that he's been pretending to be.

He grins. "Believe it or not, tough guy, we're on the same side." His eyes slide over me, something heavier than teasing creeping into his voice. "No sense tearing apart your only friend in a strange country." Ali pulls his little rock from nowhere and throws it in the air. "Besides, I don't think we have the luxury of arguing about this right now."

Jared nods reluctantly. Ali winks at me. Grabs me up into a short hug. His leather jacket presses tough ridges against my body. He smells of leather and baked grass. Jared narrows his eyes in warning, but it seems as though this time, at least, he'll let Alastair live. Ali gives us a final grin, wide and full of dimples. Then he throws himself into the tall grasses noisily, tossing back a terse, hissing, "Go east-north-east," before being completely swallowed.

Chopper blades sound louder as they track Ali's noisy progress. It's enough of a distraction. Jared grabs my hand and pulls me through the grass. "We need shelter."

Bullets fly, and we stumble through the grassy tangle toward a most uncertain outcome.

There's little time to think as we wend our way from one farm to the next. Choppers splay the sky, riding low and brushing apart the grass with their turbine blades. Then come the mosquito drones. About the size of a bird, the long-tailed surveillance drones hover in the air here and there, tracking signs of our passage. Each time one swings by, I flatten myself to the ground.

Jared stretches out against me and presses his lips into my hair. "As long as we stay hidden and don't keep stopping like deer in the headlights, we should be safe. The drones aren't armed."

We might be safe—but is Alastair?

Why did he do it? Not just drawing the soldiers away—that was plain suicidal. Who is he? Why did he come all this way, halfway across the world, to help bring me closer to my sister?

And I realize it's true. We *are* closer, Margot and me. I can feel her rising in my blood, tugging on my awareness. With each step, her presence gains strength and definition. As though that special line between us is the invisible pull of a magnet, a compass pulling me to her true north. It's an overwhelming feeling, like being flooded with rain after a year's drought. I marvel in her nearness, am nearly sick with joy and the fear that her ghostly reverberations will suddenly disappear from my flesh once again.

Margot's hand tingles with something—cold, it feels like. I feel its trace across my own fingertips. She's alive and whole.

And close.

The air fills with a chopper once more. Jared and I stop and huddle in the tall grasses. We've come to a clearing. In front of us stretches forty feet of dirt break before a thin copse of trees springs up again.

A farmer appears at the small wooden door of the farmhouse. It's squat and run-down, though the lands seem well tended to my admittedly untrained eye. The door slams behind him and he stands out sharply in a pair of dirty overalls and a red-and-white-checkered shirt. In one hand he holds a shotgun. In the other is a dinner fork. He waves both at the chopper in his field, screaming and hurling obscenities at the careless airmen.

A semiautomatic cannon pulls down from the chopper's chassis with a metallic *click*. It clicks once more, locking into place. The guns loose their bullets into the walls and doors of the small farmhouse. The farmer does a gruesome dance, his blood splaying across the door behind him. The air fills with the harsh shrieks of birds. A murder of crows streams from the trees in all directions. Jared grabs hold of my arm and hauls me into the small protection of the trees as the bullets bite into the dirt yard around the farmhouse.

Another *click*. Something screams through the air behind us before it erupts in flames. I shake myself loose and stare at the carnage. "They b-blew it up," I splutter. "They blew it up! Why did they do that?"

Jared shoves me down so we lie behind a tree trunk. "I don't think they saw us." He scans the area, keeping a practiced eye on the chopper, which hovers now above the smoke and flame as though regretting its decision to annihilate the family within.

But it's not until the metal death machine backs away and creeps in the opposite direction that Jared turns his attention to me, his expression flat and frank. A smudge of dirt sits over his eyebrow, disappearing under the ridge of his blond bangs.

I can't help it. I begin to sob. "What if we'd gone there for shelter? What if we'd been inside?"

Jared shakes his head. His fingernails—human, I note—scrabble against the bark of the tree trunk as he gets comfortable. "That farmer would have never let us inside."

It's not a comment I understand. I'm about to argue when he runs the back of his hand across my cheek, as though his senses can't tell him enough that I made it through, safe and whole.

"It wasn't about killing you or us," he murmurs. "That was about silencing potential witnesses. Whatever they want, they don't want any Lasters telling tales about it."

"How are they going to prevent that? They going to go around killing everyone? They're mad."

To my dismay, Jared shrugs. One eyebrow hitches up, making the funny smudge above it look like a caterpillar crawling over his eye. He gentles a strand of hair away from my mouth, stares at my head, my ear. "This is Russia, Lucy. Their army behaves just as ours does in Dominion."

A yawning pit of horror opens up in my gut. In other words, Jared is suggesting the army is owned by men in power. Russia's own Upper Circle. The same way Dominion's is. I feel sick at his words, as I am complicit by birth in a vast conspiracy of wealth and corruption.

I can't help myself. I heave off to the side and for the second time in a day am sick on the forest floor.

When I'm finished, Jared pulls me back against his chest. I realize I am crying—thick, stupid tears, all the more stupid for what they won't have the power to change.

"Shhhh," Jared soothes and rocks me until the sobs turn to hiccups. And as I quiet, I hear him murmur against my hair, over and over again, "Not your fault, Lu, not your fault." His voice quiets me, calms me, as his fingers tangle and comb through my hair.

Margot shares my flesh. But it seems Jared Price shares my soul.

We come upon the small shack in the woods just as the shadows lengthen and the air starts to lose the day's warmth. We've been pulling silently through the thickening forest all day. I'm starving, exhausted. So thirsty I'd drink my own tears if I had any to spare. I throw myself against the weight of a tree. After a lifetime in Dominion, it seems like an oddly decadent thing to be able to do. I look up. Birds stir noisily in the canopy above us. How could anything bad happen in a forest? It's an unreasonable feeling, I reckon, but for the first time since leaving the *Bostonian*, I feel safe. Protected.

The shack could be abandoned. The windows are dark, the blinds drawn. There's no curl of smoke from the small chimney. Jared motions for me to wait behind a large, moss-covered rock while he walks the grounds. He tunes his attention to the dirt, the plants, turning in slow circles as he goes. I reckon he has a way of spotting the tracks that others, even trained mercs, would miss. What does the world look like through his eyes?

Jared approaches the cabin door with caution, so still and quiet he could be a ghost. He slips inside. A few minutes later, he reemerges, a wide grin splitting his face.

"You look like a little boy with a new toy," I tell him, my voice sounding unfamiliar to my ears after a day of silence.

Jared grabs my hand and hauls me into his arms just before I hit the small set of stairs. "I think we've caught a break."

Jared puts me down just inside the doors. Curtains drawn, the interior of the cabin is gloomy. My eyes take a moment to adjust before I'm able to see it clearly. And then I break into a smile, too. It's enchanting. The floors are a deep red wood polished to a shine and covered in large, brightly woven rugs. A large pile of wood sits before a small fireplace tucked against one wall. The chimney is molded from a jumble of jagged gray rocks. There's a small rectangular table made from a lighter wood, three wooden chairs that would cost a fortune in Dominion if they weren't thrown for firewood.

A small kitchen is tucked into the back. It's quite modern, with a shiny sink, the countertop bare but clean. In the opposite corner of the shack sits a love seat and a chair. But it's the custom bookshelf, stacking over the doorframe and lined with books, that catches my eye. I study the strange frame until Jared wanders over and grabs hold of a leather strap I had seen sticking out of a wall but didn't understand.

He pulls. Down comes a bed, covered in a thick woolen bedspread, dark-gray with a thin strip of lighter gray against white-white sheets.

"I think they call these hidey-beds." He's still grinning as he bounces up and down on a squeaky frame. He pats the space next to him. "C'mon, try it."

I eye Jared for a long moment, unsure what I should do. Curiosity wins out in the end, and I join him on the bed. A faint odor of wet wool and mildew clings to the bedding, but on the whole, it feels surprisingly soft and thick under my hands.

"What is this place?" I say when I catch Jared watching me.

"Trapper's cabin, I think." He tosses back his blond hair, indicating the rear of the tiny home. "Saw some traps out behind the cabin." Jared regards me again, his face serious and intent. "Stay here, okay? Don't open the curtains. I'll be back in ten minutes."

"What are you—" I start to ask, but he's out the door before the words have formed.

With Jared gone, I take the opportunity to survey the small white cupboards. My stomach clenches with pain, reminding me it's been too long since we've eaten. The shelves are neatly stacked with row upon row of cans, most labeled, some not. The OldenTimes fridge with its long, horizontal handle sits in the far corner of the small kitchenette, unplugged.

The cabin air is dry, overlaid with the faintest scent of wood smoke. It's warmer than I'd have expected. But even though the furnishings are pin-neat, it's clear from the dust it's been a while since someone has been this way. It's set up for a lonely man, I decide as I look through the small shelf of books hovering over the faded cornflower-blue couch. English books and Russian crammed in together: Jack London's *The Call of the Wild* next to something called *Never Cry Wolf* and a battered, thick copy of what might be *Crime and Punishment*. A map of the region done up in bright red and blue lines, framed in sturdy wood, hangs on the wooden paneled wall next to the door. I'm busy studying the strange chevrons dotting the wilderness on the map when Jared stomps in, his feet and jeans muddier than before.

I don't know what makes me throw out waspishly, "Why are you looking at me like that?" before he's even had a chance to pull off his shoes. Maybe just because he looks surprised to see me. I bury a twinge of guilt as he laughs. It's not a sound I've heard in a while, or very often before now, I realize with a jolt. "What's got you in such a good mood?"

Jared pulls off his shoes and folds up the hems of his dirty jeans. He flashes me another heart-stopping smile, then stands behind me at the map.

My heart trips as his arm extends over my shoulder to trace a line of chevrons. "Trapper's lines," he tells me. "See how they're marked with little dots on the side?" I peer closer at the little upside-down *V*s. He's right—tiny little dots in different-colored ink mark the sides of the chevrons. "Marking their territory."

"Better than pissing on the map, I reckon, and lasts longer than pissing on the trees."

Jared's smile flares again, then dies. We're too close, his body heat smothering me in a blanket of warmth. But there's nowhere for me to move unless I want to end up in his arms. And I do—oh so badly. But not now. Not yet.

It's Jared who moves away first. "I'm just going to..." He licks his lips. "Uh—see if that bathroom has running water." He shuffles toward the small water closet tucked away behind the kitchen. His voice becomes muffled by the solid wooden door. "I turned on a valve outside that I think was the water, but we'll need to check."

I follow Jared to the door, left ajar. Inside is a small but functional bathroom: a shower stall, a toilet, a sink. A small cupboard opens to reveal clean towels.

"It's like a miracle," I say fervently, envisioning a hot shower.

Jared laughs again and turns on the tap. It spits for a moment and spills out rust-colored water for a few seconds before running clear. Washing his hands, he winks at me. "Smells okay. Maybe you could find us something to eat?" he suggests gently.

Jared is well aware that Upper Circle girls like me have no idea how to cook. Still, it's nice to know he has such faith in me. I go back to the cupboard, trying to imagine what some of the unlabeled cans might be.

We gorge ourselves on hot stew and canned peas. It might as well be heaven. And after a steaming shower, I feel almost as though the last few days, and all the horror, washes from my skin. I come out of the bathroom wreathed in steam and wrapped in a scratchy towel. I can't bear to crawl back into my dirty clothes, which I bring out and lay over the tops of one of the kitchen chairs.

"I thought I'd just look for some of the trapper's clothes," I say as I move over to the short chest of drawers against the wall near the bed. I turn and Jared is there, fixing me with a look both bright and dangerous.

I leave off on talking. I don't know what to say anymore as I become acutely aware of the thin fabric of the towel around me, the length of exposed leg and thigh and chest and arms. I run a nervous hand through my wet hair. "It's your turn," I utter in a low voice.

I'm no longer sure I'm talking about the shower.

19

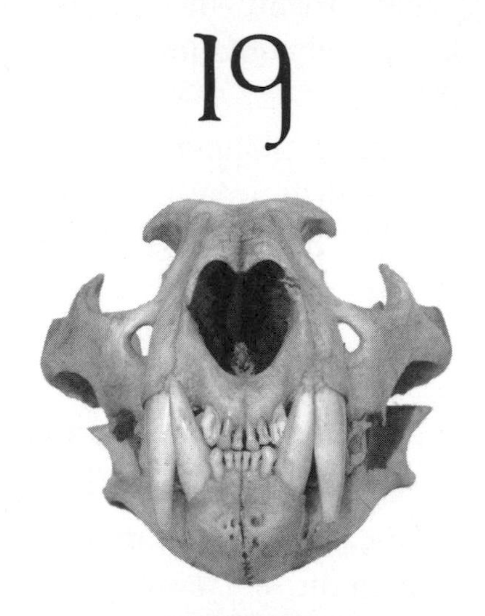

Jared lets out a breath, eyes flashing green. He eats up the distance between us in two paces but stands there, just inches from me. Not touching. Not moving. My skin tingles alerts but I have no desire to step away.

"Lucy," he says. His chest trips up and down like he's been running hard. He brings my eyes to his with the lightest brush of his fingers under my chin. "Lucy," Jared says again, but most of it is lost against my mouth as his lips take mine.

I'm swept up against the hard length of his body, his arms tough ropes, hands tangling through my wet hair. I hear tiny whimpers as his mouth devours me and I realize, as I wrap myself closer against him, they are coming from me.

Picking me up, Jared moves me to the hidey-bed. He gently lays me down before coming to lie beside me, cradling my body into his. Fire ignites in my blood as he runs his hands up my bare legs, still damp from the shower. I grab at his shirt, force it over his head. He smells like a forest now, damp and loamy and mysterious. I kiss up and down his chest, across a scar, tasting salt on my tongue.

Jared closes his eyes and arches his back with a noise I can't decipher. I stop and pull back, regarding him. He presses the palm of his hand on my chest, lighter than light, and when he pulls it away, my towel comes apart, as does the tight control I've had on my heart.

His voice is more a series of noises than language. "Lucy?"

"Yes," I say, nodding slightly in the dim light of the room. "Yes," I say again when he cocks his head as though he didn't understand.

"I don't know how..." He nibbles on my lips, cradling my face in his huge hands as my fingers trace a path down his taut torso to the fastener of his jeans. He stops to stare at me, his eyes tender and bright with passion. He shakes his head. "How to be near you." He swallows audibly. "I need you so badly my bones shake." His words echo the trill of my heartbeat, the effervescent pressure of the blood pulsing in my ears, the heat pooling in my belly and thighs.

I want him, Plague take me. I want him and I don't want to think about why he's changed his mind. Still, as he trails hot kisses down my chest, scalding me, I can't help but blurt out, "What's made you change your mind?"

He stops dead in his tracks, mouth still open on my skin. He heaves a sigh. Flips over to stare at me. "I haven't."

I pull the towel up and around me again, blushing with shame. "I don't understand. You just said—"

"I know what I said, Lu." Jared sits up and runs his hands through his hair. He pierces me with a look, eyes like emeralds.

I gape at him. *Surely he can't be serious*, my mind trips furiously. But as he continues to sit there, silent and watchful, I snap. "What is it with you, Price? What the hell kind of game do you think you're playing?" I shock myself by punching him in the arm. "Are you some kind of psycho?"

That makes him wince. I rain blows on him, my fists tiny and ineffectual against his powerful body. Until finally, he grabs my wrists and stares me full in the face.

"Stop. Stop, Lu," he says as I struggle to break free, to land another blow.

"How dare you treat me like this?" I half scream, half sob. "I never want to see you again as long as I live!"

And then I'm all-out sobbing. Still holding my arms, Jared lowers his forehead to mine and breathes deeply. "I'm sorry, Lu. I'm so sorry. It's not like that. It's not what you think."

I stare at Jared's tortured expression through wet skeins of hair, my mood fluctuating wildly between bouts of fury and shame. I don't know if I could be any more confused. "What is it, then?" I hiccup.

I gather myself together. He lets go of my hands. I expect him to pull away, but instead he cradles my face in his hands, kissing away the tears on my cheeks. He brushes my lips with such tenderness I let out another sob. Taking a deep breath, I try to harness all the pain and betrayal I feel. I level him with my coldest stare and speak once more.

"What is it, then, Jared? Why do you keep pulling away? And I swear to God you better tell me the truth this time, because you've hurt me. I refuse to play your game, Jared True Born. Give me a real reason or I am *done*." I can see that I've shocked him, pained him, even. *Good*, I think. He needs to know that I'm not messing around.

"I meant what I said." His eyes are closed but then he opens them, staring into me as though he's gotten lost. "I need you, Lu. And I need you to be whole and well, and I need to know you're safe. But if we do this—and gods take me, Lu, I want to do this more than anything I've ever wanted—then I'll have marked you."

"No you won't, Jared. What are you talking about—"

"Listen." He cuts me off gently. "I'm True Born, right? My genes take me back to the jungle, sure as Storm's take him… Well, who the hell knows with him." Jared barks an unhappy laugh. "I've got these instincts, Lu, and they drive me. And most of the time I'm in control. But when it comes to you…I'm not in control, Lu. The beast is."

"You won't hurt me."

Jared shakes his head. "No, I won't hurt you. Not physically. But how would you feel if my beast decides that you're mine and marks you as our own? Because that's what's going to happen. That's how I feel about you."

I whisper into his chest, fresh tears falling. "What would be so bad about that?"

Jared looks like he wants to cry, too. "That would be the end of it. The end of your future, of any claims you may want to make outside of me. You'd never be able to make an alliance with someone else. You'd never be able to date anyone else. Because even if I rationally agreed to stepping aside, if that's what you wanted, I don't know if I could stop myself from ripping the beating heart out of his chest and feeding it to him, Lu," Jared growls. His fingernails lengthen and he pulls them away from my flesh as though he's been scalded.

I sink down, his words penetrating my misery. Jared sits

back, too, a lost expression drifting over his face.

"How could I do that to you? How can I take you as my own, knowing that I'd be taking all other choices away from you? It's bad enough now. But if you were fully mine? It would be for life, Lucy Fox. Forever. There would be no turning back."

I sigh, my mind churning a thousand different gears at once. He's not kidding, that much is clear, and nor do I think Jared is lying to me. But I do think he's not giving himself enough credit.

I lick my lips, noting how he watches my every move. "How can you be so sure you'd be so…unreasonable?" Yet even as I ask the question, a tendril of doubt niggles at me. Life is short—but not so short for people who can't catch the Plague. Is either of us ready to make that sort of commitment? With a start, I realize just how young I am. Not a year ago I was at Grayguard Academy, finishing high school. The idea of having a boyfriend was barely on my radar. And what of marriage? Because what Jared is suggesting, what my own heart is telling me, feels a lot more permanent than a boyfriend.

My family would never allow it. The thought passes unhappily through my mind, a betrayal to Jared. And yet—hadn't I grown up fast since my Reveal? Made my own life decisions? And hadn't Jared been the one by my side throughout all of it? I clamp my eyes shut, my head reeling with confusion.

Jared shakes his head, rousing my attention. I'm not sure how long I've been lost in thought, but he's clearly been waiting to answer me. A golden curl falls across his forehead, somehow making him look boyish and lost. "I don't know.

But I feel it, the beast." His hand goes to his chest. "Right there beneath the surface. Kind of like the way you feel your sister, I reckon. And I have about as much control as you do."

"You've never really tested it," I argue.

"I don't think taking risks like that is a good idea. Not with you, Lu."

"Why not me?"

Jared levels me with a dark stare. "You know why not."

Do I? Is it because of Storm or because he cares? *Or both*, that little voice inside me insists. I don't have the answers I want—I'm not even sure I have the strength to ask them right now. The tight bands around my chest loosen an inch, and as they do so, exhaustion tugs at me. All the anger and fear of the day ebbs from my body and is slowly replaced with a dull, throbbing pain. What I wouldn't give to be anywhere but here, in the middle of a Russian forest with the one man who won't, for the sake of chivalry, have me.

Silent minutes tick between us. I lie down on the small hidey-bed, pulling Jared down beside me. He throws his arms around me like a sweater. "We'd better get some sleep, then," I say.

As if that were a possibility.

Something has changed between us yet again. Our hands are entwined as I stare moodily at his fingers, mine, winking back and forth like the lights on surveillance drones. Gone is the fear that Jared doesn't want me back. But there's nothing to replace it with—just the long, empty question mark of what comes next.

And after that?

"What about Storm?" I break our silence.

"What about Storm?" Jared repeats, clearly as awake

and restless as I am. But there's a note of annoyance there, or maybe something else I can't place.

"Are you doing this for him, too?"

"He has nothing to do with this," Jared tells me fiercely.

I angle myself to get a better look at my True Born. His chest is bare, a smooth work of art ending with a smattering trail of white-blond hair near his navel. He's thrown one arm behind his neck, the muscles taut and bulging. There is a ridge of a scar on his hipbone and, above that, a tiny, perfect mole. He is watchful, still relaxed but looking at me under a cap of curls as though he expects a fight.

And for that matter, maybe he'll get one.

"Are you sure?"

He frees his hand from mine to arrange the blanket more snuggly around my shoulders. Then links up our fingers again. "He doesn't even know."

"I don't believe that any longer."

"Why?"

"Why?" I snort in disbelief. "Because you disobeyed him for me. Because you followed me here and aren't dragging me back. Of course he knows."

Jared is somber. "I'm doing my job, Lu."

"No you're not." I put my hand to his chest. "I mean, yes, you're protecting me. And thank you. I don't know if I've ever told you how grateful I am." Jared frowns and I quickly move on. "But you've gone far and above your duty, Jared, and when we get back…"

"What?"

"I think you know what."

"Spell it out for me, Princess."

I sigh again, closing my eyes and wishing I didn't have

to say the words. “There are alliances. That’s how it works. I help Storm climb to power. He offers me protection.”

Jared sits up so fast, pinning me between his arms, that I get dizzy. His eyes spit green at me, his mouth an angry line. “That’s what you think? You think I’m holding out on you so Storm can still marry you off to get what he wants?”

“Not really.” I heave a sigh, closing my eyes. “Not anymore. I just needed to know for sure. But he is your boss. You’re always telling me to think like your opponent,” I say, finally opening my eyes. He’s still there, the alert predator waiting for his instincts to lead him. “So think like him for a moment, Jared. What would you do in his place?”

He looks like his heart is breaking as he says the words. “I’d marry you off to some important guy so I could sweep to power.”

We go quiet. It’s silent as a grave around here. I’ve never been in a place that was as empty of noise as this place is. Here there are no Lasters moaning on the street corners as their insides pull apart. None of the roving gangs in hazmat suits collecting bodies on their carts. There are no feral dogs here barking for dead flesh. No flying bullets or bombs, nor the whine of surveillance drones.

Here there is only the gentle swish of trees outside, the slight rapping of the wind at the door. Birdsong. So much twittering birdsong.

And the crushing weight of my future hanging over our heads.

For once, though, it’s not just the threat of what lies secret inside my blood. That remains a whole other can of worms.

Jared turns to look at me. “How can you think I’d hold back so Storm can marry off a virgin?” He spits out the word, as if disgusted that I even made him consider it.

"Did it ever occur to you I might need to know you're on *my* side?"

"How can you even doubt that, Lucy?" His eyes flash with indignation. "What do you think I've been doing here? Enjoying a relaxing vacation?"

"Actually, yes." I smile despite myself.

Jared's own grin teases out reluctantly, the dimples on his cheek deepening at the last second before it's gone again. "There's a lot you obviously don't understand." His words are layered with meaning.

"Illuminate me, then. I'm a smart girl. I can take it."

Jared pushes me back on the pillow, fanning my hair out and placing two careful hands on either side of my head.

"Lucinda Fox." His voice is hushed and serious, his eyes soft-soft. "Don't you know I'd tear apart a thousand Splicers and Lasters alike for you? I answer to Storm, yes, but every cell in my body answers to you, too, like it or not. He can no more order me to bring you back than you can order me to leave his service."

I stare hard into his eyes, burning blue and green in equal degree. "What does that mean?" I ask, licking my lips. My hand steadies on his chest. Jared's heart beats strong and fierce beneath my fingers. The heartbeat of a warrior.

His stare deepens until I no longer know anything outside of it. "It's like having my guts turned inside out and thrown in the fire most days. I come across your trace," he says, running a finger through my pillow-strewn curls, "and part of me goes berserk. But if I don't hear your voice or see you, I start feeling murderous. I want to break bones just to get near it. To be next to you. When you left and got on that god-awful ship. When I found your note and realized you were gone. I-I can't explain..." He trails off, and my stomach twists with guilt. I knew that he would be furious with me, but I had never intended to hurt him by leaving.

Jared's voice drops, low and shaky. He rubs at his head as though it hurts. "Do you understand? I am no longer myself, Lucy. Already I know I can never go back to that time—the time before I knew you." He blinks, misery stretching across his beautiful face. My heart flip-flops. And in that instant, I think I understand what has happened to us, Jared and me.

Like a compass, we'll always point back to each other. *But will we ever be pointing in the same direction?*

"I'm sorry," I say, tears falling down my cheeks. "I'm sorry, Jared."

He bends and kisses them, gentle-gentle, like a wish. "No," he says. And there is nothing but truth in his eyes, searing and deep. "No, Lucy. Please don't say that. However much I want to throw myself in Dominion Harbor some days, you need to know this. I feel like I never really lived, never really drew breath, until the day I met you."

I nod through a wash of tears. My chest hurts with need. I draw him closer, dissolving the pain and murmuring into his ear as his kisses move me to oblivion.

We stayed in the cabin overnight, kissing, talking, finally falling asleep in each other's arms. In the morning we woke and ate and tidied before leaving. It had been a quiet, reflective walk through the woods. We didn't say much, but then, after the night's confessions, it seemed better, safer, to keep our thoughts to ourselves.

Besides, I reasoned, *what else is there to say?* I can't change Jared any more than he can change who I am. That feral, hot part of him, the part that had taught me such violence, had also given me the greatest sense of safety I have ever known. To cut that out of him would be to take the part of him I love best.

Love? I quickly paper over the thought. I come with complications that make being with Jared nearly impossible—I see that now. Aside from my forever bond with my sister, I am bound by duty, trapped by the politics of power. Hounded by the mysteries of our blood. And as we walk, I come closer to accepting that turning me down was another form of Jared's extreme sense of protectiveness. It didn't hurt any less. But it did erase the last vestiges of humiliation.

We don't reach the outskirts of the tiny town until full dark. Only a few streetlights line a main road, dotted with tiny, sagging porches that double as stores. Not a soul walks the street. Even the dogs are asleep as I wait quietly behind a tree while Jared performs his sweep.

"All clear," he tells me before eyeing me meaningfully. "You sure you're okay with this?"

I nod, though truly I'm not okay at all. *But no use in telling him*, I think to myself as he pulls his phone from a pocket and stretches it out, searching for a signal.

We'd spoken about it, decided together. He'd finally convinced me that it was a good idea to let my guardian know where I was. And also, he'd cautioned, Storm needed to know about the Watchers' symbols, the way the army had come after us. Not to tell him would be a crime, Jared said. He didn't need to say it, but I heard the message loud and clear anyhow: *in case we don't make it.*

After a few minutes of staring at the tiny screen, apparently satisfied, Jared presses a button. Nolan Storm's face immediately fills the small display.

"Jared." Storm seems calm enough, but if you look closely you can see the tells. The sharp lines framing his lips, the tightness around his eyes.

"Storm," Jared returns casually. "Catch you at a good time?"

"Any time is good when I haven't heard from you in days."

"Well, we ran into a little trouble. Cell service really sucks out here."

"Lucy is okay?"

"I'm fine." I pop my head on Jared's shoulder so Storm can see me, give a little wave.

Storm's expression gentles. "Any word on your sister?"

I shake my head, shiver against the chill of the late-night air. I shurg. "It's more what hasn't been said. I can feel her here."

Storm curses, antlers flaring blue-white. "You need to get the hell out of there."

"We'll be to Starry Oskol by sunrise, I reckon."

"I expect a progress report as soon as you're able." Storm nods curtly.

"As soon as I'm able," Jared returns. Storm vanishes from the screen.

Jared turns, gathering me into his arms as he kisses me

lightly. My hair, forehead, cheeks, nose, lips. "That wasn't easy. I'm proud of you." He breathes in my hair and my skin. Licks my cheek. "Are you ready for this?" he asks, leaning his forehead against mine.

"No," I tell him honestly. My hands stroke the stubble of his cheeks. I lean in and suck his sensitive lower lip into my mouth. "Let's do it anyway."

20

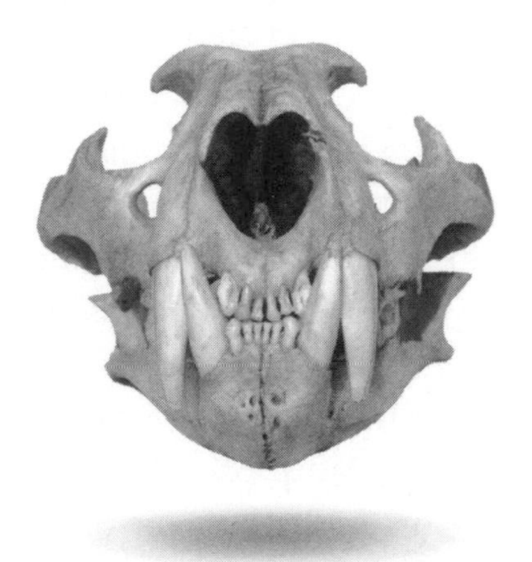

They didn't want to give us their real names, nor know ours.

"It's enough to know you are friends of Alastair's," the curly-headed husband told us as he invited us into their home through the small and overgrown garden. Inside was a perfectly charming little house. White roses sat in vases on a small country kitchen table. Plants climbed the walls, shading out the sun better than the gauzy white curtains that blew inward with the early-morning breeze.

"Call me Tom," he said, slinging his arm over the slender shoulders of his wife, who beamed at us.

"And you can call me Cilia," said the woman in heavily accented Dominion English, clasping her thin hands in front of her. "We welcome you to our home," she said formally before bustling away to bring us freshly sliced bread with oil and cheese, olives and wine.

Jared and I stared around the tiny house, its contents as mysterious as our hosts. Jared sniffed the food carefully before digging in. I examined the small fireplace, objects laid across it that I couldn't recognize. One that looked like a long hunter's knife. Two candles, a jar that looked like it was filled with salt. A small bowl set with a pestle.

"It was a new moon last night," Cilia said as she sat down across from me, drawing my eyes from the mantel. She was luminous herself, like a creature from the moon. Her hair was caught in a long braid and woven up into an elaborate bun. On her fingers were silver rings, one set with opal, the other black garnet. And beside her left eye sat the smallest tattoo of a red star. "Did you notice?" She turned her almond-shaped brown eyes on me with an air of expectation.

"Yes," I answered truthfully enough through a mouthful of bread. Jared had also mentioned the moon. A perfect night for a break-in, he'd said. Underneath the table, he squeezed my thigh. I smiled.

"After breakfast, we go for a walk," she said with a wink. "I have shopping to do."

We stroll down the block with our new friend, watchful as the patrols switch to a new rotation. The building takes up an entire city block, crouching across the space like a monstrous spider. It's fenced off like a Splicer Clinic but too large, the color of dirty metal, and with no windows. Then there are the patrols—a whole squadron of well-trained men armed to the teeth with machine guns, grenades, and, from the look of things, Tasers—sweeping the grounds in twos and threes. Cameras rotate on posts, sweeping the perimeter.

Is this where she is? I tamp down a sense of hopelessness. If Margot is in there somewhere, we'll find a way to get her out. Or, I consider as I rove my eyes over the enormous amount of security, die trying.

Unfazed, our new friend adjusts the floppy straw brim of her hat and hitches her matching straw shopping bag higher on her shoulder.

It was Tom, the careful one, who warned us about the security. He'd crossed his arms over a stocky chest, the build of a gladiator, and regarded us with intelligent blue eyes. "You'll need some cover. They've cameras everywhere and don't skimp on security. Mind you listen to Cilia when you're out 'shopping,'" he said with emphasis. "We can't afford the attention."

Jared nodded, barely looking at our host as he ate. But I could tell he'd taken the man's measure and then some. "And how is it you know where we're going?"

Tom had barked a short laugh. "Even if we hadn't gotten a note from Alastair, it's clear where you're headed, True Born." Our host cracked his fingers, then folded his arms across his chest again as his jaw worked. "Straight into the jaws of hell," he said darkly, his words tinged with his thick Russian accent.

"Starry Oskol isn't like it used to be," Cilia tells us as we leisurely stroll the entire block, then turn and head toward the open marketplace a brisk ten minutes away. The buildings rise higher here than in Dominion, many of them charming four-stories and made of wood. The scent of char overlays the entire town, as though there has recently been a large fire. "It used to be a sleepy city," she says, fishing for the English words. "Now there are many guards, much military. But I do not think it is the government in charge, if you understand me."

We reach a stall filled with produce. "We have fresh chicken and vegetables tonight," she tells us after haggling with a toothless old woman, who grudgingly hands over a chicken wrapped in paper. "Come," Cilia tells us. We walk through the market to a stall tucked in at the very back, secreted behind the shade of a large willow tree.

Cilia nods at the keen-eyed woman behind the counter. "These are friends of ours," she says to the woman, whose dark curls peek out from beneath a pink headscarf. The woman nods, unsmiling. She says nothing, but her look says it all. She rakes her eyes over us, startling turquoise eyes against dusk-colored skin. Cilia places a gold coin on the counter.

I've never seen its like. A blazing sun and crescent moon against a starry sky. "Maybe you can give them some advice," she says in slow Russian. "The kind you give to tourists." Cilia switches back to English and smiles again, her white teeth brilliant as the sun. "And some tea."

A faded magenta curtain hangs at the back of the woman's stall. She pushes us past it and beyond, into a small storage area. We don't stop there amid barrels and crates but carry on to a rusty trailer parked underneath a tree. She bangs on the door. A giant of a man with a graying beard opens a screeching screen door and hops out. He wordlessly stares at us before lumbering away to the stall.

The woman pushes us inside and ducks out, returning with

a pail of water. A live chicken struts past the door and follows us as we're motioned into the living room. Fragrant, leafy tea is set to brew on a hot plate tucked into one dark corner of the trailer. The other corner is furnished as a small living room: two chairs, one a wooden rocker, the other a threadbare green recliner. A constellation of bright bronze coins tied with red ribbons hangs from the ceiling. Upside-down bouquets of dried flowers and herbs fill in every nook and cranny.

The woman takes the green rocker. I take the other chair, while Jared positions himself so he doesn't have his back to the door.

The woman follows Jared with her eyes but doesn't say anything as Cilia launches into rapid-fire Russian that I can't follow. The woman answers, her accent different than anything I've ever heard, almost as though Russian was not her first tongue. Cilia nods, satisfied, then turns to us. "Nadya will tell you what she knows."

The woman motions at us with knuckles fat with arthritis and nods. "A big gray monster." Nadya chuckles through a mouthful of missing teeth. "The elephant has big feet." *Beeg*, she pronounces the syllables. Then she unravels for us every detail she has about "the elephant," her nickname for the long, hulking building that stretches across the town: the sentries, how many shifts for the entire building, outside and in, what times they're relieved. At Jared's prompting, she walks us through the interior layout—though she doesn't say where she's gotten her information.

It's Cilia who tells us, "They have many cleaning staff inside. Nadya has family who works there."

Neither woman mentions what they keep inside.

•••

Coming to a halt, Nadya takes my hand and looks carefully at the lines before raising her face to mine. I look up at Cilia in confusion. Who are these friends of Alastair's—fortune-tellers? Religious nuts? Sometimes the older generations go crazy over young women, though I don't know what it's like here in Russia. I've hardly formed the thought when Nadya takes a different tack, her English improving as we go.

"You understand, pretty girl. Here in Russia, the Plague was bad, very bad, long before it gets to Dominion." She shakes her head, the bottom knots of her kerchief bobbing with her head. "Listen." She taps her ear. "Here in Russia, it kill many people. Very many." Nadya reaches for my hand. Hers are chaffed and dry.

"Yes, I learned that in school," I tell her.

"You learn in school one thing. But the knowing is another. Many people left in Russia, they live in fear. They look for miracles and cures. I think maybe their miracle has come, yes?" Nadya smiles, her face a wreath of withered lines. I squirm uncomfortably. I haven't a clue what she's talking about. Neither, apparently, does Cilia, who shrugs, a look of confusion spreading on her lovely face. Jared comes to my rescue. He moves behind me and stares the woman down. But she just laughs, turquoise eyes glinting.

"You have strong protector, too. That is good. Keep him close." Nadya rises to squeeze Jared's bicep, as though testing its firmness, before sitting down again with a chuckle. Then she leans back on her tiny, threadbare chair and gives me a sidewise glance. Her expression holds a lifetime of grief. "You will need a strong protector, pretty girl."

•••

The hill isn't large, but it's dry and dotted with rocks big enough to hunker down behind. As dusk continues to fall, Jared records the movements of the guards. Not ten minutes past, we'd seen none other than Leo Aleksandrovich Resnikov exit the gray building, flanked by four hulking mercs. All five men slid into the back of an absurdly long black OldenTimes car and drove out the gate and away.

"It's all accurate, Storm," Jared now relays to the tiny screen. "Every last thing the old woman told us. Ten and two. Even down to what they're carrying. Outfitted with semiautomatic Glocks, most of them, while the outer sentries carry Uzis. Good for shorthand combat, nothing long-range. They aren't expecting tanks, just desperate people. We can slip in at ten. That's the biggest window between the sweeps."

I watch as the guards pass outside the "Elephant" and strain to listen to Storm's instructions to Jared. Storm rubs a shadowy jaw, chiseled as a block of marble. "I don't like you taking her in there."

Jared says nothing, just nods. Because of course, he agrees.

"I'm going anyway. You know I am."

Storm quits rubbing his jaw and sighs, clearly unhappy. "Yes, but I don't have to like it. Give yourselves an hour tops. If I don't hear from you in one hour forty-five once you activate the scrambler, I'm putting a team in the air."

Jared replies with a terse nod. But I have other questions on my mind.

"And what of the Watchers? Has Father Wes surfaced?"

Storm rubs at his jaw with a rueful look. "We've liberated a few more weapons caches. But oddly enough, Dominion's finest seem to be having trouble getting their hands on the Watchers and their supporters."

Something about this whole situation doesn't sit right.

"Storm, do you believe Father Wes?"

"About what, Lucy?"

"Wh-What he told Margot and me. The story of the twins who'd save Dominion from the Plague. Serena's mom."

Storm's frown deepens. "Are you asking whether I believe Serena's mother could really tell the future? I wouldn't even know how to begin answering that question, Lucy." A beat while he stares hard at the screen. "Where is this coming from?"

"I've been thinking about Father Wes and why he's doing what he's doing. But what if it's not even true? None of us ever met Serena's mother—maybe she was just a crackpot." I try to conjure an older version of Serena, though it's images of Nadya that float through my mind. How she stared at the palm of my hand as though she were reading a book. The brightness to her eyes. *I think maybe their miracle has come, yes?*

"Are there even such things as witches?"

"The Watchers believe it. But whether it's true or not? I can't really say. Serena thinks her mother was a wise woman, but I've not met any official group. There's no evidence to verify. Just a story." Storm takes a deep breath, antlers flaring to brilliant life, and cracks a small grin. "Though, to be fair, no one would believe I exist if there weren't True Born Talismans to back me up. What's brought this on?"

I'm saved from answering as the Feed breaks into long gray stripes before coming together again.

"Interference." Storm looks at something off the screen. "Alma?" he calls. "Can you tell Torch I need him, please?" He turns back to us. "Flux storm coming. You were saying, Lucy?"

"I was just wondering… The woman who gave us information today… She had coins hanging everywhere.

They looked ancient—"

Before I can even finish stringing my thoughts together, Storm cuts me off. "The Roma have been stigmatized as witches long before the Plague came around."

"You think she's Roma?"

"Sounds like."

"So she's not a witch?"

He smiles. "I have no idea. It's not as though I've had Doc Raines run any Protocols on them, if that's what you mean."

But it was Storm who'd shown Margot and me pictures of those he calls his True Born ancestors. Images of leopard-men crouching before falcon-headed kings. *We were worshipped as far back as Babylonian times*, he'd told us.

But the True Borns had returned to the world, if Storm is to be believed. The True Borns weren't—*aren't*—just a story etched in stone.

So what of all the other stories?

"I think she knew something about me," I say stubbornly.

Storm nods. "We'll discuss it when you return. And Lucy." Storm keeps his eyes, cold as winter, riveted on me. "When you get back, we're also setting aside some time to discuss your future. Yours and Margot's, should you be able to bring her back."

My hands tremble as though I've been Plague-struck. My stomach drops. Behind me, Jared sniffs. I step back from the Feed screen, not bothering to nod. He carries on in low tones to Jared for a moment or two, but I've stopped listening, head whirling.

I can't decide what's worse: that Storm will soon want to arrange my future, Margot's and mine—or that he doesn't seem at all confident that we'll be able to bring her home.

21

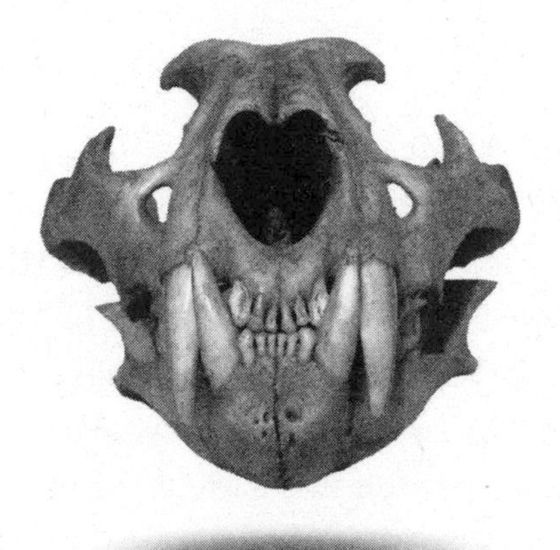

Our father liked to tell us a bedtime story about what happened when the Plague first began.

Listen well, my girls, he'd told us with gleaming, icy eyes. *People used to have different kinds of entertainment*, he'd said. *Operas, theater, ballet. Zoos.*

What are zoos? Margot had asked, wide-eyed.

Places where people brought their children to see animals locked in cages. Margot and I listened, horrified, to our father's description of lions behind bars, seals locked away in cement and water enclosures, snakes in glass pits.

Then the Plague struck, our father shouted. His fist mowed the air. *Thousands died that first year. So many they couldn't keep the zoo running properly. The animals were left alone, locked up and starving. No one to clean their cages, pick their lice, care for them.*

What happened? Margot asked, her eyes round as saucers.

I sat, her horror and my own mingling to turn me mute.

They did what anyone would do. Our father's smile was a terrible thing as he leaned over us, eclipsing the light so all we could see was the dark outline of his eyes, his cheeks. The sheen of his hair.

They did what their animal nature dictated, he murmured. *Those who couldn't escape ate their friends and died of starvation a few weeks later. Still, for months on end, there were reports of lions eating the dead in the streets. Zebras galloping through neighborhoods to the north. An elephant that rampaged through downtown Dominion until it was brought down by the army.*

There is a lesson in here, girls, he'd told us.

What was the lesson our father wanted us to learn that day?

As we wander through the "Elephant," Jared taking flank behind me, I ponder our father's lesson. We'd gotten this far, my True Born protector and me, though we had used up no little amount of luck. In the end it hadn't felt much different than when we'd raided the Splicer Clinic. We circled the block with measured steps, coming around the corner at just the right time. Jared pulled out from his pocket the thin scrap of metal that he claimed would scramble everything but aerial surveillance and flicked it on. It was noiseless as the gate guard turned the corner, lighting his cigarette. And like mice, we slipped in through the small gate opening.

But now that we traipse through the halls, I feel a little like a zoo animal loosed from a cage. I'm thinking of that story still as we turn a corner and, instead of the bank of offices the old woman had told us about, we find ourselves in a massive, empty corridor. The floors are poured concrete, painted gray but for spidery cracks spinning throughout, just like the skin of an elephant. Wordlessly we continue, anxiety flooding every pore of my body.

It takes me a dozen or so steps to realize it's not coming from me, not really. My heartbeat spikes. I take a deep breath, inhaling Margot's horror. *She's here*. She's definitely here.

I'm so focused on my sister that I step around the corner unthinkingly. Jared reaches for me. His fingers tug at the hem of my shirt, trying to hold me back. He loses his grip.

And I find myself staring into the barrel of a gun.

The barrel points square at my chest. I hear the safety click off as the soldier aims. I wince. He looks up from his scope and does a ludicrous double take.

"M-Miss," the guard splutters. In my panic, I'm barely able to take in the jumble of details: the green and beige camo of his uniform, cap pulled down low over eyes I'd as soon not look into. On the front left lapel is what I assume is his name, embroidered in black Cyrillic characters.

My legs shake but I don't have time for terror. Because there's something in the way he says that word. Something deferential and worried. I'm not seen as a trespasser. Which means—

"Would you mind not pointing that thing at me?" I say coolly, throwing him my best glare.

"S-Sorry, Miss," the solider stammers. He quickly lifts the scope of his gun and throws the safety on. I reckon he can't be much older than me, a fact I intend to take advantage of.

"I've gotten myself all turned around here in this stupid maze," I tell him haughtily. "Where the hell is the bathroom?"

The soldier's face turns a brilliant shade of scarlet. "You aren't supposed to be outside your living quarters, Miss."

I flash him my best Margot smile, pulling my hair over my ears in the way she does. "I'm not really the kind of girl who obeys rules."

"I can see that, Miss. All the same…"

"So?"

"Miss?"

"Are you going to tell me which way to the bathroom? Once I find that I'll go meekly back to my cage. All right?"

"Oh." His gun drops as he points out a door around the corner. Where Jared, no doubt, is cursing my existence. "You go back the way you came. It's kind of hidden," he tells me in heavily accented English. "I can see why you went right past it. But you really shouldn't be wandering around here by yourself. We are all armed. I'll take you, then escort you back to your quarters."

"Oh, would you?" I clap my hands together like Margot at a party, surrounded by admirers. "That would be so lovely of you." I beam at him like he's the second coming of the Cure. "This way?" I point back to where I'd come from. I don't miss the faint blush creeping over his cheeks. He nods and takes my elbow, guiding me forward.

My eyes are squeezed shut when I hear the *crunch* and heavy *thud* that tells me Jared has won the draw. I don't look behind me but wait for Jared as he pushes me back into the wall, eyes glittering green.

"Am I going to have to kill everybody here, Princess?" His words are clipped and careful, as though he's not sure what he'll do next.

I freeze against the wall, unable to do much more than nod. I mumble a bratty, "Maybe," and push at his rock-hard chest.

He glares at me a moment longer before taking my elbow and leading me on down the darker hallway.

"How good are you at playing your sister?" he says, his glance sweeping for soldiers as he tugs me along.

"You're kidding, right?"

"Does it look like I'm kidding?" he mutters, murder on his face.

I sigh, putting everything I've got into showing him what I think of his question. "*Identical* twins, Jared. We fool our own mother when we want to."

He nods, clearly not as impressed as he should be. "Good. Because I'm escorting you to your quarters, *Margot*." Jared shoves me into a shadowed doorway and eyes me dangerously. "If anyone comes, play it up. Loudly. Got it?"

"Sure," I say with a shrug.

He holds me with a stare and then disappears back the way we came from, footsteps barely registering on the gray painted concrete. It's the same color as the skies over Dominion most days, even down to the shine. Overhead, the ceilings rise at least thirty feet. Dark metal beams crisscross at the top, dotted with huge round lights and interspersed with fans. They're working, too. The air is cool and delicious on my skin.

It's been a long time since I've felt proper air-conditioning. No one has that any longer, not even the rich. My mind staggers at how much money this military fort must have cost.

And it is a military fort, I decide, albeit a private one.

Down this hallway, unlike the one we just came through, windows run in a thin stripe about twenty feet up. Like the windows of a bunker.

I try the door behind me. Locked, though I'm not surprised. Two different identi-pads wired to the door latch.

It's while I'm testing the door that I hear the clearing of a throat. I turn slowly, my eyes drifting first over the military shoes, up well-defined camo legs where the uniform doesn't quite meet the shoes, to a camo top. From under the hat, Jared peers back at me.

He folds his arms against his chest. "You weren't watching. Again." *Obviously*.

"I might be able to fool some of these identi-pads," I tell him, changing the subject. "We've done it before."

"Don't change the subject, *Margot*."

I sigh, blowing out my breath in a long *whuff*. "Fine. I messed up. Can we go now?"

"Finally." Jared nods and takes my arm, but I think I detect a sliver of a smile.

"And stop saying *Margot* like it's a dirty towel," I throw in imperiously. And damned if I don't see the smile grow a little more as we cautiously pick our way along the Elephant's trunk.

Twenty minutes later, we hit a dead end. A massive steel door stands before us, a long, empty hallway behind us. Inset in the door is a small laser platform. A blue shaft of light beams down onto the small tray, coning into a small pool.

Jared lets out a low whistle as he examines the tray. "I thought these were tall tales," he says quietly, examining the laser system.

"What does that mean?"

"It's a DNA extraction and encryption security system. So hi-tech even the hi-tech folks don't have one." Catching my blank stare, he continues. "The laser extracts a small tag of your DNA, analyzes it, works it into a sequence that it uses to create security codes, which are then used to unlock the system when that sample is reintroduced."

"But why bother with the encryption?"

Jared looks down at me. "So hackers like Torch can't get through their security system remotely."

"Oh," I say, touching the door. "It must be important, then."

"What?" Jared eyes me curiously.

"Whatever he keeps behind this door."

"Well, don't try it. If it's incorrect you could trip an alarm that sets off— "

He's too late. I throw my hand into the blue current of light. It stings and tickles in turn, not truly hurting. I find myself wondering if this is what Splicing feels like, only deeper, like an itch in your bones.

Jared snaps. *"Lucy."* He takes hold of my wrist but doesn't quite dare to pull it from the laser's sweep.

The light abruptly shuts down. Beside me, Jared tenses. The quiet hum I hadn't really noticed disappears. Then: a click, so far away and faint I look around for snipers. Before the door glides open soundlessly.

"See? I told you so," I mug with every ounce of princess I can muster.

Behind the door is a lab. It's cold inside, so cold it burns. And it's easily the biggest lab I've ever seen. Stretching on at least the length of our father's house, my view becomes obscured by banks of hulking metal machines, lab benches that stretch up a good eight feet, equipment of all sorts. Beside the door is a coatrack stacked with white lab coats. I slip one of the coats on for warmth as Jared rolls his eyes at me.

He leans down to whisper in my ear and takes my elbow. "For Gods' sake, Princess, don't touch anything."

We walk unmolested—the lab appears to be empty—until we arrive at a set of glass observation windows. I can't get a good look through the glass, but it looks like a group of wired tubs.

"What do you suppose those are?" I ask Jared.

But even as I utter the words, a man in white scrubs and lab coat appears. He tugs off a colorful kerchief, revealing thin auburn strands of hair plastering over a mostly bald skull.

Thick lines bunch up beside his eyes as the man smiles at me. "Good, you're here. I thought you'd be another hour or more," he says quickly, the words strung together in perfect, if slightly odd-sounding, Dominion English.

"Here I am," I reply. I adjust my legs to stand slightly akimbo, the way my sister does when she's bored and restless. "So?" I prompt.

"Come on, then. We've lots to do today." He sends me a curious glance over his shoulder. "You're in a chipper mood for once."

Jared and I follow the man down a maze of benches, finally stopping in a small Protocols area. I groan inwardly.

Jared grabs my elbow and gives me a hard look.

"Sit," the man says. I do so, slowly, giving myself time to make out the name written below the security tag.

"Dr. Evans," I say gingerly, "do we really need to do this today?"

The man bustles around loading his instrument tray. "Now Margot," he chides, "you know we do this every Tuesday."

The right name, then. A short huff of relief escapes me.

The doctor waves an imperious hand at Jared. "You may go now, young man. She'll be at least an hour here."

Jared shakes his head. "Sir, no sir." He clips his heels together exactly the way we'd seen the guards do when they switched off shifts. "Orders are to remain present today, sir," he says, his voice dripping with military respect.

A long moment draws out as the doctor regards Jared carefully. "Okay, young man, then you stand over there. We respect privacy around here," he orders. Jared steps back.

And once again I find myself trapped in Protocols hell.

We've been put through Protocols every year of our lives, Margot and I. Testing of our skin, our hair, our organs. Measuring and extracting DNA samples, blood samples, urine samples. They say that with the proper monitoring, they can detect with almost complete certainty if—more like when—a body will be eaten by the Plague, that ticking time bomb lurking in our cells.

In the past year, though, we were put through Protocols more times than anyone else we've known. We thought maybe they just weren't telling us that the Plague had us in its diamond-sharp sight. We thought one of us, at the very least, was a goner.

It hadn't happened. I'd as soon say the real reason behind all the Protocols has yet to surface. *But apparently they are still putting Margot through them.*

The doctor pulls out a syringe and a couple of tubes. He'll draw plenty of blood, then. But when he pulls out a DNA gun, I start to inwardly quake. *Is Margot sick?*

"Doctor Evans." I tug on my hair nervously. It's what Margot would do. "Is that really necessary?"

The doctor stops and puts down the gun. He drops a hand on either side of the Protocols bench he has me on and levels a look at me. "I know you don't like this, Margot, but—"

"I'm just not feeling well today," I blurt out.

The doctor frowns, reaches for a thermometer. "Perhaps the shots were too strong."

"Uh, yeah," I say. "I've been poked and prodded so much I'm beginning to feel like a human pincushion. Honestly, Doctor Evans, I can't even recall what the shots are for, there've been so many."

The doctor sets down the thermometer with a sympathetic look. "Margot," he chides softly. "We talked about how you and your sister were born, remember?"

My throat suddenly closes. "You know I wasn't quite myself. Tell me again," I whisper. It's a gamble, but it works. The doctor settles himself beside me, giving me a chance to study him more closely. The lines on his face are unusually thick, slabs of flesh that fold and crease. No one in the Upper Circle would live with such lines. Or live so long. "Well, you'll recall I first met your parents when they were very young, around your age," he starts. His face is kinder than I'd first thought, warm with memories from the past.

"It was my greatest triumph," he tells me with gleaming eyes. "The DNA we seeded into the zygotes—you and your sister, of course. Pure genius."

The hairs on the back of my neck stir. My stomach roils, the sick rising. A heavy tread thuds toward us. *Jared must have smelled my distress and is on his way over*, I think to myself.

"I—I still don't understand what it's about," I tell him honestly, mind reeling. How can we be genetically engineered? How could they not have told us?

What exactly did they seed inside us?

"Why did they do it?"

The doctor's face suddenly crumples, the lines sagging down over his frown as his eyebrows knit together. He pats his lab coat distractedly, looking for something. "I hate what he calls you," he mumbles, fishing out a pair of OldenTimes round wire spectacles.

"Why?"

"You are not *korova*." He rolls out the Russian word for "cow." "You are a perfect specimen, a true merger between nature and the magic of science, far better than anything we've managed before. You and your sister, such a perfect twist to the story when I heard." He laughs, tugging his glasses off and wiping them with a polka-dotted handkerchief. "Nature has the last laugh."

"I don't understand, Doctor Evans. Why does nature have the last laugh?"

I feel Jared rather than see him round the corner as the doctor pushes out the words that will change everything. "You and your sister. Lock and key. He can only complete one part of his project with you, Margot. For the other, he needs your sister, does he not? Lock. And key."

My mind roars, the blood so thick in my ears I think I've gone deaf. *Lock and key*. The tiny birthmarks left behind when they separated us. One in the shape of a lock's barrel, the other the thin lines of a skeleton key. Sick with the thought, I nearly miss the doctor's next words.

"And of course, all those babies—they will be useless for what he truly wants."

Babies? What babies? My thoughts instantly drag back to Margot and what the Watchers stole from her all those months ago. "So why is he doing it, then?" I play along, knowing exactly who "he" must be.

But the doctor just shrugs, a gone-gone gleam of madness in his faraway eyes. "He'll never be able to synthesize a stable drug from just one DNA set. But he can harvest some of what he needs."

"For a cure?" I breathe.

"A cure?" The doctor pulls back, surprised, and grabs a DNA extractor. "Ha! My dear girl, why create a cure when you can make drugs that control the symptoms? People will live in hell, but he can almost indefinitely delay the final stages of the Plague. Think of the money he will make."

Examining me like a favorite puppy, the doctor sighs. "Pity we were never able to reproduce the results we had with you two. Still, he's hopeful one of the Specials will show some promise."

Specials. He's talking about babies. I want to retch, but I catch the telltale deep-green of Jared's eyes. It's time to leave before the doctor meets his maker.

Just as I shove off the table, I catch Jared stiffening again, pulling his camo cap farther over his eyes. A muscle in his jaw jumps. Not good news, then. Seconds later I hear them, too, the ringing of loud footsteps down the cold, barren pathways of the lab.

They draw closer. And by the time I realize that two sets belong to a pair of armed soldiers, who fall into attention at either side of the nearest exit, I'm staring into the face of a third man: the smug, handsome face of Leo Aleksandrovich Resnikov.

22

"There you are, Margot." The smooth lilt of his voice haunts my nightmares. A shudder works its way through me. I clench my fists, trembling, so that I won't reach out to slap him.

This is the man who stole my sister.

I expected him to look different somehow. But here he is: the same swarthy complexion, the same dark eyes. His hair, which had been down to his shoulders last time I'd seen him, is pulled back in a slick ponytail. I detect the odd gray streak through the sides. The lines around his mocking, lying mouth.

He frowns. "I was looking for you."

My hands grip either side of the Protocols bench while I shrug. What would Margot say?

I coyly glance up at him through my hair. "I was looking for you, too," I croon. Then curse myself—what if Margot's hair is different now? I've grown it in the last few months, so it's longer now, almost as long as hers was.

But is it enough to fool this man?

The doctor steps between Resnikov and me while I frantically search the room for Jared. He's gone. I can't seem to see him anywhere, though maybe that's a good thing for the moment. Even the doctor seems to have forgotten him. A lucky break.

I'm keenly aware that the last time Jared and Resnikov saw each other, Jared wiped Resnikov's strange twin, Richardson, off the face of the earth.

Sweat beads on my back, rolls down my armpits. *Where the Holy Plague fire is Jared?*

"Just need her for another—oh, probably an hour or so."

Resnikov's voice cuts like a whip. "You're finished for today, Doctor." He tilts his head back and regards me, his lips a tight line. "Margot, it's time for you to get back to your quarters now."

I shrug again and push off the bench carefully, the way Margot would do to avoid breaking her nails. Smiling with what I hope is Margot's abundant charm, I tell the snake at my side, "Let's go, then. Bye, Doc Evans."

The doctor waves distractedly as I let Resnikov lead me out of the lab, his pet soldiers following behind like armed lap dogs. We pass bench after bench, each one empty save for equipment—genetic analysis equipment, screens for DNA microscopy. Tall fridges for storing samples. But in the shadows of the lab, Jared is nowhere to be seen.

No one finds a True Born who doesn't want to be found, Storm told me once. I never thought I'd one day pray that was true.

Resnikov tightens his grip, now an iron band around my

arm. I don't respond, don't even look at him as he murmurs, "I thought I told you not to go wandering around by yourself."

It's only then I look into his face. He's handsome—or handsome enough, I reckon. But as cold a prince as I've ever seen. And I detect a darkness there, lying buried deep in his soul. But I want him to see the truth. So I blink, tell him, "But I wasn't alone." A cloud passes over Resnikov's face until I say, "One of your pet monkeys brought me down there."

He grumbles, but his grip eases. I leave my arm in his, remembering that Margot was always less creeped out by Resnikov than I. We move quickly down the hallway before stopping at a set of identi-pads. I watch as his eyeball is scanned, his DNA extracted and analyzed. It's more secure than the most popular Splicer Clinic, I think to myself. Meaning, he's clearly hiding a lot. Maybe the doctor is right and Resnikov really is working up a partial cure. The door snicks open and Resnikov leads me over the threshold into another wing, this one decorated like a home.

But when the door snicks closed behind us, guards left outside, I realize that not only am I alone with the man who helped destroy my family—we're likely to run into my sister at any second.

And worst of all: my best weapon, in the form of one undoubtedly pissed-off True Born, is locked outside.

"You look different today, *Krasavitsa*."

Resnikov stops and takes my chin in his fingers, studying me in the recessed lighting of the living quarters. I don't get more than a glance at my surroundings, but my initial impression is one of wealth and ease: a chandelier of spun crystals hangs twenty feet above our heads, tracts of Persian carpets woven with delicate white flowers set in a blue field line the long hallway, also dotted with treasures and tall wooden doors.

What does "krasavitsa" mean again? My brain frantically filters through the many phrases a diplomat's daughter knows, from "Pass the dinner rolls, Your Eminence," to "Where did you get that lovely dress?" It's thinking of the bored diplomat's wives in all their finery that brings it back. My mind stutters to a halt.

Krasavitsa. Beautiful girl.

I force myself to look back at him, the man who stole my twin. Scrubbing the hatred from my features, I smile flirtatiously. "So do you."

Resnikov grabs my wrists and tugs me gently toward him. There's a glint in his eye I don't like, especially when he places one of my hands against his chest. His heart thumps loudly beneath my fingers. Slack-jawed, I dare not pull away, even as he draws me closer, closer.

When his lips brush mine, I think I might be dreaming. It's gentle at first, the warm, dry whiskey scent stealing over me. Then his mouth slants slightly. It comes down to claim me.

I'm trapped. And I'm kissing my enemy.

It's Resnikov who breaks the kiss a second later. He touches his lips a little ruefully. "I do seem to lack all control when it comes to you."

I reckon I've stumbled upon a secret my sister is going to have to spill when I find her. And then I'll throttle her. Blinking in shock, I step back and stare at my sister's captor, hoping my anger doesn't show.

His next words tumble out with a sigh. "You're angry," he says, bringing my fingers to his lips. "I promised I'd give you more time."

"My sister," I choke out, incoherent with rage. I realize my mistake immediately but it's too late to try to cover up. The best I can do is to bluster through.

But Resnikov just nods, as though he was expecting this kind of outburst. "Yes, I did promise. Like I said, my sources saw her in Dominion about a month ago. She did receive your letter." Resnikov lets my hand drop and leans against a wall, arms crossed. He regards me warily from under hooded eyes. Like a fighting lover, I realize.

Luckily, he mistakes the reason behind what I assume is my ashen hue.

"Don't worry so much, darling." He smooths a hand against my hair. "I promised I'd bring you your sister, and I will deliver that promise." His dark eyes probe my face as he cups my cheek gently, his fingers splaying the length of my jaw. "My dear, I hate to leave you, but I have urgent business I need to attend to. Don't forget. If you want to see your parents again, you'll do as I wish."

I nod, numb, and watch his broad back stride quickly toward the living quarters door.

"You don't have to do this," I call out, my voice breaking slightly. I curse myself for pushing it too far, for breaking character, and pray that he will take it in stride. People hear what they want to, after all.

His hand freezes on the doorframe. He turns back to me, an unfathomable look on his face. "*Maya dorogaya*," he drawls. *My dear*. "What has gotten into you?"

But I shake my head, find myself stepping toward him,

my whole body quivering. "You don't have to do this. Please."

Resnikov steps forward, almost as if he's unsure of himself. And there's something to the way he looks, as though I've pierced through the thick armor of his heartlessness. *Not me*, I remind myself, *Margot.*

"We've been through this, *dorogaya*." His voice scrapes along my skin as he reaches out and caresses my cheek with a soft finger. "*Dorogaya*," he says again, his fingers tracing over the skin of my cheek, "*krasavitsa*. You are so beautiful, do you know that? I am the luckiest man in the world. But we are doing this, Margot. You and I. Our children will grow up in a world where cures and miracles exist."

I can't help it. Hot tears leak out, my throat closing and opening like a fist. "There are already miracles in the world, Leo. I'd as soon they were free and available for everyone."

A shadow crosses his face. "But that is not an option, Margot. Is it?" Iron coated in silk. His hands tighten in my hair for a moment before he lets me loose. I nearly stumble back. And then he's quickly to the door, opening it with just the wave of his hand.

One-way security, then. That will come in handy, I think as I sag to my knees in relief. I sob, trying to catch my breath, my wits. My body feels as though it's been hit by electricity.

I'm distracted then by a pinch at my wrist. I look down in wonder. Something niggles at me. I look up. And stare into a mirror reflection of myself, dressed in pants and a blouse, tousled auburn curls falling to her shoulders.

"Some love scene, little sister," says the mirror. "I never knew you were such a fine actress." A smile breaks out over the reflection's face, an echo of my own.

Margot.

23

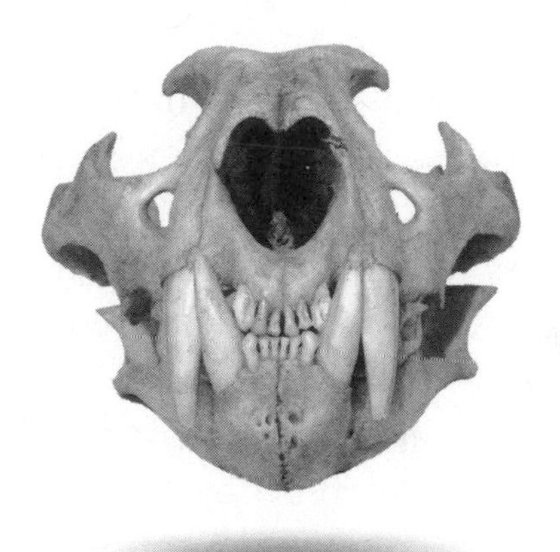

I can barely stand, but I manage to stumble to my feet and run to her. We don't need words, Margot and I. Quiet-quiet, as we've always been, we take inventory of each other.

Margot touches my hair, longer now. I tap at her cheek, feeling its echo on my flesh. Sound and well. Her arms come around me, and we both flood with the feeling of completion. *Lock and key*. Blood and bone. My sister and I are one. And in that instant, all the pain and the fear I've endured is worth it. I'd risk a thousand more soldiers if it meant my sister and I never had to be apart again.

"What the Holy Plague fire are you playing at, Margot?" I say when I can speak again.

"Shh," she says. "Not now. Is Storm here?" She glances expectantly over my shoulder at the door.

"No," I whisper. "It's just Jared and me. And a new friend

who's hopefully waiting for us outside."

Margot keeps her beautiful blue-gray eyes locked on me. "We need to be careful," she tells me, so serious it breaks my heart. "He'll never let me go."

"What have they done, Mar?"

She shakes her head. "You mean Father and Mother?" Margot tips her head back, an angry scoffing laugh darkening the room. "Don't you know?"

My sister's beautiful face twists into an ugly mask.

"We're their greatest investment. We were born for this, all right. But not for whatever those witches thought. You know what we were born for, Lu?" And now I see it, the storm of tears welling up in her eyes. "We're cows. Genetic cows. Cash cows. Call it whatever you want. They made us so they could control the whole world."

My body goes numb. "What do you mean?"

"They have a word for it, you know. *Korova*. Cow. That's what the soldiers call me when they think he can't hear."

I've never heard my sister sound so bitter. "Margot," I say, wanting to comfort her.

But for the first time in our lives, Margot shakes me off. "No. We need to go. Now."

The grim look in her eyes gives me chills. But when she touches her arm, then mine, I know she's okay. I know my sister's mind as well as I know my mind. *And she has something to show me.*

"Take me, then." I tell her. Two minutes later, with a hastily stuffed backpack, we set off.

•••

The massive room smells like oil and antiseptic, airless and fetid at the same time. "What is this place?" I whisper in our special way. Margot taps her wrist. A warning to stay silent, stay vigilant. Guards could be near.

A few seconds later, she turns back to me, takes my hand in her own identical fingers. She leads me a few paces beyond the dark silver corridor marked with glaring biosafety hazard signs.

"Promise you won't freak out," she says under her breath.

I nod, but she seems to hesitate a second longer. *"Margot,"* I bark.

She snaps out of it, leading me around a corner. We don't have to crouch any longer. On either side of us loom huge machines. They run in rows down a room as large as an airplane hangar. Machines that push up toward the vaulted ceilings, then back down again.

I clasp her hand tighter. Tap one finger. Margot turns and taps the side of her face beside her eye. *Watch carefully.*

It must be a factory of some type, though it's quieter than any factory I've ever seen before. Polished metal throws off reflections here and there, making me think I'm seeing things. Cold white plastic with dark-red serial numbers crown row after row of conveyor belts, bolts, and arms.

A machine like a Splicing gun bears down on tray after tray of what looks like micro-wells. The gun pokes down into the wells, seeding something microscopic before lifting up again. It repeats in the next tiny hole, over and over again, repositioning itself like a flamingo about to feed.

Margot calmly walks me past this strange marvel and over to a machine that spits out coated bottles of liquid. I can't see it but I know there's a trick here. Is the splice-gun material going into the tall vials?

Margot's eyes are huge in her head. "Where is he?" she asks, meaning Jared. I shake my head, unable to speak. Vial after vial pushes into carrying trays, which are then dipped through a liquid-nitrogen vat, coming up frozen.

"Margot, what are they doing?" I don't recognize my voice, a strange rumble.

She doesn't answer, though. Just lets loose my hand and threads her way through a gap in the machinery, cutting across the massive production floor.

I follow Margot to the other side of the factory. Light from a small control room spills out across the polished cement floor. She motions to me before pressing herself against the wall. I do the same, watching her carefully for clues. We are there for I don't know how many painful heartbeats when something brushes up against my arm. I jump, barely holding back a squeaked scream. A hand flings out and grabs the back of my head, another flying across my mouth.

And I glare into a remarkable pair of emerald eyes.

Margot nods at Jared just once, as though she expected him, her face drawn and pale. She points at the window and Jared nods, giving me a wicked smile before leaning down to my ear.

"Now behave yourself, Princess." His breath tickles my ear. "There's a team of those fake True Borns posted right outside." I suck in a breath, my whole body quivering. A heartbeat later he's released me. I stumble back toward the wall.

Jared leans across me, leaving a trail of hot awareness across my body, and taps Margot's arm. He gives her some sort of signal I can't see, but I can feel her nod. Jared's body coils like a spring as Margot holds out her finger. A jolt of blue light coats her hand and a door lock light turns green.

The door slides open. A feral scream rips the air beside me.

And chaos is loosed in the form of Jared Price.

Margot and I flatten ourselves against the wall as Jared pounces past us into the control room. In the space between heartbeats, a wet sound cuts off the terrified cry of whoever sat in that booth. A pulsing alarm blares through the room, making me jump. I try to grab onto Margot, but she keeps her face turned toward the door. Then, like a shadow, she slips into the control room.

"Margot," I call after her, my voice drowned out by the shrill siren. "What are you doing?"

She returns a second later, looking haunted. Jared appears behind her, a dull gleam of satisfaction coating his face along with fine droplets of blood. He takes his T-shirt and wipes his face. Only, the blood smears. I stifle a gag and follow my sister, who breaks into a run down the length of the production floor.

Jared stays behind me, grabbing my hips and holding me up when I threaten to stumble. We reach the small door just as Margot has slid it open with her DNA, and we follow her into another long room.

Only this room is different.

This one is filled with row after row of glass canisters, at least ten that I can see. Each foot-wide glass canister rises at least six feet in the air. "Margot," I call out, but she disappears around a corner. As if she'd hear me over the alarm anyhow, still blaring and clearly wired for every room. Someone will come for us soon. In the meantime, I watch as something whirs from the black pumps that seal the top of each. It sounds like a pump, but the canisters are so thick with murky liquid that I can't quite make out what's inside until I step closer and see the hazy outline of a tiny skull—

Babies. They're making babies.

My mouth flops open as Jared slams into my back.

"Oh my God," I say, feeling sick and crampy all over. I sway to the side, feeling the world tilt crazily on its axis. Jared says nothing, just pats my back and looks like he could rip the room in two.

"Margot. That way?" He points to the right. I nod when I hear a man's voice yelling from that direction.

"Hey, you can't be here— Wait, don't touch that!"

Jared leaps around the corner, fingers sharpened razors. A bloodcurdling scream comes from someone, but I can't tell if it's Jared's or the guard's. A gun discharges, the sound tinny and musical. It cuts into one of the glass canisters, which explodes into a million pieces. Thick, mucous-like pink fluid spills out onto the floor, along with the contents of the jar that lands in a tiny, unmoving heap. The air quickly becomes saturated with a smell I've never experienced before—a cross between the sea and the iron-tinged scent of blood.

I know I need to move, need to get Margot. But I'm frozen to the spot. *Special children in a world where children would be special.* Because it's finally occurred to me just what these babies are.

These are the fruits of what was stolen from Margot in the Splicer Clinic.

Her eggs. Her babies. Being harvested for their DNA.

...

Time stills, and though I must be imagining it, my ears fill with the sound of a ticking clock, each tick as heavy as a drumbeat. I walk forward slowly, careful to step around the tiny bundle of flesh on the floor. I reckon I know better than to try to revive it or comfort it. This baby is already dead—if it was ever really living.

Margot screams, but I still walk calmly, slowly. *Shock*, I think to myself. *This must be what it feels like.* As I turn the corner, Margot is locked in the embrace of a tall, thin giant of a man.

Haven't I seen this giant before? I question my sanity and blink. But no—it *is* the same figure, or one remarkably like the one Jared killed in the Splicer Clinic all those months ago.

But he was dead, my mind sorts out logically. Dead, but the image of Richardson and his doppelganger, Resnikov, floats past my eyes.

They're doing far more than DNA extractions here.

A tall man with absurdly large muscles in a dark shirt and a neck the size of a tree trunk has Jared poised above his head. He hurls Jared onto the floor, and I hear a giant *crack* as Jared hits. I jerk forward, not sure what I'll do yet, but my feet hit something in the way.

The body of a guard lies on his side, white eyes unstaring. But locked in his hands is a gun. And a gun is something I can use.

I wrench the barrel from the dead man's fingers. They're tough and stiff. I have to snap one back to free the trigger.

The gun is heavy as I strap it around my neck and look behind me to make sure there are no guards swarming there. It smells like fire.

I raise the gun, checking the safety, and stare past the metal hinge with one eye closed. "Stop," I say, but through the chaos, no one hears me. "Stop!" I yell, just as Jared is thrown again, this time against a pipe. It cracks with a resounding *boom!* and hisses steam as Jared slumps to the ground.

The muscle man turns, grinning. I hit him while he's still taking his first step toward me. *Always so sure the girls won't fire, aren't they?* my mind whispers crazily. He's spun by the bullet, a hole opening in his shoulder as my arm turns numb. I want to drop the heavy gun. But I know that if I do, we're all doomed.

The giant stalls, Margot between his hands like a little mouse. I aim for his head.

"Let her go." I still feel as though I'm swimming. The world is tinged with that surreal sensation that comes from being underwater.

Jared stirs, and I see the muscle man lunge for him, despite his wound. I fire once again, this time missing him on purpose.

"I won't warn you again," I yell.

Jared gets up and shakes it off. The giant stares at me, an expression of bemusement on his face. "Same." He points a long finger at me. "Same." He points at Margot. His teeth are too short, in places missing altogether. When he speaks, the words tumble out childishly, as though he's just learned to talk.

"That's right. And you do not want to hurt her. Your boss will be *very* angry."

Muscle Man whispers urgently at the giant. I turn the

gun on him and fire into his leg. The recoil knocks me back, but I keep my feet as the man screams and falls.

Jared is suddenly before me, a trickle of blood oozing from his nose. He gently pulls the gun strap from around my neck. "Okay, okay," he coos. His hair is clotted with blood on the right side, as though he's been bashed but good.

"No it's not." I fight the overwhelming urge to sit down.

"Stay on your feet, Princess," he snaps, though his eyes survey every inch of me in a single glance. Making sure I'm whole. "Margot," he calls. "Take a step to the left. Slowly, that's it."

She does. The giant looks like he wants to argue, but he's still busy. His eyes travel between Margot and me again and again, as though trying to pinpoint our differences.

"Sister," I tell him. The giant nods, as though I've said something wise. A shot cracks out from behind me and the giant crumples. "Why did you do that?" I scream, horrified. But the look on Jared's face says bloody murder.

And steam is quickly filling the room.

Margot comes toward me. "The pipe's been hit. I think the room is going to fry."

"Gee, you think?" Jared answers testily.

"Well, do something to help it along!"

Jared throws the gun to one side of his body and crosses his arm. "I don't take orders. And we're not burning this place down with you both inside it."

But Margot's rising panic and anger give me all the incentive I need. The gun hangs loosely around Jared's frame, so it's not such an effort to grab it and point at the large black machine that the broken pipe feeds into. My fingers twitch on the trigger. Jared tries to slap my hands away, but it only presses the trigger down faster. Round after round flies into the machine, shredding it. Fire belches from its side, but the bullets keep flying, hitting the pipes crawling from floor to ceiling, more canisters, more machines, until finally Jared rips the gun from my reach.

"What the hell are you doing, Lu?" Jared yells. He freezes, listening to something our ears can't pick up. "Get out of here. Now." He pulls Margot and me toward a door that the giant and muscle man must have come through. Margot holds out a shaky finger. The blue light spills over her skin, taking too long, too long while the fire blooms behind us.

The door finally snicks open. We're about to step through when a voice cuts through the flames and chaos.

"Margot."

Resnikov looks untouched somehow—by the flames or the violence all around him. Margot turns white as a sheet and starts to shake. Fear and pain stab through my heart until I'm gasping for breath.

"Margot, don't leave. You can't leave. *Te mne nujno, maya Dorogaya*." He takes a step forward, the inkling of a hand raising.

Whatever blood was left in Margot's face drains. I can feel her grow faint. Before either of us can say or do anything, Jared shoves us through the door. The metal quickly slides it shut behind us.

A massive rumble shakes the building.

Jared forces us into a run through the corridors. There are guards everywhere, most running toward the baby factory. But despite the omnipresent scream of the alarm, or maybe because of it, no one stops us. It doesn't hurt that he's still dressed in soldier fatigues and is strapped with a semiautomatic rifle.

"It's this way," Margot urges, pushing us toward an utterly nondescript door. We push the bar and stumble out toward the inky gray skyline of Starry Oskol.

Margot doubles over, sobbing for breath. I reach out and touch her back, and she grabs my hand. I feel it then. Feel her lungs burning for oxygen, for fresh air. Air she hasn't breathed for months now, I reckon.

Jared's eyes are green coals as he eyes the top of the Elephant, buckling with heat. "No time," he says. One eyebrow cocks up. "You need me to give you a lift?" he asks Margot.

Straightening her spine, Margot shakes her head. We half walk, half run to the gates where two sentries are on high alert. Visors pulled down over their eyes, they train their guns on us as we come forward, but they don't make any other overt moves.

"Explosion," Jared tells the sentry. "Boss Man said evacuate the jewels." Jared tips his head to both of us, then back at the building.

The sentries stare at each other, obviously unsure. Jared taps one booted foot on the ground, drawing the sentries' eyes. It's an explosion of force, so fast I barely catch it—the gun butting first one head, then the other. They both go down in a heap, where Jared stares at them for a moment.

"The boots were a dead giveaway," he says, stepping over them and unlocking the gate. "After you, ladies," he says.

We walk the streets silently, Margot and I clasping hands. No one stops us. Those who cross our path lower their eyes or move across the road. It might have to do with the bloodstains all over Jared. Or the dark, murderous look on his face.

We're only a third of the way to Cilia and Tom's when we turn a corner and a rock flips through the air, catching our attention. The lean form lounging against the wall leaps forward and catches it.

Margot stumbles. The dark-haired man grins and catches her elbow.

"I see you found your sister," Alastair throws out conversationally.

"Where have you been?" I nearly yell.

Alastair eyeballs us, his eyes raking over Jared. "Missing all the fun, it seems. Though I don't think we'll have long before there's more." He motions to the Elephant, now with a fine sheet of fire and smoke rising from its back. "Come on," he says, "we can't go back now. I have a boat lined up. I think you'll like this one," Ali says, offering his arm to Margot like a gentleman.

Margot taps her cheek twice. *Where did you find this one?*

I tug a lock of her hair. *Later*, it promises.

Just then the Elephant booms, balls of fire careening from its roof like streaking comets, turning the world into a black, white, and red nightmare.

24

It took more than two weeks to make our way back to Dominion. Two weeks of Margot looking over her shoulder. It was only once we were safely on board the hulking cruise ship—this time the *S. S. Liberty*, taking its moniker from a long-ago name for Dominion—that the endless, stuttering conversations between my twin and I finally began.

"I don't want to tell you," she repeated, as though keeping silent would protect her from the bad dreams that had her sitting up and screaming night after night.

"No matter what," I reminded her. That has always been our pledge to each other. Lock and key.

"What did the doctor tell you?" I ask one night as I brushed Margot's hair.

"About us? He said we were made. We're Splicer babies."

Her laugh was hollow. "Though what I don't get is what happened. He kept saying it had a mind and will of its own. They think the experiment failed, you know…whatever it was they were doing with us."

What are we?

"What of the babies?"

The moment I say it, I know she can't bear to speak of it. Her heart beats in my throat like a terrified bird's. She stills my hand on her hair.

"I—I can't."

"It's not your fault," I whisper, though she knows it already. I change the subject as quick as I can. I scrub at my mouth with the back of my hand. "Gods, I can't believe Resnikov kissed me."

Margot giggles. Still, there's something off about her reaction. The cord between us, that knowing, grows taut and strange. *What did he do to her?*

"Do you think we'll ever be free of them?" She sighs and sinks down on one elbow, watching me with bright eyes.

"Who—our parents? I'm not even sure we'll ever see them again. Are you?" I don't have the heart to ask whether she thinks they've all been destroyed, those Specials. There will be time enough for me to pry the story out of her.

Margot surprises me with her ferocity as she snarls back, "It's the one thing I'm certain of. They'll come for their investment."

And what investment was that? We know only that they wanted to make money. Like as not, we've been seeded with some sort of snake-oil cure. *Like nano*. I recall the way our blood seemed to call to each other. Was that part of it—part of our parents' master game? Only time will tell—time, and

Doc Raines's lab. I decide not to press Margot. She needs to learn to trust others again, to open up at her own pace. It's not something that can be forced.

Through the long nights on the ship, I put together the pieces of the puzzle that I do know: the nanotechnology of the magic bombs. How our own blood behaves at the nanoscale. I tell her of my social outings with Storm, the sweaty ugliness of Theodore Nash.

I say nothing of Jared and our tacit understanding.

And I tell her of Ali. "Have you seen that stupid pet rock of his? He'd rather carry that around than a spare change of underwear." I laugh.

"Don't mock him, Lu," Margot tells me seriously. "There's something different about him. Can't you see it?"

I roll my eyes. There was plenty that was different about my new friend, though I'd not be so rude to put a name to it. And for some reason, unknown even to myself, I don't mention Ali's odd sleight-of-hand that has me wondering whether I'm seeing strange.

"Sit down, Lucy," Storm commands, his eyes gray as a sea. It's a useless command. Now that I am once again surrounded by luxury and safety, I find I can't relax—not while, outside Storm's walls, people are falling like dominos.

Margot is already seated, back straight as a rod. Face still and anxious. She hasn't been herself since we fled Russia. I can feel her scars, heavy and deep, even if I can't see them. Storm leans himself against the broad oak desk in the room he uses as his office, arms crossed, and stares at us both. I'm distracted by his reflection, the horns rising majestically from his skull, more visible to me in the glass than the shimmer of air that seems to fold over him.

I tuck in beside my sister on the white leather couch. Pick at a scab on my knee I didn't know was there.

Storm gathers himself. "I told you we were going to discuss your future. And yours, Margot, now that you're here." Margot nods, her eyes as round as saucers. "I think you might have gotten the wrong idea about me being your guardian before," Storm says to me now. "It's not optional. I don't make idle threats. And I don't let my charges run off and do anything they wish." He raises an eyebrow now to Jared, who leans against the opposite wall beside the door and scowls. The room is so quiet that the clock can be heard, ticking over Storm's head.

"I won't get married," I blurt out.

But instead of being angry, Storm just shoves his hands in his finely tailored trouser pockets and uncrosses his feet. "Why do you think I want you to get married?" His chiseled jaw catches the watery light, obscuring his features.

"I *heard* you, Storm."

A beat of silence. Then: "You heard, but you didn't understand. I'm going to say lots of things I don't mean in public. I'm going to do so because I need information, and I need leverage. And you two are the perfect levers."

"So you're going to use us, then?" Margot blurts out bitterly, then claps a hand over her mouth. "S-ry," she mumbles through her fingers.

But Storm just smiles. "No, Margot. We're going to help each other. You must have a lot of questions about yourselves. I think we can take a stab at answering some of those. More importantly, before anyone thinks of getting married, there's something else you two need to do."

Margot and I stare at each other, our faces identical masks of puzzlement.

"I think it's time you two went back and finished school," he says with a slow, sweet smile.

It's after midnight when I wake, knowing my room has been invaded. My dreams had been filled with blood. Blood covering my eyes, obscuring my view. Blood turning me numb.

When I feel wet across my cheek, I brush my skin, thinking I'll see red. A light clicks on. Jared stands at the door.

"Must have been a bad one."

I take a few ragged breaths. "You didn't wake me."

Jared tilts his head and stares at me as though I'd spoken birdsong. He languidly crosses the room before sitting beside me on the bed. He's in sweats and a plain long-sleeved shirt, the buttons at the neck open to expose his skin. I wonder what he was doing before coming in, whether he was coming to check on me or had been walking by and heard me.

His voice is raspy, as though he's been yelling for days, rather than quiet and withdrawn as he has been. "I never know. I *know*, but I mean…I never know if I should wake you." He means the Seeing dreams. Somehow he knows.

One hand raises as though to stroke my hair. He stops, lets it drop. My eyes finally adjust enough that I can see the pained look in his blue eyes. The dark shadows beneath, the hollowing planes of his cheeks.

We stare at each other for what seems like an eternity. Until I can't stand it anymore. *I can't do this*. I panic. It hurts to keep my distance from him. It hurts me more knowing he can and will.

"Well, I reckon we don't have anything further to discuss, then, do we?" I shoo him with my hands. "Time to go now."

"No. Wait." Jared stares at me in open-mouthed surprise. "I…"

"What?" My eyebrow cocks up in a perfect imitation of his own.

A shock of blond hair falls over one of his eyes. He looks down, maybe only just realizing he's taken my hand.

"I don't understand it myself." His voice softens to velvet. He leans closer, his breath now a warm breeze against my lips.

"Oh?" I say again, pulling back.

"This is what I've figured out. When you're with me, I know you're safe. So you need to stay with me."

A pause while I consider. "I won't let you be just my bodyguard."

"Well, we'll have to negotiate that."

I narrow my eyes at the True Born. *We'll see about that*. "And what about if I go off to school? Or when I get married? You were worried about that before." I swallow and lick my lips. Jared's eyes light in fascination, watching my every movement.

"Well," he says, seconds before his lips touch mine, a butterfly kiss that sends electricity ricocheting through my body. "I'm more worried about you getting through a school year. We'll have to see about the rest."

His lips come down a second time, claiming my mouth fully. My belly dips as blood roars through my veins.

He pulls back. Jared's eyes glitter green, and his magnificent chest heaves under the thin white material of his shirt. "We still can't tell Storm. Not if you want me to remain alive. I can't be here all night," he tells me in a panic-edged voice.

"So go." I push him away. Jared stays where he is.

"Storm told me you and Margot are going through Protocols tomorrow."

"Yes."

"We'll get to the bottom of whatever's going on, Lu."

"Maybe." It comes out like a squeak. I'd rather be electrocuted than have Margot and I go through Protocols, as Jared is well aware. But there's no other way we can solve the mystery of what they've seeded in our blood…or what it is our parents and Resnikov hoped to use it for. And why now, when they'd had eighteen years to use us like blood cattle… Had something woken in our blood just prior to our Reveal? The thoughts swirl round and round in my brain, keeping me wakeful. All told, we left Russia with more questions than answers.

Jared still makes no move to leave.

"Well?"

"I can stay here for a little while longer. If you like," he tells me after a long beat. "Until you fall asleep."

"Okay," I say, oddly soothed. "I'd like that."

The nightmares had been recurring all night. And each time, just before the blood flowed, I saw the terrible face of Father Wes.

Jared leaps over and tucks me against him. He's warm

and solid, spicy and hot. Immediately I feel sleep steal over me. "You know you'll fall asleep and wake up with a crick in your neck," I tell him as his hands thread through my hair.

Dominion is still quiet, though I'm told the Watchers continue to scurry around in the dark, planning gods know what. But, right here and now, there is Jared. Jared and me.

"Yeah, probably." I can hear the smile in my True Born's voice. "Go to sleep, Princess. I've got you."

And so I do.

ACKNOWLEDGMENTS

It bears repeating that books are born into the world only through the efforts of a community. A very special thanks is owed to my editor, Liz Pelletier, who through this series has taught me so much—not just about writing better books, but about what lies at the heart of this story. I want to give a "group hug" to the entire Entangled team, in particular: Heather Riccio for keeping track of me, Melissa Montovani for her awesome support, and Stacy Abrams, whose keen editing has made this book so much better. You have been so supportive, kind, and friendly—thank you. I also want to thank my agent, Robert Lecker, who has been an incredible pillar of support (I'm so relieved that I'm turning out to be a good investment!). A special thank-you to Fernanda Viveiros and the rest of the Raincoast Books team for being my Canadian cheerleaders. I am so proud to be represented by this label in Canada. Thank you also to Courtney Graham and Melanie Windle, the lady geniuses of Glamazon Pictures, who continue to ask such interesting, provocative and important questions, and another shout-out to the inimitable Irwin Adam for the Russian lessons. I have been so lucky for the unflagging support of my family and friends through all this book stuff. Thanks, guys—love you all. Finally, I want to acknowledge the many remarkable scientists at the Institute of Biomaterials and Biomedical Engineering at the University of Toronto who shared their research with me, spawning the "sci-fi" elements of this series. I have been at times inspired, awed, confused, confounded and terrified by the insights you have shared with me, and I am a better storyteller for having crossed your paths.

Don't miss where Lucy's story began in

TRUE BORN:

And don't miss the stunning conclusion to the True Born trilogy in

TRUE STORM:

Read on for a Sneak Peek!

1

All our lives, the Harvest Moon Masque was but a fairy tale for my twin sister, Margot, and me. The Masque follows the last of the country harvest, attended by the elite and upper crust in Dominion's Outskirts. It had been my sister's dream to dance at this riotous ball in a matching gown and mask. So it's a bitter-tinged irony that I'm here instead, without her.

The rules of Dominion's Upper Circle society aren't followed out here. Here, at Senator Theodore Nash's sprawling plantation home in the Outskirts, surrounded by verdant green fields I've never seen the like of, the country folk follow their own gods. The Plague may be gobbling up these people, same as in Dominion. But here the wealthy farmers, their mercs and field hands, seem less worried about the death and starvation that perch on each street corner of NorAm's capital city. Out here, under a stretch of endless gray sky, people may die, but they don't starve by the bucketful. Here, Lasters and Splicers aren't so different.

Lasters are those near certain to die from Plague—or the empty bellies and hard times that come hand and hand with it. Lasters don't last. Splicers survive. The wealthy Splicers attend Splicing Clinics, where new DNA is sewn in to take over from that spoiled by Plague.

In Dominion, there's no mixing of these social worlds. The Lasters are our servants. They are the mercs who guard, our cooks, our caregivers, while Splicers—those from the elite Upper Circle, like me—take up positions as politicians, socialites, doctors, and lawmakers. Splicers run our world. Splicers will inherit the earth. Or so it seemed, once upon a time.

I know better now.

If anyone is to survive this brutal Plague and its endless destruction, it's to be the one group that I've not seen in and around Nash's country estate.

Laster, Splicer...*True Born.*

To be True Born means you can't catch the Plague, though you're a pariah in so many other ways. They say True Born DNA has all but jumped back in time. A natural defense mechanism against the wasting sickness, they say. True Borns have special rogue DNA that has burrowed back into our ancestral past, turning some into what we all once were: not fully human. Some True Borns have the strength of cheetahs or the speed and grace of gazelles. Some have the hirsute bodies of our furry ancestors and some the scaly skins of our reptilian cousins. Near all I've met, I reckon, are extraordinary in some way. Hated and feared by all, too.

But here, in Nash's well-appointed ballroom, it's only rich and poor, Laster and Splicer, who dance side by side. As level as death itself.

Margot would love the romance of the Masque: the high and mighty of our elite world hobnobbing it with the sons of farmers. As for me? I love it a lot less, though likely because the romance of the evening is not coming alive in the arms of my current partner, Gordon Preston the Third.

"Y'know, you sure are the prettiest little gal," the Third slurs with a half note of surprise. He slips his mask up on his forehead and blinks at me owlishly. Drunk as sure as I'm a Fox. Gordon has not been withholding on a number of things this evening, booze being one of them. His identity being another—despite the nature of the event we are currently attending.

What he hasn't told me is anything useful. Though I play the role of flirt and ingénue, I'm here less to dance than to gather information for my guardian and leader of the True Borns, Nolan Storm. I've buttered up Preston the Third in a thousand delicate and flattering ways, all to have him answer a handful of questions: Have people in the Outskirts heard tales of a new, miracle cure for the Plague? Do the farmers trust the newly elected Senator Nash? Are the Outskirts at all worried about the reach of Dominion's rabble-rousing preacher men?

He's hummed and hee-hawed and grown so bold as to tell me not to worry, as he and his papa will protect me and the rest of the pretty gals of Dominion's Upper Circle. In other words, so far all I've really pulled from the Third is a lesson in lechery.

"Y'really not going to tell me? 'S just yer name." He jostles my arm as though I'm joking.

"No. It's a masqued ball, Gordon. We don't reveal our identities until midnight. We've been through this."

My partner eyes me wolfishly. "You're gonna to tell me your name. 'Ventually."

"Nah." I shake my head. "Spoil the fun." I'm ready to disappear, certain that even if Preston the Third has any information that would be useful to the True Borns and me, he's too glogged to give it to me. But farmers' sons, I'm coming to learn, are persistent.

"Where y'goin'?" he whines, halting me with a surprisingly strong grip on my arm. A shiver of apprehension rushes through me. Gordon's hair is a messy dark mop, bunched and pinched where his black mask rides up. His nose falls like a thin, sharp blade, but it's the curl of his bloodless, thin lips that I don't like, the sharp slant of his cheekbones. More than anything, I don't like the gleam in his black-black eyes.

I don't bother to smile from under my violet mask. He's too far gone to notice politeness anyhow, I remind myself. I had let Gordon lead me into a quiet alcove off the main dance floor, hoping the relative quiet would help him focus. Now I realize my mistake.

Gordon Preston the Third has begun to focus on only one thing: getting fresh with me.

I glance out from the alcove with its marble benches and exquisitely detailed walls and ceilings. In the ballroom proper those ceilings rise a good twenty feet, high enough to have a band play on a little stage overlooking the dancers, who whirl as one under the bright crystal chandeliers. *It really is like a dream*, I think to myself. A lovely, old-fashioned dream. A dream where no one dies, shaking and sickened by the Plague. A dream where there are no poor, no desolate survivors.

And no Gordons, I think to myself wryly.

"Well, terrific to meet you, Gordon. Thanks for the dance," I chirrup brightly and take a step away. Any young man of breeding would recognize this as a clear signal that his presence is no longer requested by the lady in question.

Gordon, apparently, skipped this particular etiquette lesson.

"You ain't leavin'." Gordon lunges at me.

I recoil in shock, but it's too late. The thin strap of my dress snaps under his clumsy paws. I take another step back, holding the front of my dress. It's a fitted bodice, unlikely to fall. Still, I feel exposed, vulnerable to eyes and wagging tongues.

I glare daggers at my partner. "Oh, you didn't just do that. Who the hell do you think you are?"

Eyes glazed with as much excitement as drink, Gordon gives me a belching half sneer. "Oh, but I jus' did. Ev'y'one knows you Upper Circle girls are fast."

"You lecherous, arrogant ass!" I call Gordon out as he reaches for me again. My hand comes down automatically in a well-formed, defensive chop. I enjoy his surprised howl as I mentally scroll through all the ways I will murder him. Before I can make a second move, though, a shadow appears behind Gordon. It moves so fast, so silently, I almost miss it. Then one long finger reaches out and taps Gordon on the shoulder.

"May I cut in?" a voice rasps from behind a midnight-black mask. The candlelight from the wall sconces bounces off the tall figure, the pearly light absorbed by the black velvet of his suit. He's tall, lithe, and cuts the kind of dashing figure that makes girls feel dreamy.

Gordon frowns at the intruder. "I don't th-think," he sputters in protest.

But by then the masked man has inserted his more muscular frame between Gordon and myself and swept into a low bow before me. He wears his hair in the way common to the men here: slicked back and swept to one side. The mask covers most of his face, drawing shadows down over his lips. Even the color of his eyes is a secret, hidden by the dim lighting of the alcove.

"My lady, if you would care?" the masked figure trails off and extends a hand to me.

I take the solid fingers in my own, their flesh hot as coals against my own, and allow myself to be pulled into an alcove waltz. His steps are slow but sure, and when he turns me, I spy Gordon fuming at us from a distance.

"Is he still watching?" that voice purrs into my elaborately upswept hair.

"Yes."

"Good," rasps the voice.

Moments later the masked man's lips come down and sear me with a kiss I feel all the way to my toes. He pulls back a fraction of an inch while my breath hitches. Green-green eyes cut through the darkness. I sigh and lean my forehead against his tuxedoed chest, feeling the familiar shiver of comfort and crazy overtake me.

"I thought you'd never show," I murmur.

"And miss all this fun?" comes the man's sarcastic reply.

My partner turns me in time to watch Gordon storm off in a huff. A hand lightly skims the skin of my collarbone, causing a revolt of sensation to ripple through me.

"You okay? I thought I was going to have to decapitate him," my dance partner says, staring at me earnestly as he tucks the broken strap into the bodice of my dress.

"That would have spoiled my fun. I had it covered, you know. And anyway, Storm wouldn't have liked that."

"I don't care what Storm would like," he purrs with anger. "If that boy had laid so much as another finger on you, I was going to feed every single one of his digits back to him."

I sigh again and let my True Born partner twirl me

around. "Storm *really* wouldn't have liked that. I'm supposed to be gathering intelligence, not body counts."

Tense and ready for war, the True Born graces me with a terrifying smile. "You know what I think about Storm sending you off on recon."

I stop dancing and place my hands to the hard muscles of the True Born's chest. "We've been through this." I sigh. "Who better than me? All I'm doing is asking a few questions to people I would ordinarily be associating with. I can look after myself, you know. I'm not some helpless damsel in distress."

"Dammit, Princess. I know that. Doesn't stop me from wanting to do very bad things to anyone who so much as thinks about hurting you." My partner pulls his mask away from his face, revealing the cut and chiseled cheekbones and absurdly full lips of Jared Price. I try to calm the flutter of my pulse at the sight of him, but I'm about as successful as I was at pulling intel from Preston the Third: not at all. Instantly I'm lost in the glowing green of his eyes, a sure sign he's about a whisker away from either ripping someone to shreds or dragging me into a shadow and kissing me senseless—that last would be my choice. But though I know Jared is one of the most dangerous creatures in this house—a close second only, I reckon, to my guardian, Nolan Storm—I'm not afraid this panther man will hurt me.

At least, not intentionally.

Mine. Not mine. My heart trips through the familiar ebb and flow.

I blink, forcing back the thought along with an unexpected welling of tears. Our situation is complicated. Jared is Storm's man. Though I don't think he'd give me up for Storm—should

I ever be stupid enough to ask that of him—he'll be cautious about giving in to what some days feels like a Flux storm brewing between us. And then, everything is made more complicated by who I am. By *what* I am.

Whatever that may be.

"Don't look like that, Lu," Jared mutters as he curses under his breath.

"Like what?" I blink at his too-handsome face. The curved planes of his cheeks. The perfect softness of his lips, so strange in contrast to his killing nature, and the tiny scar that sits right beside them. But it's the eyes that hold me mesmerized. Jared isn't like most True Borns. When he's calm and human, his eyes are an indigo-blue sky filled with promises. When he's stirred, when his True Born nature is called, the monster that claws itself to the surface and screams like the hunting cat it is, his eyes turn a vivid emerald-green. Like they are now. Those eyes momentarily blur before me as a tear gets tangled in my lashes. So soft and swift I almost don't notice it, Jared scoops up the tear and stares at it like it's a miracle. I watch, blushing and confused, as he kisses the damp drop from his finger.

We've stopped moving, though I hardly notice. I only know the hot strength of his hand on my back. Only the tug of my heartbeat, a steady drum gone haywire, and that peculiar scent of his, musk and cinnamon, that makes me feel at once calm and safe and utterly out of control. I don't even know if he's aware he's pulling me closer, tighter, his head tilting toward me as though he can't help but meet my lips with his own.

"What'd you get?" A bright voice pops up between us. Jared growls.

Not two hairs from us stands a gorgeous redhead in four-inch stilettos. Her low-cut sheath dress hides nothing from the imagination—save the pistol strapped to her inner thigh. Storm's assassin, Kira, cuts a pretty picture, but I'd as soon not cross her. I've seen what this True Born can do with a stiletto.

"Nothing, I'm afraid." I grimace and try to step away from Jared, but he holds me fast and glares at Kira.

"Our friend had a few too many," Jared drawls, looking pointedly at my dress strap, which has pulled loose once again from Jared's fix. "Do you have a pin, Kira?"

The gorgeous woman rummages through a tiny beaded handbag and pulls out a pin. "Ta-da!" She smiles and hands it over to Jared.

Jared's eyes cross as he concentrates on the tiny pin. "Hold still," he tells me. Despite his preternatural dexterity, I'm somehow not reassured.

"Do you know how to work these things?" I ask nervously.

A lock of slicked blond hair falls across his forehead as he stops to grin at me, a pure boyish grin that turns my guts to mush. "Relax, Princess," he tells me. "Can't be harder than surviving an arena fight. I got this." His fingers skim the skin beside my shoulder, leaving behind a tingling wake of sensation. Jared looks in my eyes and for a few long seconds I reckon the pin has been forgotten. With three quick twists, he wrangles the pin into the thin black strap of material. Though it's fixed well enough for now, he shrugs off his coat and drapes it over my shoulders.

"What's this for?" I ask as my chilled flesh is suddenly enveloped by Jared's extraordinary heat, his scent tripping through my senses.

"In case the pin comes loose," he tells me with a dark look.

I can read murder written there, wrestling with something just as primitive: as though just by draping me in his jacket he claims me before all these country politicians and their reckless sons. But then the tall, lithe warrior laces his fingers through mine. And as he tugs me through the crowded dance floor into the heart of the darkest men of Dominion, my feet, like my heart, are light as air.

The True Born winds me through the buzzing, busy ballroom, up a marble staircase that rises into a curved balcony where the band plays something bone-jarring and sweet. He ducks me past them, into a black-and-white-tiled hallway. We flow past several pairs of armed men, none of whom seem to be concerned by us. They'll know which guests are which by now, I reckon. Jared's coat barely keeps me warm amid the arctic chill of the room I'm ushered into, flanked by two mercs in matching navy suits. They don't wear earpieces, these country mercs. Then again, I don't suppose they'd have to.

Criminals are sent here to the territories of Dominion, the Outskirts, to till and water the fields and harvest food, to be sold in the city. But once their sentences are up, many prefer to stay, putting to use their hard lives and harder bodies as the personal security to the Upper Circle elite. They say the mercs are reformed, more loyal and trustworthy than most. Still, when I pass the two mercs and one of them looks at me with the inklings of appreciation, I shiver with unease.

We pass through a heavy oak door and into a hallway lit only by candles shoved into wall sconces. The tiny flames make the hallway seem warm in contrast to the voices raised in anger coming from a room beyond. We follow the argument to the end of the hall and step into a brightly lit room fit for royalty.

Our host looks dapper for a dead man, I'll give him that.

"Ah, there. See? I told you she was fine," cries Theodore Nash. The new senator for the Outskirts lounges back in his chair with the smug satisfaction of a man who has everything. He's got a cigar in one hand and a snifter of spirits in the other, while his bow tie has come undone and hangs down alongside his neck like a deflated balloon. The tux, though, is impeccable, and though he doesn't don a mask like the dancers in the ballroom, I'd swear his is the most deceptive of all.

Because just a few weeks ago, Theodore Nash sat before us sweating and patchy, clearly about to hurl into his end days: Plague-struck. Today, though, he's fine.

I can tell when they'll fall sick, when they'll die. It's one of my gifts. Or curse, more like. Sure as Sunday, Theodore Nash was halfway to death last time I saw him. Today, he sits calm and happy as you please, cheeks bright with health, eyes shiny and clear.

No one who Splices would look that good so close to death's door. So why does Nash seem so healthy?

Nolan Storm pulls himself from the desk to greet me. Though his voice was not among those I heard, I can tell my guardian is angry. A swirling, spectral wrack of antlers rises into a crown over his head. Molten silver eyes, one of his most peculiar traits, roil like a storm-tossed sea. In his suit he looks like a prince of the Upper Circle. But as his foot impatiently stamps the floor, I see him for what he really is: the most powerful True Born in Dominion and beyond.

"Well," drawls Nash. "I think that pretty much concludes our business for today. Wouldn't you agree, Mr. Storm?"

Storm looks as though he'd prefer to rip Nash's head from his shoulder, something I'm certain he could do in ten seconds flat. Instead he dips his spectral crown in assent. It's a strange sight, and stranger still to think that I can see the weight he carries when others can't. Only a handful of people can see them. Only True Borns and me.

His father was the First, we're told. The first of the True Borns, maker of Kings. Storm once showed Margot and me a stone etching, tablets from Babylon carved thousands of years ago. In the stone, trapped for an eternity, there were leopard men and men who looked like Egyptian deities: half man, half beast. Though our genomics professors will tell us that our DNA devolved to allow some small part of humanity to survive the Plague, Storm tells us a different version of history.

True Borns are the old gods returning, Storm says. They come back when needed, the ancient DNA reasserting itself into family lines and allowing the children of gods to reign once more. And Nolan Storm, my guardian, would be king of them all.

If he can survive the two-faced wrath of Theodore Nash, that is.

"You were worried about me?" I ask, confused. "I was downstairs dancing with a boy named Gordon Preston. The Third," I add.

Nash snorts a laugh. "Ah, Preston. Such a fine boy. See? I told you everything was fine."

"You tell me that, Nash. But then you muck it up by sounding vaguely threatening."

Nash makes a show of feeling hurt. "I would never," he says unconvincingly.

"At any rate, our business is concluded. Wouldn't you say?"

"Yes, you're right. I've made my decision. The water project contract is canceled. Effective immediately."

Storm's voice is deceptively flat. "Jared, escort Lucy to the car, please."

Jared tugs my hand, but as I brush by Storm I whisper under my voice, "Please don't kill him." The subtle upturn of Storm's lips answers me. And then I'm swept from the room like a leaf, past the men with big machine guns and ill-fitting blue suits.

Jared escorts me nearly as far as the long, wide entrance that empties into the massive ballroom when I stop and squeeze his tuxedoed arm. "One more dance, Jared. Please?" I plead.

And maybe it's the moonlight. Maybe it's the glitter on the mask. But for just about the first time since I've known him, Jared Price doesn't snark before doing as I've asked. Instead he sweeps me into his arms.

The band strikes up a stirring song, and the packed ballroom, filled with the very *crème de la crème* of high society in and outside of Dominion, executes the steps in unison. And while I've observed that the country folk of the Outskirts are not quite as fashionable as Dominion's Upper Circle, Nash's home could certainly give some of Dominion's senators a run for their money.

Gold braid plaster edges the exquisitely wallpapered

walls of the ballroom. The rugs are the most sumptuous money can buy. Huge, ancient vases, the painted kind that used to store grain, run the length of the long entrance hall with its highly polished marble. And hovering over all that wealth are a half dozen three-tier crystal chandeliers. Still, I can't help the feeling that something is *off* about the whole place, right down to the polished servers wielding silver trays overloaded with food.

"Notice anything interesting about this place? " I ask my partner, who hasn't bothered to pull his mask back down over his beautiful indigo eyes that simmer with a hint of emerald as he looks back at me.

"Yes," Jared replies seriously. We stop moving. I try to mentally adjust to the sudden shift between us. He looks at me as though he's dying of thirst, and I wonder if my face betrays my confusion.

"I'm serious," I say, clearing my throat. We sway, our bodies just touching. I can feel the pull between us, a current as sure as electricity. And just as able to shock me.

"So am I," Jared rasps. For a moment I'm caught up in the emerald sheen rolling over his eyes, a dead giveaway that he's caught up by some strong emotion. Sometimes I think that's what he feels for me. Other times, I remember that Jared Price will never lay claim to me. I'm a girl from the Upper Circle, intended to make a brilliant match—a political union. No hearts and roses for me. And Jared Price is my merc.

And once again I'm about to show just how different our backgrounds are, I muse with an inward sigh. I turn and run my gaze back down the hall, trying to scratch away at my instincts.

"What did you see in the gallery?"

Jared frowns down at me. "Lots of those urn things."

"They're not urns," I tell him.

"Well, cups, then. Cups for giants."

I hold back a smile. *"Vases,"* I correct. "What else?"

"Some paintings. Mostly these country scenes that look like they're from a thousand years ago."

"Exactly," I say as clarity washes over me. Jared continues to look mystified.

I ponder the scene before me. "Country scenes. Country vases. It's the perfect country seat, isn't it?"

Jared looks around him at the glowing opulence. "Well, yeah."

"You know what comes with country seats like this?"

The True Born shakes his head, amused. "I bet you're going to tell me."

I cock an eyebrow, giving him a haughty look. "It's a country *seat*, Jared. This is an ancestral home. It certainly looks like it's stood right here for generations. So where are they?"

"Who?" Jared's hands reflexively curl tighter around me.

"His ancestors. His family."

No portraits of long-dead patriarchs with their silvering hair and rounded country bellies line the halls. No idle housewives in finery stare down at the guests from the walls. The pictures are all expensive, yes, but not personal: There are only paintings of harvested wheat, ploughs, fields…

Nash was an upstart in the last election. He was an unknown, some third-rate senator who all but barreled over his competition. From nothing to king overnight.

What I still didn't know is, is that normal for the Outskirts?

I go up on my tiptoes and whisper in Jared's ear, "Where are all the dead relatives, do you reckon?" before giving his earlobe a not-too-gentle nip. I leave off the puzzle for now, knowing it will be easier for me to figure it out later. When I'm not so distracted by my proximity to Jared.

He doesn't pluck me away, but as I lean back, his eyes shine green. "Do that again and I'll—"

"You'll what?" I taunt. Grumbling under his breath, Jared closes his eyes and shakes his head. "You'll what?" I ask again, though this time I loose a silky voice on him as I run my fingers up his tuxedo-shirted chest, down his stomach. I slip two fingers between buttons. Along with the raised ridge of a long, puckered scar, the heat rising from his skin fascinates me. I close my eyes and feel as though I'm being washed out to sea as our bodies drift together across the floor.

Jared claps a hand down over mine, stopping my explorations, though our *détente* lasts a moment longer. His chest heaves a little more than usual, as though he's been running. But it's enough to shame me into stopping.

If we go any further I'll claim you. And then there will be no more choice for you, he'd said to me. We were in a cabin when he said those words, thick in the Russian woods. It would have been so easy to take advantage of me—to be with me, a willing and all-too-eager novice. And he didn't because he cares.

But there is no choice for me, I think a little bitterly. I am Lucinda Fox, daughter of Lukas Fox, the power behind Dominion's closed curtains. Daughter of Antonia Fox, social queen of the Upper Circle. My duty has always been clear: to make a good match that will help further my family's ambitions, to take care of my twin sister, Margot. It isn't fair for me to toy with Jared any more than it is for him to toy with me.

"I'm sorry," I tell him breathlessly.

Jared just shakes his head at me, lips pressed closed and flat, as he laces his fingers through mine and guides me off the dance floor toward the front door.

Grab the Entangled Teen releases readers are talking about!

Bring Me Their Hearts
by Sara Wolf

Zera is a Heartless—the immortal, unaging soldier of the witch Nightsinger. With her heart in a jar under Nightsinger's control, she serves the witch unquestioningly. Until Nightsinger asks Zera for a prince's heart in exchange for her own.

No one can challenge Crown Prince Lucien d'Malvane… until the arrival of Lady Zera. She's inelegant, smart-mouthed, carefree, and out for his blood. The prince's honor has him quickly aiming for her throat.

So begins a game of cat and mouse between a girl with nothing to lose and a boy who has it all.

Winner takes the loser's heart.

Literally.

Frequency
by Christopher Krovatin

Five years ago, Fiona was just a kid. But everything changed the night the Pit Viper came to town. Sure, he rid the quiet, idyllic suburb of Hamm of its darkest problems. But Fiona witnessed something much, much worse from Hamm's adults when they drove him away.

And now, the Pit Viper is back.

Fiona's not just a kid anymore. She can handle the darkness she sees in the Pit Viper, a DJ whose wicked tattoos, quiet anger, and hypnotic music seem to speak to every teen in town… except her. She can handle watching as each of her friends seems to be overcome, nearly possessed by the music. She can even handle her unnerving suspicion that the DJ is hell-bent on revenge.

But she's not sure she can handle falling in love with him.

entangled teen
an imprint of Entangled Publishing LLC